I0545484

ADVENTURES AT

DEAD RIVER

DILLON GARRISON

A Morningside Publishing Book
Payson, Arizona

Adventures at Dead River

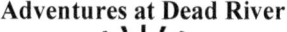

A Morningside Publishing Book

Text Copyright © 2016 by Val Edward Simone
All Rights Reserved.

Printed in the United States of America

Library of Congress Control Number: 2016919559

Printed Version
ISBN 978-1-936210-60-2

Cover Design: Val Edward Simone

For more books please visit:
www.morningsidepublishing.com
www.ekidslandpublishing.com

MORNINGSIDE
PUBLISHING, LLC
PAYSON, ARIZONA

Dedication:
To the next splendid adventure

With Special Thanks To:
Editor
Rita Samols

Musical Inspiration
Inka Gold
Secret Garden
Ernesto Cortazar II

CHAPTER 1

The hat sat alone on the rock not far from the dead tree, along the dead river, in the dead hot heat of the sweltering midsummer desert.

The gathering mass of black clouds teased a cooling deluge. Tease was about all they ever did in these parts this time of year. And it was the tease of a whore's eyes: if you wanted to play, you had to pay. But in the desert you paid with sweat and blood instead of coin. Of course, if you played out here long enough, you ended up like the river itself — *dead or dying.*

On this day it was no different. The clouds refused the kindness of rain, and the desert burned.

Sometimes, though, the desert sizzled. A bead of sweat from a man's brow dripping onto desert rocks in the middle of the day sizzled. As did a rushing gush of blood from his bullet-torn body splashing onto those same rocks.

Blood, water, there was no difference. Everything baked, burned, or sizzled in this miserable expanse of forsaken land.

To the steely, piercing eyes of U.S. Deputy Marshal Eli Alva Carson, someone had recently played in the desert. And that someone had paid the full price for the privilege.

He didn't have to wonder what he would

find when he looked. Whoever the hat belonged to was dead; no one willingly left their hat behind. Not out here in this desolation of scorching sands and baking rocks. No, sir, not on a day like today. Not on a day that threatened to challenge the heat of Hell itself.

But that's how life had existed out here through the ages, if one could call what happened out here *existing*. A better word for it would be *enduring*. Life had endured despite everything the wretched desert had thrown at it. Forever, it seemed, life here had been under the threat of annihilation. It could be said that the only thing flourishing out here was threat itself.

But soon, with the coming of the railroad, this barren wasteland would feel the unrelenting force of change. Life would move through it much faster, crippling its ability to wreck the living the way it did now. Eventually, the desert itself would have something to endure — the harsh reality of being tamed.

Marshal Carson didn't ponder these thoughts for long. Those changes were still a ways off. The railroad wouldn't be gouging its way through these parts until next year.

He was more concerned about this day. It was going to be one of those days when he regretted his decision to take on the job of Deputy Marshal for the Arizona Territory.

At fifty years of age, he was old for a lawman. Most of the other hard-driven lawmen had already left their careers far behind by the time they'd reached their early forties, when the pain of the saddle and the unforgiving trail life had already worn them down to mere shadows of bolder, stronger, tougher men who now lived only through memories while they hurt all over.

Carson was a difficult man to pound into submission, but the vision of riding a rocking chair had been looking more and more appealing over the past year. With each strenuous moment the beckoning of retired life called more loudly.

Kneeling on the large outcrop of rock to pick up the hat, he scorched his knee. *Miserable desert!* he thought, drawing his knee back quickly and rubbing the pain away.

"It's a despairin' place for any kinda life out here," he muttered, wiping his shirtsleeve across his brow. "You're a nasty bit of land. But I reckon you'll soon get yours. And you deserve it."

He spoke the words aloud, but it was only the desert that heard them. He was alone. No one in their right mind would be out in this heat, these badlands, so far from normal life. Not if there wasn't a good reason for it — "good" being a relative term, of course.

So what was *his* good reason for being out here on this atrocious afternoon? There was none other but the saddled, partially devoured dead horse lying next to the road with a bullet hole between its eyes, the crawl marks leading away from the carcass, and, of course, that god-awful blood trail that had led him through the dry and dusty wash of Dead River to the flat outcrop of sandstone where he had found the hat.

Earlier, the six-team stagecoach driver, Ben Jonas, had spotted the rotting carcass as he drove his exhausted team across the blazing desert toward Holbrook. He'd brought the team to a stop, setting to furious flight the many vultures that had gathered to enjoy a rare desert feast, and called back to the coach for Marshal Carson to come have a look. He enticed the marshal out of the carriage by saying, "I think I might have an adventure out here for you, Marshal."

Having responded to a telegram from Sheriff Moncrief in Gallup notifying Carson of the capture of Red Darrington, once a low-level but now a notorious California criminal, Carson was, at that moment, on his way back to Holbrook with Red as his prisoner.

Red's lesser crimes included cattle rustling and horse theft. And while those were hanging offenses, no one had pursued Red on those charges. Two head of cattle and a horse taken during one of his drunken escapades were hardly worth the effort, especially since all three animals were recovered unharmed.

There was also the interesting charge of *wanton, lude, and lascivious behavior*, which intrigued Carson. And being a most insightful and inquisitive man, he knew there just had to be an interesting story connected to that charge. But he resisted asking Red to explain it, not wanting to exchange anymore words as was necessary with a criminal in his custody for fear of losing his wary edge.

Until recently, though, Red had been nothing more than a barely tolerable nuisance. But he had crossed the line and was now wanted for murder.

He had been captured while attempting to disappear from the eyes of the law up in the shadowy eastern canyonlands, the mountainous region in the northeastern part of the Arizona Territory near the borderland of New Mexico. With his outlaw ways having finally caught up with him, he was now being escorted out to Sacramento for his trial by Marshal Carson. The marshal was none too pleased about the escort duty.

Under favorable weather conditions and over level terrain, a six-team stagecoach could travel an average speed of five miles an hour and cover sixty to seventy miles a day. But not out here. Between the killer heat and the hilly landscape, the stage would require the better part of three days to cover the ninety or so miles from Gallup to Holbrook.

The past day and a half had worn heavy on Carson. Red talked incessantly. The conversation was boring, trivial, and often sprinkled with wild threats to the marshal's safety and security, delivered in a manner Red considered to be hilarious — but threats even Red knew to be ludicrous. He'd been yammering all day long. Carson had tried to ignore him, but he was nearing the point where he was considering cuffing Red to the back of the stagecoach and dragging him into Holbrook.

Between Red's yammering and the hammering of the incessant heat, Carson leapt at the chance of an adventure.

Just hearing the word *adventure* excited him. He loved adventures. Anyone who knew the marshal also knew about his enthusiasm for adventuring. He had told nearly anyone willing to listen how eager he was to vault headlong into a journey of the exciting and the unknown on a moment's notice.

But the adventure he had envisioned vanished the moment he stepped down to the ground next to the dead horse and directly into the furnace of the desert.

He shot Ben an irritated look.

"This ain't the kind of adventure I had in mind, Ben."

"I reckon that depends on your attitude regarding it, Marshal."

"There's nothin' wrong with my attitude. It's the circumstances you choose to call an *adventure* that I find troublin'."

Ben Jonas chuckled.

The honest but horrid truth of the matter now settled in on Carson's brain. Since he had officially witnessed the scene, he would now be required to follow up with a formal investigation after he had gotten his prisoner back to Holbrook and locked away.

Why had he taken that blasted oath of the U.S. Marshal Service while unaware of the extreme weather in this part of the Arizona Territory? Why hadn't he just stayed in Denver, where he was born and raised? Why hadn't he retired there as he'd originally intended, six years ago? If he had, he most likely would be sitting comfortably on his front porch right now with a cup of freshly brewed coffee in his hand, watching the world pass by, at ease with the choices he had made for living his life.

Well, he reasoned unsatisfactorily, he had willingly taken that oath five years ago, along with the job, and he now had no choice but to solve this new mystery.

"Adventure, my rooty-tooty," he mumbled.

Carson squatted down and put his hand on the horse between its forelegs.

"Still a bit on the warm side, Ben, but that could be the effects of the sun, I suppose."

"Give me a chance, Marshal, and I'll leave you warm by the side of the road, too," said Red from inside the stagecoach. Then he cackled.

"Red, you murdered a man for a five-dollar pot at a poker table. You been jabberin' and smart-mouthin' me nonstop for the last day and a half. You think you're the clown of the trail, but I'm tellin' ya, Red, you ain't funny, and I'm sick of all yer jabberin'. Now, I'm stuck with ya for another day and a half and I'm tired of ya, Red, that's the truth. I'm plum tired of yer big mouth. So give me just cause, Red. Please. Give me cause to lay you out here next to this horse and claim self-defense. Would that be okay with you, Ben?"

"Self-defense, Marshal? Absolutely. I'd swear to it."

Carson stood up and moved to the head of the horse and squatted once again as Red's cackle ceased abruptly.

"You hear that, Red?"

"I heard," came the sullen response.

"Good. 'Cause you smart-mouth me again and I swear I'll shoot you dead just for the peace and quiet gained on the ride back to Holbrook. Do I gotta remind you that you're wanted dead or alive?"

"No, sir. You don't gotta remind me of that."

"Wonderful. Now sit back and shut yer yap."

Red Darrington grimaced as he sat back and clamped his mouth shut. Not even a dyed-in-the-wool criminal fancied being out in this desert, alive or dead.

"This blood is pretty much baked, Ben," Carson said, sticking his index finger into the thickened pool. "And the carcass has been gnawed on a fair bit by the buzzards. My guess is all this happened earlier today, maybe this mornin'. But heck, with the sun cookin' everything like it is, it coulda happened yesterday, too. I'm surprised the animals ain't fully got to it yet. But I'll bet it'll be pretty much et up by tomorrow or the next day, or just as soon as the critters get a good whiff of the rotting meat."

He stood up, pulled a handkerchief from his coat pocket, and wiped his finger.

"It's just bad luck — dirty, darn bad luck, I'm sayin'," he muttered, knowing that he would have to venture back out into this wicked, blistering heat to locate the source of the blood trail.

He didn't have to guess where such a search would lead him, either — to a sunbaked, rancid body that, by then, would be more or less devoured by the creatures of the high desert.

He looked up at the stagecoach driver.

"I reckon I might as well see where this blood trail leads, as if I don't already know."

"Try to see it as an adventure, Marshal."

"You and I need to have a chat about what either of us might call an adventure, Ben."

Ben Jonas chuckled again. He'd known all along this would be nothing akin to an adventure for the marshal; he just enjoyed playing his part in the running joke between them.

"We'd be mighty glad to wait on ya, Marshal," he said, with a sly smile.

"Yeah, and I appreciate that, Ben," replied Carson with a hint of teasing sarcasm in his voice.

After his discovery of the hat, Carson walked back to the stagecoach. He stopped just below Dell Longarm, the stage's shotgun rider, and studied the hat.

"Did you find ya a body to go with the hat, Marshal?" Dell asked.

"Nah. For now it's just the hat."

"I reckon you'll have to come back out here, then."

"Yeah. I reckon so."

Carson pointed to the horse.

"That saddle don't look none the worse for wear, Dell. Might as well collect it. Ain't no use lettin' a useful saddle like that rot out here with the horse."

"Sure thing, Marshal. I'll take care of it." Dell jumped down from the coach seat.

Carson shook his head.

"It's just dirty, darn bad luck, I'm sayin'."

He slapped the hat against his leg.

"Ben, a part of me will sure be glad when they finish layin' the railroad through these parts.

But there's another part of me that realizes how much the railroad is changin' this country. I think the changes are comin' too fast for this old man. Lawman's work is changin'. Attitudes of folks is changin'. The whole world is in the midst of a great change. And I find myself wonderin' if I'll be able to keep up with them changes, or will they just leave me in the dust of the past altogether in short order. I'm certain to miss ya both when the use of stagecoaches comes to its end, but I can't say I'll miss the slower ride through this hell none too much."

"You ain't wrong, Marshal," replied Ben Jonas. "Things are changin' fast. To be honest about it, I think before too long the stage lines will be finished altogether throughout the country. But for now I hear tell the Benson-to-Tombstone coach might be expanding the service down to Bisbee. I reckon I'll get on with that outfit for a time at least, but I hear the summertime run is even hotter than here."

"I don't envy ya none, Ben. But I'll tell ya, the sooner I get outa this area, the better."

Dell smirked as he began uncinching the saddle from the horse.

"Now then, Marshal, sounds like you don't favor it none out here."

"That's the truth of it. I surely don't. Never have."

Dell's eyes scanned across the desolate landscape.

"Yeah, it's a bad piece of work, alright."

"I'll say this, Dell. Ain't no kinda lovin' god created this place. It's the spawn of some hellish evil, 'cause I've never seen a place more worthless and prone to dyin' in all my life."

Carson stepped away from the stagecoach and stared out over the expansive ruination.

"Is there a problem, Marshal?" asked Dell, picking up the saddle.

"A problem? Yes, sir. There *is* a problem, Dell. It's called Dead River. And it's this blasted good-for-nothin' desert — this open, dried wound in the earth that ain't never gonna get healed. Ain't nothin' good ever happened out here, and I don't suppose it ever will. This is an end, not a beginnin'. When you find yerself out here hurtin', you're at yer end."

"Well, I reckon you might be right about that, Marshal. This horse is ended, for sure. And with all that blood, I expect there's someone out there in the midst of it who's at his end as well."

"I reckon so."

"I'll tell ya, Marshal, I've lived out in these parts most of my life and I've grown to despise this place."

"Well, I fear if we stay out here any longer than we have to, Dell, it just might despise us right back."

"Yes, sir, I reckon it will. It's just ornery enough to do that."

Dell dropped the saddle onto the cargo deck at the back of the stagecoach and moved toward the front. He glanced up at the blazing sun. "I don't think the sun's gonna do us any favors out here either."

He shook his head as he climbed back up into his seat and reached for his shotgun.

Carson grabbed the door, then stopped. He turned his head and stared once more at the stark, empty surroundings.

It ain't to *no one's* favor out here, Dell. To be out here at all is just dirty, darn bad luck, I'm sayin. 'Cause the wind blows unmercifully, the sun bakes the livin', and the sand flies about like clouds. No, sir, ain't no favor to be found out here for the livin'. This desert is only fit for dead things, or dyin' things, or things that don't even know if they're dead or dyin'."

CHAPTER 2

Unlike the county sheriff's larger, multi-celled jailhouse, Marshal Carson's thirty foot square office building, with its single jail cell, built sparingly out of brick and wood, sat alone on a lot at the south end of town.

Marshal Carson had existed quietly but happily at his desk during all the years that he had been assigned to that small office.

Across from him, on the other side of the room, was another, smaller desk with two wooden chairs for his deputies. Behind him, was a wood bookcase filled with books.

The cell, which stretched fully across the west side of the room from wall to wall, was currently occupied by Red Darrington, who sat quietly on his bunk.

Deputy John Slims strode into Carson's office. The long, lanky deputy was an affable character who seemed to smile all the time, no matter the circumstance. His upbeat nature contrasted often with other people's demeanors, but he was always welcomed wherever he went. In the town of Holbrook, John often stood out for his ability to find joy in most every situation.

So it was no surprise when he sauntered through the door with a wide grin.

"All saddled up, Marshal. Got extra canteens, provisions, and ammunition on the packhorse. Whenever you're ready to go."

Carson, leaning far back in his chair, feet on his desk, cocked the toes of his boots to one side to see his deputy better. He raised his hand from off his stomach and sipped the lukewarm coffee from a gnarled and dented tin cup, his favorite.

He yawned and stretched his arms out wide, careful not to spill a single drop of the precious elixir.

Returning his hands to his stomach, he turned his tired eyes once again to the bubbly deputy, who looked eager to begin the journey.

"Stop it, John. Yer gaiety is downright exhaustin'. You plum wear me out just watchin' you shuffle about all the time with that smile on your face and that spring in your step." Carson chuckled at his lighthearted jab.

"You know it's just my nature, Marshal. You about ready to get after it?"

"No sir, John. I can't say I'm ready for this at all, but if we're gonna do it, let's get to it."

"It's somethin' I could do alone, you know. There ain't no need for you to go out in the desert, Eli. It's just lookin' for a body. I reckon I can do that without any help."

"I wish I didn't have to. I've spent too many of my better years in the saddle huntin' down desperate and wicked men only to find mostly bodies at the end of the journey. I'm tired of findin' bodies, John. I would like to see more *life* before my time comes and I go shufflin' off into a final cloud of my own dust."

"I don't reckon anyone gets used to seein' bodies, Marshal, and I know no one would think less of ya if ya didn't want to go out in the desert on this search. Everyone knows you're high in years."

"I took an oath, John. Years or not, I took an oath to do a job. I give my word carefully and I take my word seriously."

"I know that. But it's wicked out there, Marshal. The desert kills hearty men just for the sport of it. Five years of this is enough for any man like you out here. And at yer age, you don't need to be goin' up against this wicked world no more anyway."

"Tell me, John, how much more wicked would this wicked world be if a person could ignore a noble duty without conscience, disregard a promise made without consequence, or fail to take action against evil without a righteous reckonin'?"

"You know I can't speak on high-minded things like that, Marshal. I don't have a mind for such thoughts."

"You're wrong about that, John. You have a first-rate delvin' mind. Just give yourself time to discover your true self. And never shirk your responsibility to yourself. Do that and you'll be just fine."

"Thank you, Eli. You've never shirked your responsibilities, not that I know of. And I reckon you wouldn't be shirkin' them none now if you assigned me to the task of investigatin' that dead horse and such out yonder. I can handle that heat better'n you can."

"No doubt about that, John. But it's my job to do. I won't lie to ya, it's gettin' harder for an old man like me to do this work. But it's what I signed up for. It's what I get paid for. Besides, it's been a while since you and I hit the trail together. Who can say? It might even turn out to be some interestin' kinda adventure by the end of it."

"There you go! I suppose you *could* think on it as an adventure."

Carson smirked.

"I'd be kind callin' somethin' like this an adventure. I *do*, however, have in mind a real adventure — an extraordinary adventure, a lively adventure, an adventure truly befittin' my adventurous spirit, I'm sayin'. Yes sir, a grand one to recollect on in my future years, before my memories fade, my body withers, and the only adventure remainin' will no longer be wondrous, but dark and final."

"When did ya start talkin' so dark-like?"

"It ain't intended to be dark, John. Just thoughtful. You know, in a philosophical manner."

"Well, yer philosophy has been tendin' a mite toward the dark side lately, Eli. I can't say I favor it none."

"You don't, do ya?"

"No sir, I can't honestly say I do. And besides, it don't fit well for the man I've known all these years to go talkin' that way. I expect you got plenty of good adventures left in ya before you're done with this life."

"I hope you're right, John. I reckon seein' that horse yesterday and knowin' what I'll soon find for lookin' just finally got to me. Yes, by golly, you're right. There's no cause to be so tenebrous."

"So what?"

"So gloomy, John."

"Gloomy. Yes, sir. No need I can see to be that way."

"Okay, enough chitchat. Let's hit the trail."

Marshal Carson swung his legs off the desktop and let his boots drop to the floor in one fluid motion. He rose from his chair and drank the last of the now cold coffee.

He set the dented tin cup back on his desk and looked over at his other deputy, Jimmy Johnson, who sat quietly on a chair in the corner of the office.

"Don't trust nothin' Red tells ya, ya hear, Jimmy?"

Jimmy was the quietly dependable and capable sort, often left in charge of watching over prisoners while John and Carson went off on their adventures hunting down and transporting criminals around the territory.

Although as affable as Deputy Slims, Jimmy displayed little tolerance for men of desperate and corrosive natures. He winked a lot at the men behind the bars, but it was not a friendly wink. It was a purposeful reminder that while they were in his care, their lives were constantly in danger of being snuffed out.

"Not a worry, Marshal," replied Jimmy. "He'll be right here when you get back."

Red Darrington smirked. "Knowing that area we was in two days ago, you'll be lucky to make it back at all, Marshal — dead or alive." Red again graced all present with one of his cackles.

Carson turned stabbing eyes to Red. "You hush yer mouth, Red, or I'll by God and holy green grass hush it for ya."

Red quieted, knowing that his attempt at impetuousness was no match for the stark reality presented to him by Marshal Carson.

"Well, I was just sayin'," said Red.

"And I've just about had enough of yer *just sayin'*."

Carson fell silent, placed his hands on his hips, and stared down at the floor, calming himself.

After a bit, he raised his head and stared at the outlaw.

"How did ya lose that card game, Red?"

"He had a better hand."

"But *you* was the one doin' the cheatin'."

"I know that. I know that."

"But, Red, you was also doin' the dealin'."

"I know. I was there."

"Then how could you lose?"

"I gave him the wrong cards."

"I swear, Red, you ain't got the brains the Good Lord gave a peanut. I'm gonna send you straight to Sacramento for your trial on the first available stagecoach just as soon as I get back. And with you bein' wanted dead or alive, I shouldn't have to remind you how much easier on me it would be to ship yer carcass in a box out to Sacramento. For all yer smart-mouthin', I just might have the box strapped to the top of the coach and leave the lid off it so the buzzards can pick the eyes outa yer head along the way. Would you like that, Red?"

"No, sir. I don't believe I would."

"Are you gonna behave yerself, then?"

"Yes, sir.

Red Darrington sealed his lips. He pressed his back up against the cool brick, knowing it was the only thing in the county that would remain cool during the coming afternoon.

"Hopefully, we'll be back in four or five days at the most, Jimmy." Carson stared at Red as he spoke. "From the amount of blood I saw on the ground, whoever it was didn't get very far. I expect we'll come upon a body, or what might be left of it, sooner rather than later."

"Just worry about yerself, boss. Red and I will be just fine here." Jimmy winked at the prisoner. Red lowered his glance from the deputy and wisely, for once, offered no cackling response.

Marshal Carson picked up his saddlebags and tossed them over his shoulder.

"Okay, then. We'll be seein' ya, I reckon," he said, dreading the thought of going back out into the desert.

CHAPTER 3

Carson stepped out into the already sweltering early morning air. The heat from the sun just peeking over the horizon smacked him across the face like a hot frying pan.

"It's just dirty, darn bad luck, I'm sayin', John. That Red is about the dumbest outlaw I've ever run up against. He gets my blood to boilin'. But at the same time, his antics get me to chucklin' so much, I almost have to leave the room sometimes for fear he'll see me laughin' and take that as encouragement to continue."

He glanced up at the cloudless sky and shook his head.

"I'll tell ya, though, it's too darn hot for either."

"Good morning, Marshal Carson."

The sweet young female voice startled him. He didn't expect to hear such a tender and refined voice out here in the territory, so far from cultivated society — and certainly not this early in the day.

He turned his head and noticed the very pretty woman standing on the boardwalk across the street. She raised a hand in greeting and began walking toward him, replete with parasol and looking fresh as a cool morning in her bustled powder-blue dress, white ruffled shirt, blonde hair pulled back in a bun secured by a powder-blue hat, and bright blue eyes.

"Good mornin', Miss," he called back. "You're up early."

"Early bird catches the worm," she replied with a warm and bright smile as she continued crossing the street.

Carson chuckled. "I've never thought of myself as a worm before. A skunk perhaps, a scoundrel maybe, a tired old man for certain, but never a worm. But I see your point. And now that you've caught me, who might you be?"

"I might be your greatest jubilation or your worst tribulation."

"Oh, my! Sounds excitin'."

The young woman reached the boardwalk on the marshal's side of the street and stepped up onto it.

"Perhaps so, but I would hope that your final judgment regarding such might rest upon the consequences adjudged from the indomitability of your unrivaled potentiality. A conclusion, I hope, based upon the preponderance of evidence delivered *pour le dépliement de découverte*."

John had never seen a woman as pretty as this one. Her voice was like the voice of an angel sent down from on high, although she spoke in a song-like language unknown to him.

"Oh my," he said, eyeing her beauty appreciatively. "What's them funny words she just said?"

Carson patted him on the shoulder.

"It's French, John. It means *'for the unfoldin' of discovery.'* What she's sayin' is she hopes I'll arrive at a conclusion as to whether she has come as jubilation or tribulation based upon the unwrappin' of a mystery. I don't know what mystery she's referrin' to, but I'm excited to find out."

"She sure is pretty, Marshal."

"She is indeed, John. That's a fact." Carson was unable to take his eyes from the dazzling young woman who had come to a stop before him. "And she's a highly educated young woman, too."

"Why, what a kind compliment, Marshal. Thank you."

"And one well-earned, I'm sure. *Le dépliement de découverte*, indeed. Of course, in determining the most suitable technique of examining any theoretical supposition, one must necessarily disqualify any prejudicial attitude toward the elaborated methodology itself, requiring an extended period of consideration."

"Indeed," the young woman replied with a grand smile.

"And, of course," Carson continued, "any presented evidence, despite the preponderance, or lack thereof, may influence my reaching a considered opinion regarding the eventual veracity of such a provisionary conclusion."

"Oh my stars," said John. "They got their own language goin' on."

"Indeed again, Marshal." The young woman continued. "Let us then immediately undertake the discussion essential to defining the limits of any exclusionary measures regarded as uncomplimentary to such evidentiary procedures necessary to effect the undertaking of an appropriate investigation."

"What the *heck* did she just say?" asked John.

"She hopes I'll like her and she would like to discuss us takin' on an investigation."

"Why didn't she just say that?"

"She did, John. She just said it real pretty."

"So this is business then?"

"I think so, John."

"It's difficult for me to be sure, Marshal."

"At times, appropriate business stratagems are the most difficult to construct," said the young woman, "but also the most rewarding if managed properly to their conclusion. Wouldn't you agree, Marshal?"

Carson chuckled, then bowed to the young woman and smiled.

"I would, Miss. Please step into my office. I would be most delighted to discuss your stratagems with you."

Carson continued chuckling as the young woman nodded gracefully, passed him, and stepped through the doorway.

"I can't rightly say for sure," said John, "because I didn't understand but a word or two, but I do believe you two was havin' some fun with each other. Am I right about that?"

"We were, John. We were. And I do believe this might turn out to be some kind of an adventurous and wonderful day after all."

"Might be, if I can survive the conversation."

The young woman walked around the office until she stopped and studied the contents of the bookshelf behind the marshal's desk.

"Where did you get your education, Miss...?"

"Lizzie May Allen, Marshal. And that would be Smith College, in Northampton, Massachusetts. I graduated two years ago."

"You're college educated?" asked the marshal. "My, my, I haven't ever spoken with a college woman before."

"Well, Marshal, although more often than not we are beset by the prevailing primordial attitude of most men, there are some women in this country who are possessed of higher ambitions than simply making dinner and making babies."

"Darn it all, Miss Allen, ain't you just delightful."

"Thank you, Marshal. But perhaps, out of respect for your deputy's sanity, we should dispense with any further illusions of pretense."

Carson chuckled.

"Well, Miss Allen, while it's true that eloquent words are not currently counted among his many strengths, John is one of the most capable deputies I've ever had. And there's no one I trust more. This other deputy here is Jimmy Johnson. An equally capable man."

Jimmy removed his hat.

"Howdy, ma'am. Marshal's right. You sure do talk pretty."

"Thank you, Mister Johnson." Lizzie nodded politely. "Pleased to make your acquaintance."

She turned her eyes back to John.

"John, is it, sir? John what?"

Holding his hat to his chest with both hands, the deputy stepped forward and smiled. "John Kevin Slims, ma'am. It's an honor to make yer acquaintance."

"It's an honor to make yours as well, Mister John Kevin Slims," Lizzie answered with a sparkling smile.

"Aw, shucks, ma'am. Ain't no need to go callin' me mister. Most folks around these parts just call me John or Slims, or deputy. I reckon any of those would do nicely, comin' from you."

"Then John it is. Please call me Lizzie, John."

"Yes, ma'am…ah…Lizzie, I mean. That'd be just fine. Thank you, ma'am."

Red Darrington stood up and moved to the bars of his cell with a lascivious grin and lips parted to utter a salacious comment.

Carson pointed his finger sternly at the outlaw.

"Stagecoach top, buzzards."

Red got the message immediately and returned to his bunk, silent as a mouse.

Carson's attention returned to Lizzie.

"Stagecoach top, buzzards? My, Marshal. I do believe there's an interesting story there somewhere."

"You have no idea, Miss. Well, now that you've forever captured the hearts of my deputies, as well as that no-account scoundrel's, how, may I ask, did you hear about me?"

"From His Honor Wallace P. Perry, Territorial Judge in Gallup, New Mexico."

"I see. And how is Judge Perry?"

"Bristle Bottom is doing just fine and asked me to say hello to you for him."

Marshal Carson laughed for several seconds before continuing.

"Bristle Bottom! I haven't heard him called that in ages."

"My father and he were childhood friends. It was my father who gave him the nickname."

"You don't say."

"Bristle Bottom?" asked John, wide eyed. "You call a judge Bristle Bottom? Right to his face?"

"I do," replied Lizzie.

"My word."

"How'd he get the nickname?" asked Carson.

"According to my father, he got the name from accidentally sitting on a porcupine when he was a young boy. It bristled his bottom pretty thoroughly, apparently."

"I'll be. I heard of 'em. Porcupines, that is. Ain't never seen one, though. Where was this?"

"Where I grew up. In Massachusetts."

"Son of a gun," said Carson. "I didn't know he was from up yonder. I had wondered how he got that name, though. Miss Allen, you're a pure delight."

"He had many good things to say about the *philosopher* marshal, too."

Carson laughed.

"Philosopher marshal? Did he call me that?"

"He certainly did. He said you were one of the best marshals that ever existed. He also said you had a quote, unquote 'special spark for living and the brightest mind to see it through to a glorious conclusion.'"

"Well, I don't know if that's true. I think he was just bein' over-generous with his words. But now, what might I do for you, young lady?"

"My brother is missing. I'd like to hire you to find him. Judge Perry said to ask *you* about it."

"I see. Did he forget to mention my status as a U.S. Deputy Marshal and not a Pinkerton detective?"

"He did not."

"I see. Well, I am sorry to disappoint you after such a munificent endorsement from old Bristle Bottom, but I have important territorial duties to perform. In fact, we was just goin' out yonder into the desert on an investigation when you fortuitously arrived to delay our departure."

Lizzie noticed the hat on the marshal's desk — the one he had found in the desert two days earlier. She gasped.

"Dear me! That's his hat!" She moved quickly toward it. She picked it up and turned it over, studying it.

"This is Billy's hat, Marshal! Do you know where my brother is?"

"Billy, you say? Your brother's name is Billy?" asked Carson. "Oh, dear Lord. Please, Miss Allen, take a chair for a moment, won't ya? I'm afraid I've got some bad news."

Lizzie dropped into the chair, still studying the hat, while Carson sat down on his desktop.

"Ain't no way I can put it any gentler. That's where we're headin'. There's a dead horse out yonder on the trail, Miss Allen. And there was a bad blood trail leadin' away from the horse. I have to tell ya, there was a significant amount of blood — a fatal-lookin' amount, I'm afraid."

"What makes you think it might be my brother?"

"The blood trail led me to an outcrop of rock, where I found the hat."

"Did you find his body?"

"No, ma'am. That's why John and I are headin' out to the site. We're gonna do our best to find it. You're welcome to stay here in town until we get back. Shouldn't take more than four or five days, I expect. No more than six for sure."

"I'll be going with you, Marshal."

"I'm afraid that's not possible, Miss Allen."

"Call me Lizzie, please. And I'm going with you. I have to find him."

"Ain't no place out there for a fine young woman like yourself. I'm afraid I have to insist on you stayin' here."

"Don't you be fooled by my fancy speech and fine clothing, Marshal. I was raised on a farm with three brothers. I was the youngest child. I can shoot and ride as well as any man — better than some, in fact. I'm going, and that's that. If you'll give me some time to change, I'll purchase a suitable mount and equipment, and we'll be on our way."

"A farm ain't the desert, Miss Allen. There's things out there that can kill ya dead in minutes."

"And if they're not careful, I'll kill *them* faster than that."

John began to chuckle.

"It ain't funny, John," said Carson.

"I ain't laughin' at the circumstance, Marshal. It's just that I'm understandin' everything bein' said now."

Lizzie chuckled.

"What education do you have, John?"

"Well, ma'am, I got through the sixth grade all right, I reckon. Had a little trouble with my learnin' past that point. No matter, though. Had to quit anyway. Pa needed me on the farm."

"And you never went back to school?"

"I tried, but by the time I could go back, the teacher said I was too old for learnin' any more of my words and numbers."

"That's a shame, John."

"It's okay. Like the marshal says, can't everyone be smart, else you won't know who the smart ones are.'"

"I suppose, in some strange way, that makes sense. But I expect you have other gifts that those who can read don't possess."

"Yes, ma'am. I reckon I might."

"Learning to read is easy John. I'd be pleased to teach you to read."

"That's a mighty kind offer, ma'am. I'd like that very much. Thank you, ma'am."

"Lizzie, John. Call me, Lizzie."

"Yes, Lizzie, ma'am."

Lizzie chuckled.

"We'll have to work on that, John."

"Yes, ma'am. Thank ya, ma'am...Lizzie."

She turned her attention back to Carson.

"I'm registered at the hotel. I'll change my clothing and we can be off within the hour."

"Miss Allen."

"Lizzie, Marshal. Please."

"Miss Allen, you're not goin' out there with us. I'm sorry, but it'll be close quarters. It wouldn't be proper, you travelin' out into the desert with two men you just met, in the first place. In the second place, it's too hard, hot, and dangerous if you ain't mindful of life in the desert. And third, and I do apologize for my *primordial attitude*, but we don't have the means to entertain a woman's ways out there. It's hard enough on us menfolk. The facilities of an arid desert are not meant for a woman's delicate sensibilities or necessities. If you catch my drift."

"I just told you how I was raised, Marshal. Now, if you're afraid I'll show you both up, well, I apologize, but that isn't my problem. I am going. He's my brother, and I *will* help find him."

"Ma'am," said John, "I don't mean to be rude about this, but he might be et up a bit. He's been out there at least a coupla nights now, and you know them desert critters..."

"John, you're a very kind soul, but I'm well aware of what condition his body might be in if he's dead. I've seen my share of blood and things eaten. I'm not as fragile as that. I'm not one to come apart over such things."

"Miss Allen," said Carson, "I understand you might be harder than you look, but it's *my* investigation and I'm afraid I can't have you out there with us. Stay at the hotel. We'll go find your brother and bring his body back. And make no mistake about it. He's dead. The amount of blood I saw out there, it can't be no other end for him. I'm sorry."

"You can't stop me from searching for my brother, Marshal."

"You're right about that, I reckon, but you won't be travelin' with us. And that's final."

CHAPTER 4

The sapping heat of the long day had Carson and John tuckered out.

Their horses were hobbled and the men lay on the ground, their saddles under their heads. Except for the blaze of the campfire, darkness had engulfed them, and the eerie sounds of desert night life offered only a disquieting rest.

John awoke with a start, sniffing at the air. He glanced over at Carson. In the glare of the campfire, he saw the old marshal laid out on his back, the fingers of his hands interlaced over his chest, snoring loudly, completely unaffected by the unnerving night noises.

The hellish heat had been particularly hard on the marshal. He hadn't even felt like eating supper, which would have consisted only of a piece of jerky and a hard biscuit anyway. It was all he could do to set his saddle and blanket down on the ground as his bed and bid his deputy good night before passing out.

"Marshal?" whispered John, rising to a sitting position.

There was no response from Carson, just his continued rhythmic snoring.

"Eli…Eli. Wake up, Eli."

The marshal didn't stir. John picked up a small stone and tossed it over the tops of the dancing flames of their campfire and struck Carson in the chest. That awakened the marshal with a jolt.

He bolted up into a sitting position, drawing his revolver. "Wha...what?" he mumbled.

"Eli...do you smell it?"

"Smell what?" replied Carson, his head still partially steeped in slumber.

"Take a whiff, darn it all. Do you smell it?"

Carson sniffed at the air.

"I do now. Smells of smoke."

"Heck smoke. It smells of somethin' cookin'."

"You're right, John. Someone's cookin' somethin' nearby. We best have us a look."

They crouched low and moved toward the enticing aroma. As they neared, they heard the light crackle of a fire and could see a flickering orange light reflecting off the rocks around the end of a large boulder.

They crept closer until a voice called out.

"Supper's ready, boys. Are you going to skulk about amongst those rocks in the dark, or are you going to eat?"

The marshal and John cut each other a surprised look as they straightened up and walked around the boulder to find Lizzie May

Allen, attired in men's clothing, her hat slung on her back. She was sitting on a rock near a campfire, dishing food from a large pot onto a metal plate.

"What the heck?" said John.

"Hello, John," said Lizzie. "Are you hungry?"

She held out the plate and a fork.

"Oh, my! Yes, ma'am, I surely am." John took the plate from her hand and raised it up to his nose to take in the seasoned fragrance.

"Mmmm. My, oh my! Smells wonderful."

"Good. Sit down and eat, then. How about you, Marshal?"

"I'll be," said Carson. "How did…"

"Mister Johnson at the livery stable in town. He set me up with the full rig."

"Lordy, that smells good. What is it?"

"Well, Marshal, I didn't have a lot of time to prepare, so you'll have to settle for fried potatoes and rattlesnake, but it's properly seasoned and it should fill you up."

"Rattlesnake?" asked John. "Where did you…"

"They hunt at night, John. It wasn't hard to find him…or is it her? I'm not sure which it is, but no matter. Call it supper now."

Lizzie dished up another plate and handed it to Carson.

"Okay, Miss Allen," said the marshal, taking the plate from her. "I can admit it. You whupped us. You whupped us fair and square. But how did you track us all the way out here? We left long before you did."

"If you reasoned yourself to be a man of stealth, Marshal, let me set you straight on that point. You're not. You left a trail a blind man could follow."

"But you had to arrive long after us. How did you get your camp set up so fast?" The marshal rolled his eyes at the fine flavor and smell as he shoved a forkful of food into his mouth.

"When you're out hunting with baby brothers whining about their empty bellies, you learn to set up camp quickly."

"I thought you said you was the youngest."

Her eyelids fluttered. Carson noticed, but he made no comment.

"I am, but most men act like children at times — especially my brothers."

Carson laughed.

"Okay, okay. I had that comin'."

"You did, sir."

Morning arrived on time for itself, but it came much too early for Marshal Carson. He and John had moved their horses and equipment to Lizzie's campsite very late the night before. After a compelling and exhaustive campfire conversation, Carson fell asleep, but he hadn't gotten all the sleep his aging body needed.

He stirred a moment, moaning with the realization that he had to get up and back on his horse and trudge through the building heat of the new desert morning.

"'*A sleeping man lives no adventures*,'" said Lizzie, seated on a rock in front of a blazing campfire, scrambling eggs in a frying pan.

"Do adventurous dreams count?" Carson asked with a yawn, his eyes still closed.

"No," she replied. "'*Adventures dreamed are not adventures lived.*'"

"That's true, I s'pose. But a very wise man once said that '*a well-rested man is able to more fully appreciate his adventures.*'"

"Oh, really?"

"Well, I ain't sure if he was a wise man or just a tuckered-out old man."

"I see. And just who might that be?"

"Me."

Lizzie giggled.

"I thought as much. But how about this? '*A man resting too long gets buried.*'"

Carson chuckled as he rolled over and sat up. He forced his eyes open and smiled at Lizzie.

"I get the point."

He yawned again. Then he sniffed at the air, which was filled with the aroma of biscuits, bacon, and eggs. He smiled.

"I swear, Miss Allen, I could wake up each and every mornin', from here on out to my end, to that smell. … Is them *eggs* I smell?"

"It is."

"Cookin' in bacon grease?"

"Bacon getting crisper by the second."

"Where did you get eggs out here?"

"Do you really want to know?"

"No, not really. Smells great, though."

"Did you know that your snoring sounds like growling, Marshal?"

Carson chuckled again as he got up slowly from his blanket.

"Yes, ma'am. I'm afraid I've heard that many a time before. My apologies," he said, shaking the feeling back into his aching legs.

"Well, it's better than a fire at keeping critters away at night. I'll say that for it."

"I regret it if I kept you awake with my indecorous sleepin' habits."

"Please, Marshal, next to my brothers and my father, you were silent as a lamb. Now, how much farther do we have to go today?"

"We should be at the horse by noon or so."

Marshal Carson shook his legs again to assure himself that indeed blood was flowing through his veins and arteries. He was about to nudge John awake with the tip of his boot when Lizzie held up her hand to stop him.

"Please, Marshal. Let him sleep for now. I was hoping that we might engage in a sequestered conversation for just a while longer."

"Certainly, Miss Allen."

Lizzie filled a plate with biscuits, bacon, and eggs and handed it to the marshal. He took it and sat down next to her on the rock.

"I thought you a woman of broader ambitions than cookin' meals."

"I am, but I have to eat, too, you know. And I can't very well count on you two to do it right, now can I?"

Carson chuckled.

"You *are* a mystery, Miss Allen. A grand, illustrious, and ever-changin' one, to be sure. But a mystery just the same."

"One of the charms of being a woman, Marshal."

"Yes, ma'am. I hear ya."

"It's going to get mighty tiresome, you calling me ma'am or Miss Allen all the time. Can you please just call me Lizzie?"

"I'll try. But I'm old and cantankerously set in my ways. It's difficult for a man like me to change."

"No need to be so negative."

Carson smiled.

"Truly said. My apologies. But I'm a man of hardened ways."

"My father was, too."

"Well, my hardened ways have led to many mistakes, so I reckon you could say I'm a man of many mistakes as well, Miss Allen. That's just the truth of it. And we all have to live with our mistakes for a lifetime, don't we?"

"I suppose so. But you don't seem to be a man of many mistakes, Marshal."

Carson smirked.

"If only that were true."

"Okay. Tell me, then. What mistakes do *you* have to live with?"

"What mistakes do I have to live with?" Carson repeated, filling his mouth with a bite of biscuit. "All of 'em, Miss Allen. The mighty and tiny alike. All of 'em I made while I've walked my path through this life. Now, I reckon history will have to judge my mistakes as bein' noteworthy or not. But as I see it, my only real duty, the real duty of anyone, is to continue to walk my path in the hope that I'll learn how to make fewer mistakes as I go."

"You're an enlightened man. I suppose it's true that we all have to live with our failings for a lifetime. And I also suppose that that is the ultimate purpose of learning. But I suspect, Marshal, that you've put many of your mistakes well behind you by now."

"Hardly, but the way I figure it, it's all about what ya do with the learnin'. If ya have the knowledge and fail to act on it, all learnin' comes to nothin' but a big maybe. And in this world,

Miss Allen, maybe don't get ya nothin' but maybe."

"Perhaps on the outer skin of it, that might seem true. But I believe that simply acting on knowledge isn't enough. If you apply your learning absent a definitive purpose or goal, or simply apply what you've learned in the wrong direction, you can fail as dramatically as doing nothing."

"That's true enough, I reckon."

"My daddy used to tell me that a goal without a plan is like a fart in a windstorm. It has little chance of surviving the breeze."

"Oh, dear."

"Pardon me, Marshal. Raised in a family with four men, remember?"

Carson chuckled.

"Yes, ma'am. I do recall."

"Marshal, I have another observation I'd like you to comment on, if you will."

"Sure. What is it?"

"You seem to be an educated man. I find myself wondering why you choose to speak so colloquially, as if you lack an education. Why is that?"

"I have no formal education to speak of, Miss Allen. Not college learned, like you. But I read a lot. And I know lots of pretty words and their meanin's. But I don't like usin' them around most folks. If I do, I come off soundin' high minded, and I don't fancy doin' that. It's been my experience that most folks don't take kindly to them that knows more than they do. So sometimes seeming dumber is the smarter thing to do."

"You *are* very wise. I understand completely. An educated woman seems to horrify most men."

Carson laughed.

"Yes, ma'am. That is the truth."

"Why do you think that is?"

"I don't reckon there's much mystery to it. An educated woman is difficult to control and manipulate."

Lizzie chuckled.

"Exactly, Marshal. Tell me something else, please. Why aren't you married?"

"An educated man is difficult to control and manipulate, too."

Lizzie laughed. "Okay, I had that coming."

Carson chuckled.

"I've always tried to convince myself that I wasn't the stay-at-home kind of man that most womenfolk look for in husbands. But the naked truth of it is this. I'm better at dealin' with outlaws than I am at dealin' with the suffocatin' needs of a woman."

Carson grinned as he continued. "Besides that, I can shoot an outlaw if they rile me too much."

Lizzie burst into laughter. After she settled down, she looked into Carson's eyes.

"You're everything Judge Perry said about you, and more. But it seems to me you could be so much more than what you are at present. A judge also, perhaps."

"Oh my, not me. I ain't judge material. And I'm too old to go changin' my ways now."

"If you don't mind me asking, how old are you, Marshal?"

"I'm fifty feeling like eighty."

"You're a young-looking man for your age, Marshal."

"Why, thank you, Miss Allen. In fact, just yesterday a rock said I looked younger than dirt. Dirt, however, was incensed by the rock's comment."

Lizzie laughed again.

Carson continued to shovel food into his mouth.

Then she became serious.

"Can I trust you, Marshal?"

"Miss Allen, my age alone should answer that question."

"Oh?"

"Yes, ma'am. A man doesn't get to be my age unless people trust him. The untrustworthy don't usually make it this far in life."

"Ah. I suppose you're right about that as well."

"Is there somethin' you need to tell me?"

"Maybe, Marshal. But for now, we'd better wake John up and get his belly filled too before we move out."

She looked up at the cloudless sky, pink with the coming sunrise.

"It's going to be another hot one, I think."

"Yes, ma'am. That's normal for these parts at this time of year. And where we're goin' ain't gonna be any cooler. It's just dirty, darn bad luck, I'm sayin'."

CHAPTER 5

The Dead River wash was a slow, arduous thirty-mile ride northeast of Holbrook toward the lower foothills of the eastern canyonlands.

Thirty miles was not normally far for a horse ride, but the scarcity of both water and shade made any trek across its crumbling surface all the more intimidating. Anyone who wasn't intimidated was usually dead or dying.

In the already unbearable swelter of the early morning, Marshal Carson's bandana was soaked to dripping, but he wrung it out and wiped his face with it just the same, knowing it wouldn't be the last time.

"It's just dirty, darn bad luck, I'm sayin'," he mumbled, swaying in his saddle to the rhythmic saunter of his horse.

John heard the marshal's remark and ignored it. He had heard those words from the marshal's mouth countless times, and he'd always guessed they were meant for no one in particular and didn't require a response.

He wiped his own face as well and then glanced at Lizzie May Allen, riding easily on her mount. She was a tough one; she showed no sign of weariness or discomfort from the heat or the saddle. John was impressed.

His thoughts returned to the marshal.

"So tell me, Eli. What kinda adventure was you thinkin' on when we was last discussin' it?"

"I don't know exactly, John. But this one ain't come to resemble anythin' like I had in mind."

John Slims chuckled.

"No, I reckon it ain't. But if ya *could* go on an adventure of yer own choosin', what would ya like it to be?"

"Well, somethin' memorable, I reckon. Yes, sir, somethin' that the memory of it will stay bright and shiny in my mind's eye when I'm in my rockin' chair on the porch. How 'bout you, John?"

"Treasure, of course!"

"You'd like a treasure-seeking adventure?" asked Lizzie.

"Yes, ma'am, I would. Been a fancy of mine ever since I was a youngin'. Don't remember where I got the notion of it, but I still have dreams of findin' me a long-lost treasure sometimes. Is that a crazy thing to say?"

"No crazier, I suppose, than any other adventure."

"Speakin' of treasure, John," said the marshal, "I heard tell the Spanish conquistadors hid gold somewhere around these parts. Well, more to the truth, it was them Jesuit priests that hid the gold."

"Priests? You mean the prayin' kind?"

"The very same."

"Don't that beat all. How long ago was that?"

"Oh, heck. Some say that was back in the 1600s. Some say it was long before that, maybe even back in the early 1500s."

"Give me a moment to think on that a bit, Eli. You say it was 1600? It's 1880 now, so that would make it…well…"

"Don't hurt yourself, John. It was a long time ago. Just leave it at that."

"I reckon that would be best. Workin' numbers makes my head ache."

Lizzie chuckled. "We'll have to teach you more about numbers, too."

"That would be nice," replied John.

"Anyway," continued Carson, "I heard it said that the priests got ordered out of the territory by the Spanish king. He wasn't happy that them holy fellas was stingy about sendin' him his fair share of the gold. Well, sir, them boys grew a mite ornery about havin' to leave such a rich land behind. So before they left the area, they buried the gold in different parts of the territory. And they took the knowledge of the locations with 'em when they left."

"They didn't leave no map?"

"No, John. There ain't a map nowhere to be found. At least none I ever heard of."

"Ain't that somethin'. So you're sayin' there might be gold stashes somewhere out here?"

"That's what I'm sayin'. If them stories is true. It'd be somethin' to find, I reckon."

"So, could that be your great adventure, too? Trackin' down a gold stash?"

"No, John, I'm too old to go searchin' through these mountains for that sorta thing. My old bones is havin' a hard enough time in this saddle."

"How do you think someone goes about startin' a treasure-huntin' adventure, Eli?"

"I can't rightly say. I reckon that's why we're out here trackin' down a dead body, 'cause we don't know how to start a better adventure."

"How 'bout you, Miss Allen? What sorta adventure would you like?"

"To be honest, John, I haven't ever given it any thought. And right now I'm more concerned about my brother."

"Of course you are," said Carson. "I do apologize for our lack of propriety and compassion."

"No need to apologize, Marshal. It's my concern, not yours."

"Not true, Miss Allen. Findin' the killer or killers is among my highest priorities. And I intend to find him, or them, if they can be found."

"I appreciate that, Marshal. I really do. But it's my father that I'm really worried about. He's not in good health. I fear that the revelation of my brother's demise might have a terminating effect on him."

"If you don't mind me askin', what was he doin' out this way, your brother?"

"We were supposed to meet in Holbrook two days ago. When he didn't show up, I became worried."

"I ain't pryin', you understand, but why was you meetin' out this way?"

"I can't tell you that right now, Marshal."

"Why is that, Miss Allen?"

Lizzie's eyelids fluttered and then she stared vacantly.

"Miss Allen?"

"Yes?"

"I asked why you can't tell me the reason you and your brother was intendin' on meetin' out this way."

Lizzie's eyes turned toward Carson. She blinked and smiled as her gaze focused.

"Because I don't know myself the reason why. My brother sent me a telegram to meet him in Holbrook with all due haste and that he would explain more after we met up."

"Well, that's mighty intriguin'."

"Intriguing, yes, but I'm concerned about why he didn't show up."

"Yes. That's troublin'. May I suggest then that we err on the side of caution and proceed carefully until we discover the truth of the matter?"

"Agreed, Marshal."

As Marshal Carson had predicted, it was about noon when they came upon the horse carcass. Also, as predicted, it had been half devoured by a variety of desert creatures. What was left was a mess and hardly resembled a horse anymore.

Marshal Carson reined his horse to a stop next to the carcass and peered down at it.

"I expect your brother's body to be in a similar condition by the time we find it. Best prepare yourself, Miss Allen."

"I already have, Marshal."

Carson touched the sides of his horse with his boot heels and steered it along the path toward the large outcrop of rock where he had discovered the hat next to the dead tree three days before.

Within minutes they were there. Carson stopped his horse and slid down off the saddle, dropping the reins to the ground.

He walked around the outcrop, searching for any marks. None were immediately in sight.

"Is this where you found the hat?" asked Lizzie.

"Yes, ma'am. It was just layin' there." Carson pointed to the spot where he had found the hat.

"I don't see any blood, Marshal."

"There ain't none, Miss Allen. Weren't no blood here the other day, neither."

"There ain't no shortage of it trailin' over to here, Marshal," said John.

"I know. It's like he got to here and just stopped bleedin' altogether. Peculiar, ain't it? Mighty peculiar."

"Maybe he patched himself up after he got this far."

"Sounds reasonable to me, John. But where did he go from here? Look for more crawl marks. With this much blood loss, I don't see how he rose up and walked anywhere. But he left this rock headin' in some direction, that's for sure."

John Slims and Lizzie Allen slid down to the ground and dropped their reins into the sand as they began a slow walk around the area. Their eyes mimicked the marshal's in searching for any clue as to what had become of the man who had worn the hat.

John discovered a small length of rope that had been cut. He picked it up as possible evidence. But it was Marshal Carson who spotted the footprints in the sand just off the edge of the rock outcrop to the south.

"Over here!" he shouted. "I see it, but I ain't believin' it. He walked away — ran, even."

They retrieved the reins to their horses and led them along the path of the footprints for a couple hundred yards and passed a large boulder before coming to a sudden stop.

Their search was over.

The man's body lay facedown in the sand. His head was turned to his right. His eyes were gone — pecked out by birds — and the body had several other gnaw marks on it.

All in all, though, it wasn't as bad as Marshal Carson had expected. He reasoned that the horse was more appetizing to the larger critters than the young fellow was.

Lizzie came upon the body and stared down at it.

"It's my brother. It's Billy," she said, tears filling her eyes.

"I'm real sorry to hear that," said Carson.

Lizzie knelt down beside the body. She placed her hand on its back and sobbed.

John walked around the area for several minutes and then stopped.

"How could he run this far from the rock? I don't see how, myself. Not with all that blood loss. It just don't seem possible."

Carson, still studying the body, spotted marks on the man's wrists.

"Look there, at his wrists. He was tied."

"Prob'ly with this," said John, holding out the piece of rope he'd picked up.

"Where did you find that?"

"Back at the rock."

"Yes, sir. That makes sense."

John walked to the body.

"It does. But Marshal, how did he make it all the way over here? That's a long way to run, bled out like he was. And there ain't no blood trail out to here. That don't figure at all."

"It *is* a mystery, John. And not one to pleasantly cogitate on."

"To what?"

"To enjoy thinkin' on."

"No, sir. Not pleasant at all."

The back of the man's shirt was stained completely red. A large hole just left of the spine looked like an exit wound.

"Forgive me, Miss Allen," said Carson as he dropped to one knee. "I don't mean to be indelicate, but I'm gonna have to turn the body over."

Lizzie stood up and stepped away, still sobbing and mumbling softly to herself.

"Billy, Billy, Billy. What happened to you, dear brother?"

Carson patted the corpse's back.

"It's just dirty, darn bad luck, I'm sayin'."

"Yes, sir. Bad luck for sure," repeated John.

Carson slowly rolled the body over. The pool of blood had soaked into the desert floor directly beneath it. After wiping away the bugs and spiders that had collected in the bloody bullet hole, he was reassured that the wound in the back was an exit wound. The front of the man's shirt was just as blood-soaked. The Marshal parted the shirt and took note of the bullet hole.

"Forty-four forty, I'd say. One shot. Well, John, we got us a murder investigation for sure. Darn it all. It's just dirty, darn bad luck, I'm sayin'."

"Marshal," said Lizzie. "Could I have a moment alone with my brother, please?"

Carson stood up.

"Certainly, Miss Allen. Of course you can. John, let's you and I step away and allow Miss Allen her chance to do some grievin' in private."

"Sure thing, Marshal. Miss Allen, I do co...co...commiserate with yer loss, ma'am."

"Thank you, John."

"Well said, John," said Carson. "That was very eloquent."

"That means nice, right?"

"Close enough, John."

"It's a long hike for me, but I'm gettin' there, Eli."

The two lawmen stepped around the nearby boulder as Lizzie knelt beside her brother's body and began mumbling again.

"Well, Eli," said John, "you're right. This ain't the kinda adventure I had in mind either."

"No, sir. It sure ain't."

John peeked around the boulder to see Lizzie searching the body and going through the corpse's clothing. But he didn't think it odd enough to say anything to Marshal Carson. He stepped back and shook his head.

"Ain't a good thing, findin' yer kin in this fashion."

"No, it surely ain't. I'd hate to find *my* brother this way."

"I didn't know you had a brother, Eli."

"I don't, John. I was just sayin' I'd hate to find my brother this way if I *had* a brother."

"Ah, got it. Yes, sir. That would not be a good thing."

Lizzie stepped around the rock. She had stopped crying and was calm.

"Thank you, Marshal. My grieving is done. I appreciate the moment of privacy."

"Did ya find what you was lookin' for?" asked John.

Marshal Carson looked sharply at Lizzie.

"No, John. I'm afraid there was nothing left behind."

"You searched the body, Miss Allen?" asked Carson.

"I was hoping there might be a memento of his that I could bring back to my father. My father would have liked something from his youngest son. But alas, he'll just have to get along without anything tangible to remember his son by."

"So you didn't find anything on the body?"

"Nothing, Marshal. How sad it is to die with nothing, don't you think?"

"Yes, ma'am. Truly a shame. Your brother had little in the world, I take it?"

"He left home with nothing, Marshal. I suppose it's also what he achieved in his shortened life and will take with him into the next life — nothing. My father will take this news hard, I'm afraid."

"I reckon so," said Carson.

The three walked back to the body. Carson pulled a folded tarp from the packhorse and spread it out next to the body.

"Well, John, let's get what's left of him into the tarp and strap him to the packhorse. I'll take the arms. You take the ankles."

John did as he was told and gripped the ankles hard. Then he yelped.

"I'm bit!" he said, rubbing a spot on his left hand.

"What got ya, John?"

"I don't know, but I got a puncture. Maybe a scorpion. But where did it go? I don't see it."

"Let me see your hand."

John showed the wound to the marshal. Carson studied it for a few seconds and then shook his head.

"You wasn't bit, John. You was poked. Check his cuffs."

John reached down and turned the man's pant cuffs down. He gently ran his hand over the material and discovered something hard and sharp.

"Lookie here, Marshal. You was right. There's somethin' in his cuff."

John pulled out his knife and slit the stitching in the cuff and then gasped as a rough-shaped, stamped gold coin-like object fell to the ground. He picked it up and again pricked his finger.

"Ouch! Son of a gun got me again."

He stared at it in awe and then looked up at Carson.

"It's gold, Marshal! Pure gold!"

"Let me see it, John."

The deputy carefully handed the oddity to Carson.

"That's what I was looking for, Marshal. May I have it, please?"

"You was lookin' for this?"

"Yes. My father gave it to him just before he left home. May I have it, please?"

"Just a moment, Miss Allen. Let me have a look at it."

"There's really nothing to see. It's just a keepsake given to him by my father."

"Yes, ma'am. You said that."

Carson turned it over and over, studying it. It was coin-like, but cut in half in a zigzag fashion. The cut edge was rough, resulting in sharp points at the ends of the cut.

"Sure is odd lookin', ain't it?" asked Carson. "I've never seen anything like it before."

"And you won't ever again," said Lizzie. "It's one of a kind. My father made it himself. Now, may I have it, please?"

Carson held onto it.

"What do these strange markin's on it mean?"

"My father didn't say. He just made it that way."

"It looks to be the opposite of another. Where's the other half?"

The young woman's eyes fluttered a second and then she smiled at Carson.

"My father has it. He said it would never be whole until Billy brought his half of it back home."

"He favored your brother, did he?

"If a father can have favorites, Billy was his."

"I imagine that stung a bit, huh?"

"My father never left any of his children wanting, Marshal. It's just that Billy lit up his face more than the rest of us."

"I wonder if that's what got him murdered."

"I hardly think half of a small gold piece would be worth murdering someone for, Marshal. Now please, may I have it?"

Carson thought about it for a moment and then handed the object to Lizzie.

"I reckon you're right. It hardly seems worth killin' someone over."

"Thank you, Marshal. My father will appreciate the return of the keepsake."

"You might have told me about it before, though."

"I'm sorry. I didn't think it necessary. It's just a keepsake."

"I suppose so. Okay, John. Let's try this again."

"Marshal," said John, "I know I ain't the smart one here, but how did it get into the cuff of his pants?"

"I reckon he sewed it in."

"Why?"

"Do you have to ask? It's gold!"

"I get that, but why sew it into his pants?"

"To hide it from bandits, I suspect."

"But if it's only got a little value, why go to the trouble of hidin' it at all?"

"There are many forms of value, John," said Lizzie. "Although there's little monetary value in it, I think he recognized the sentimental value of it and didn't want to lose it or have it stolen by someone who didn't appreciate it the same way he did."

"Yes, ma'am. I reckon you're right about that. Makes sense now. Okay, Marshal, let's go."

CHAPTER 6

The chilly desert night had settled in upon them as they sat around a warming campfire.

"I'd rather we was on an adventure where they ain't no dead bodies," said Marshal Carson as he stared into his cup of hot coffee. "It just don't seem like a good adventure draggin' a body around with ya. No offense meant, Miss Allen."

"None taken, Marshal. I can't say this is fun for me either."

"Maybe this could become a good adventure if we changed our minds about it," said John.

"Well, ol' Ben Jonas told me that very thing the other day. I'm certain you're both right about that, if we lowered our expectations about any adventure we might embark upon. But I'd hate to do that, John. Havin' high expectations about an adventure is what makes it an adventure, in my mind. Lowerin' the expectations of it just cheapens the whole experience. But then again, there is a certain degree of uncertainty and happenstance anytime one embarks upon a journey into the unknown, I reckon."

"I reckon so, Eli."

"Besides that," continued Carson, pointing at the tarped body tied across the packhorse, "he's gettin' pretty ripe for *my* likin'. The sooner we get him back to town, the better. Livin' things don't last long out here in this wretched place, so I reckon it's fittin' that things not livin' don't last no time at all."

"But we're doin' a good thing, ain't we, Eli? I mean, it's a kindness we're doin' for him, not leavin' him out here to get all et up, ain't it?"

"I reckon so, John."

"Then maybe what we're doin' is a good sort of adventure in that respect."

"You're always seein' the good side of things, John. I think it's a wonderful talent you have. And you're right. Maybe this is a good thing we're doin' after all."

"Maybe doin' this might earn us a better adventure later on. I mean after we get him back to town, maybe a dandy adventure'll find us."

"You have a nice way about you, John," said Lizzie. "You make me feel good just being around you. Thank you."

"Welcome, Miss Allen. It's just my nature, I reckon."

"It's a good nature to have."

"Maybe you're right, John," said Carson. "Maybe a fine adventure will present itself one day. But I'm too darned old for most adventures anymore. I like to think on 'em now and then, though. It's a fondness I have. Books call it a *fantasy*. I reckon that's what my life has become now — a fantasy, an unattainable reality in this life."

"You know, Eli, you're talkin' more and more like you're gonna die soon. And I'm here to tell ya it ain't so. I reckon you got lots more life ahead of ya. So I'd appreciate it very much if you'd stop talkin' like that. Makes me mighty uncomfortable."

"I'm sorry, John. But I'm long past my prime for this kind of work. Ain't many men I know of worked this job as long as I have. But you're right, and I'm sorry. I don't mean to bring ya down with my continual penitential consternations."

"Now what does peni...peni... What the heck you sayin' now, Eli?"

"I don't mean to sound sorrowful, John."

"Then why don't you just say that?"

Marshal Carson and Lizzie burst into laughter. Finally Carson gathered himself and, wiping his eyes, said to his deputy, "Sorry, John."

"Darn it all, Eli. That's what I like most about ya. You're a smart man. And with Miss Allen here, well, I reckon I ain't never been around smarter people ever. I'd like to someday be just like you two. I even tried readin' some of the books on that shelf in your office. But tarnation if I can get but a few paragraphs into 'em before my eyes go blurry and my head goes to achin' from all them big words."

"I didn't know that, John."

"It ain't somethin' I'm proud of, Eli. Bein' around you makes me feel stupid and unworthy at times."

"It pains me to hear you talk like that, John. *'To read with diligence; not to rest satisfied with a light and superficial knowledge.'*"

"There you go again, Eli."

"Calm yourself, John. They're just fancy words for a simple idea, written by a Roman emperor by the name of Marcus Aurelius a very long time ago. An idea I believe to be a good, wise, and worthy goal for each of us."

"What the heck are you talkin' about, Eli?"

"He means," Lizzie interjected, "to simply read all you can, John, and never be satisfied knowing just a little bit about this world. Read and learn all you can about what's important and then use that knowledge to change yourself and the world around you if you can. To make it a better place, or at least one more fitting to live in for a time."

"Exactly," said Carson. "And keep learnin', John, until you know as much as possible about the world you live in. That's all them words mean. But how powerful is knowledge, John? How wondrous is it to know things that matter most?"

"How am I s'posed to answer questions like those? How can I learn what matters most when I don't understand the words I try to read?"

"Readin' words on a page is easy enough," said Carson. "That's just learnin' to read. *Understandin'* what you read, that can be difficult, and that's the same for a lot of folks. But nothin' is impossible if you have it in mind to succeed. Until you have the learnin', though, don't fret about it. *'For how should a man part with that which he hath not?'*"

"Is that somethin' from that Marcus guy again?"

Marshal Carson chuckled.

"Yes, John," interjected Lizzie again. "And it just means don't worry about what you don't have anyway. Learn what's important for you to live a good life. If you can do that, you'll do just fine and everything else will work itself out."

"Does this Marcus fella have a book?"

"He does," answered Carson. "And when we get back to town, you're welcome to it."

"Will ya help me with the big words, Eli?"

"I will," replied Lizzie. "I'd be honored to do so."

"That'll be just fine, Miss Allen. Yes, ma'am, that'll be just fine."

"Listen, John," said Carson. "I've been thinkin' for a good long while about somethin'. I think it's time I share them thoughts with ya.

When this investigation winds down to its inevitable conclusion, I think I'll make a change in my life. I believe I've had my fill of totin' dead bodies around. And to be honest, I think I've had my fill of bein' a lawman. I'm goin' lookin' for greener pastures and a slower life."

"Can't say I find fault with you for thinkin' like that, Eli. But I hope you'll change yer mind about it. I like workin' with ya."

"I like workin' with you, too, John. But I've been thinkin' on it a good long while. The events of the past days have only spurred me into takin' it more serious. I think it's time I move on before this changin' world tosses me off the ride to land someplace not of my own choosin'. Time is come that I get to retirin' and makin' tracks to that ol' rockin' chair."

"Well, I recall you talkin' about it some last year. But I thought you'd gotten such nonsense outa yer head back then. I can see them thoughts ain't left ya though. Now, I won't go to arguin' with you regardin' it. And I reckon I gotta accept your decision, but I don't have to like it none. And that's all I have to say about it."

"I didn't mean to rile ya, John, expressin' my thoughts on the matter like this. But I'm glad you're done talkin'. We need to get us some sleep pretty quick."

"Fine. Have it your way."

"Fine."

"Fine!"

The marshal sipped his coffee with a chuckle.

Deputy Slims awoke to the aroma of coffee brewing. He turned over and saw Lizzie Allen and Marshal Carson sitting by the fire, sipping from tin cups.

"How long you both been up?" he asked as he crawled out from under his blanket.

"Oh, an hour or so," answered Carson.

"The coffee smells good."

"Well, get yourself over here and have a cup."

"Think I will. So, what you two chattin' about now?"

"Just chattin'," said Carson.

"We've been talking about lots of different things," added Lizzie.

"Like what?"

"Nothin'," said Carson. "Everythin'. It's complicated."

"'Nothin'. Everythin'.' Don't tell me, then. I don't really wanna know. I was just bein' polite."

"Sorry, John," said Carson with a smile. "In the moment, we was just discussin' how we found her brother in the state he was in. It ain't been what you might call *good mornin'* conversation."

"Hold on, Eli. If you're gonna talk about that, I think I might need me a cup of coffee in my hands first. It's hard enough for my mind to keep up with you when it's fully awake."

Carson chuckled.

John walked over to the campfire, yawning. He grabbed the empty tin cup sitting on one of the fire pit rocks and poured himself a cup of coffee, then sat down across from Carson and Lizzie. He sipped the coffee, shook his head, and spit his mouthful of coffee out onto the ground.

"Lord almighty, I got sand in my mouth, my eyes, and my nose. And I think I could plant potatoes in my ears."

"It *did* end up a mite windy last night," said Carson. "Like I said before, this ain't a place that's kind to life. It's just a place that kills it dead and buries it over. I know I've only lived out here five years and maybe it's just I ain't got used to it yet, but I don't think I ever will. And quite frankly, I don't care for it none."

"I reckon that's true enough. So what about her brother?" asked John.

"I've just had some strange thoughts on the matter," said Carson, staring into the flames of their campfire.

John waited for Carson to continue. He didn't.

"Well, you gonna tell me about it, or am I s'posed to guess?"

"Sorry, John. Been thinkin' on him bein' tied up like he was."

"Why is that?"

"His hands was tied, and I find that mighty peculiar. How does a fella with his hands tied ride a horse all the way out to here?"

"Maybe they was tied in front and he had hold of the reins."

"Lizzie said those very words. But think about that. If you're gonna secure a man, would you put him on a horse and willin'ly give him control of it?"

"I see yer point. So you think his hands was tied behind him?"

"Makes more sense, don't it?"

"Yes, sir, I reckon it does."

"Then how did he get a horse all the way out here without bein' able to steer it?"

"Someone led his horse out here, I reckon."

"Exactly, John!"

"I see yer point on that, too. It *is* strange, now you mention it. So you're thinkin' he weren't alone out here?"

"Someone shot him, John. I reckon he weren't alone."

"I mean someone led him out here and then shot him?"

That's my guess. And stranger still is who cut him loose and why?"

"I ain't followin' you on that part."

"Why untie him at all? If you want him dead, just shoot him and leave him where he falls. No reason to untie him and then shoot him, is there?"

"None I can think of, Marshal."

"Unless it's some kind of sportin' thing. Give him a chance to run. Nah, that don't make sense either. He was shot right next to his horse."

"Right! That's right. Who you think did this, Marshal?"

"That, John, is part of the adventure of bein' a lawman, ain't it? And just the part I ain't gonna miss."

"I don't have a mind for investigatin' like you do."

"We all have our strengths and weaknesses, John. But I sense there's much more to this adventure than just a simple killin'. I expect we'll find somethin' much deeper. It's dark, I tell ya."

"Well, we got us a fire, and sunup will be here shortly."

Lizzie chuckled.

"Not talkin' about that kinda dark, John. I'm talkin' about people kinda dark. The kinda darkness that seeps into a person and eats the life out of 'em and leaves 'em with a troubled soul."

"Whew! That's thinkin' beyond me, Marshal. I'll leave them sorta thoughts to you. We need to get goin'. We got a hard ride back to town and I believe it's gonna be even hotter today than yesterday."

"They're all hot days out here this time of year," said Carson. "It's just dirty, darn bad luck, I'm   sayin'."

CHAPTER 7

The early morning air was already uncomfortably warm, and the clear sky promised to make the heat more oppressive as the day progressed.

The two lawmen and the young woman had ridden quietly for some time when John's mind could no longer contain the barrage of questions within him.

"What do ya think makes some people so good natured and others so evil?"

"Where did that come from?" asked Carson.

"I've just been thinkin' why someone would kill a young fella like Billy."

Well, John, I believe that's a ponderable question that might be difficult to answer in only a few words."

"Do ya think people is just born either good or evil without 'em havin' any say in the matter?"

"I ain't sure, mind ya, but I believe we might all be born the same and it's more the full collection of choices we make throughout our lives that makes us go either way."

"So you don't think some are s'posed to be one way or the other?"

"You talkin' destiny vesus fate, John?"

"Heck, Eli, I don't know *what* we're talkin' about."

Carson and Lizzie laughed.

"Sorry, John. You just have this way with particular phrases sometimes that tickles my funny bone. But what you're sayin' is important, the way people is. I think it's all a matter of comin' to it bein' either destiny or fate in the end. But I believe it all begins with *perception*."

"What does that mean?"

"It means that some folks have a certain sensitivity or awareness about the things around 'em. People see the same thing but they have different views on it because of their different sensitivities. For some, life is a wondrous journey — an excitin' adventure. For others, life is a torturous ordeal. Now, it troubles me to think that the kind of life we live here is all that might ever be. That living good or bad is just somehow based on simple dumb luck. But it's hard for me to accept that some folks are only meant for a good and easy life while others are meant to only have it so difficult and sad. Maybe the quality of our life depends on the choices we make while we're livin' it. And that might depend on our perception, our sensitivities to the things around us, while we're makin' those choices. You follow that, John?"

"I think so. Yer sayin' how we see the things around us might determine the choices we make. And it's them choices that might determine how we live out our lives?"

"Spot on, John. But maybe, instead, our choices don't matter at all. Maybe it does, after all, simply come down to just the lot we draw right before we're born — good luck or bad luck. I don't know which is right and which is wrong, but it comforts me some to think that we might have a say in how we live and maybe even how we die. Of course, maybe we don't have no say at all. Maybe, in the end, our only reward is just gettin' through this life to its end."

"So you don't think destiny plays a part in our lives, Marshal?" asked Lizzie.

"I can't say, Miss Allen. But I expect that some born into this world ain't meant to live here long. And they pass on. Some, it seems, live too long. I think bein' born is grand enough, but it's our departure that leaves the greatest mark on all those left behind. The greatest gift we can leave anyone is a good memory of our good self."

"But what about destiny and fate, which you mentioned? What's the difference? How do they play their parts?" asked Lizzie.

"If you're gonna keep pressin' me for a definitive answer, then I think some have a destiny. I think others just fall to their fate."

"What's the difference?" asked John.

"Simply put, I think those who plan their lives well achieve their destiny. Those who fail to plan fall to their fate."

"That scares me, because I don't think I have a plan for my life."

"Sure you do, John," said Lizzie. "You still plan on being a deputy after Marshal Carson retires, don't you?"

"Yes, ma'am, I reckon I'll keep doin' what I'm doin'. I don't know what else to do."

"Then you have a plan, John."

"Yes, ma'am, I reckon that's so. Thank ya kindly for that. Now I feel better."

The trail through the rocky hills was narrow, forcing them to ride in a single file with Carson leading the way. In Carson's mind it was a dangerous trail, an easy spot for an ambush.

No sooner had the thought entered his mind than a bullet hit the dirt next to the marshal's horse, followed by the sound of the rifle shot.

"Behind them rocks over yonder, John!" yelled Carson, already reining his horse toward a nearby outcrop of sandstone.

Another bullet struck the ground near Marshal Carson's horse, kicking up dust and bits of shattered rock that impacted the side of his face like the sting of a scorpion. The packhorse carrying the body of Billy Allen bolted away with such a start that the reins slipped from John's hands.

The last he saw of the packhorse, it was galloping toward town.

Three more shots rang out and missed them before they were all safely behind the outcrop. Then a continuous barrage of bullets came at them. Some whizzed harmlessly by overhead while others ricocheted dangerously close to them off the boulder. They were safe for the moment but pinned down, and they knew it. They weren't going anywhere anytime soon.

"Who you think's doin' the shootin', Marshal?"

"Thankfully, someone as yet unskilled in the art of sharpshootin'."

Bullets continued pelting the sandstone block, but were terribly off line and represented little immediate threat to the three of them.

"You're right. They ain't too good."

"Be glad of that, John. But if they've got a lot of ammunition, they don't need to be good — just persistent and lucky."

"Who are they, Marshal?" asked Lizzie, nonchalantly.

"In case you missed it, we ain't yet arrived at the introduction phase of our relationship. And I don't think I'd care to stick my head up and try for it right now."

"Well, whoever they are, they're terrible at this business," she said matter-of-factly.

"Yer takin' all this rather calmly, Miss Allen. You been shot at before?"

"Once or twice, or thrice. But by a lot better than whoever is out there now."

"Them bullets is hittin' everywhere but where they should."

"I still ain't complainin', John. Now, I don't know who hired such a sorry lot of assassins, but so far it's been to our good fortune."

"And I expect our good fortune will hold out," said Lizzie. "My goodness, with these boys here, I just might take a nap till they're finished shooting."

"I'm glad to see they ain't botherin' ya none, Miss Allen. I, however, ain't all that steady about it."

"We're dealing with idiots, Marshal," she said.

"Hey, Eli," said John. "I'm just wonderin'. Are we experiencin' destiny or fate?"

At this point, John, I'd say it might be a bit of both...or neither."

"I was lookin' for somethin' a bit more positive from ya, Eli."

"Well, then, let's see if we can coax destiny to our side."

"Okay. How do we do that?"

"First off, we need a goal."

"A goal?"

"Somethin' to aim for. Somethin' you'd like to see accomplished. Somethin' realistic, though."

"Well, I'd like to not get shot. Is that realistic enough?"

"Sounds like a good goal to me. Now we need us a plan."

"To be honest, Eli, I ain't got one."

"No plan?

"Not presently."

"That's too bad, because as Miss Allen pointed out earlier, a goal without a plan is like a fart in a windstorm."

"Okay. I got one."

"Good. So what's your plan?"

"No plan, Marshal. Just a fart."

And John farted.

The slow, rhythmic, continuous gunfire sent bullets ricocheting all around them for several more minutes, forcing Carson to revisit their situation.

"John, if we're gonna hope to get outa this predicament, we need a plan real quick."

"How about we let them run out of ammo?"

"I like that, John, but I can't speak to their willingness to accommodate us on that plan. I think we need to force an end to this quick-like. I don't wanna be here after nightfall. It'll take away the advantage the rocks give us durin' the daylight."

"Sorry, Marshal. I still can't think with all them bullets flyin' around. Them boys sure do have a lot of ammo."

"Yes, they do."

"And that just might work against them," said Lizzie.

"How's that?" asked Carson.

"Marshal, they're doing more shooting than looking. I don't think they're even taking the time to aim."

"Go on, Miss Allen, I'm listenin'."

"They're shooting like madmen. They're not paying close enough attention to what's going on around them, I'll bet."

"Okay…so…"

"So, Marshal, I think I have a plan."

"I hope your plan don't get us killed," said John.

"Well, I think we can all agree on that, John," replied Lizzie. "Now, I do believe, from the rifle fire, that we have two sharpshooters up high in those rocks. Three at the most. I think we should flank them."

"I know what that is," said John.

"How do you know about such tactics, Miss Allen?"

"Let's just say that although I've been shot at, I'm still here. Now let us move on."

"Fine."

"John, you go to the left and Marshal, you go around to the right. Both of you be sure to stay hidden as much as you can until you have a good line of sight on the shooters."

"Got it," said John.

"See that boulder up there, John? The big one with the shelf?"

"Yes, ma'am."

"Think you can make it up to there?"

"Yes, ma'am. I reckon so."

"Good. If you can make it up there, you'll be above them and have a superior firing position."

"I see that."

"Marshal, can you make it to that clump of boulders there, about halfway up to their position?"

"I believe I can, Miss Allen. But I'm a bit beyond my rock-climbin' days and that clump is still gonna be below 'em quite a bit."

"That's fine, Marshal. John's my ace in the hole anyway. If you can draw their fire, they'll be looking down at you. I'm hoping John will have a clear line of fire down on them before they know they've been out-maneuvered. John should be able to eliminate them from his superior position in no time."

"I'll be," said Carson. "Miss Allen, you and me are gonna have a conversation about this when I get back."

"Just make sure you *do* get back, Marshal. I should be able to keep them busy from here until you boys get into position. Once you do, I would expect this ordeal to be over very quickly. Now get going."

"If this don't beat all," muttered Carson as he turned and began slinking his way through the rocks.

"Heck, Miss Allen, you seem pretty good at this stuff."

"Enough chitchat, John."

"Yes, ma'am."

"Okay, let me take a few shots at them to get their heads down and then you hurry on up through those rocks there."

"Anything you say, Miss Allen."

Lizzie cocked the lever of her Winchester carbine.

"Here we go now," she said.

She stood up and began firing slowly and steadily at where she thought the assassins were. From the errant return fire, she confirmed that there were three riflemen and they were bunched up together on the lowest stack of rocks about 150 yards away.

Lizzie did her best to hit her target, but the assassins were hunkered down too low to get a good shot at their heads. The best she could do was to lob the bullets directly in front of them against the rock in the hope that the splinters of both sandstone and lead would cause them to keep their heads below the rock until John got into position.

"Okay, John. Go!" she said.

Keeping in a crouch, the deputy began working his way through the line of rocks leading up to the stone shelf Lizzie had indicated.

Carson worked his own way through and over boulders leading up to the chosen clump of rocks. His old, worn-out body moved slowly.

Lizzie's shots did keep the assassins' heads down, so they were unable to see the lawmen slip through the boulders and up to their destinations.

John's young and lanky form flowed smoothly over the rocks, like water, and he was soon nearing the shelf of rock he was aiming for, while Carson had to work to get his body to perform climbing that was much better suited to a man half his age.

Lizzie stopped firing to reload, and the assassins quickly began their own salvo upon her position once again. With a fusillade of lead splinters screaming over her head, she found it difficult to rise back up and return fire after she had reloaded.

John and Carson stopped climbing when they didn't hear the report of Lizzie's rifle. They assumed she was reloading and so they kept low until they could hear her rifle blasts anew.

John had nearly made it to the boulder with the shelf, but was forced to stop when Lizzie's rifle fell silent again. All he could do was to wait nervously.

Carson, also nearing his targeted position, stopped and waited for Lizzie to begin firing. His heart pounded from the effort it had taken for him to climb over the large boulders. But he ignored the pounding and forced his body to work.

About a minute later they both heard the shots from Lizzie's rifle.

John started up toward the boulder one more time and then realized that although he was very close to it, he was unable to get around the boulder to the shelf itself.

There was no side access to the shelf, only a sharp drop-off a hundred feet or more to another boulder. The only way to the shelf, as he saw it, was to scale the rock from behind up to its top and then drop down onto the flat stone.

Doing so, however, would almost surely expose him to the assassins while he negotiated the drop onto the shelf. It wasn't a good plan, but it was the only practical solution immediately available. And knowing that Lizzie would soon run out of ammo again and have to reload, he didn't want to be caught out in the open.

Soon, he hoped to hear Carson's distracting fire on the assassins. He glanced back down and saw Marshal Carson nearing his own targeted position.

In doing so, John lost count of Lizzie's shots.

He had a choice to make. Go now and hope he got into position before her rifle was empty, or wait until her next barrage began.

He thought about his climb one more time, but no other way to the stone shelf presented itself to him except to go straight for the summit.

"Goal and plan," he whispered. "Destiny or fate. Here goes nothin'."

He tucked the butt end of his rifle under the back of his shirt and crawled up the rock until he reached the top.

Lizzie's rifle quieted, and the assassins, boldness renewed by the silence coming from her position, opened up unmercifully.

Peeking over the top of the boulder, John found himself in a superior position to the assassins just as Lizzie had said — looking down on them at about a forty-five-degree angle.

Heck, he thought, *this is even better than the shelf.*

Crawling forward just a wee bit closer to the edge, he spotted one of the assassins aiming down at Lizzie's position, firing rapidly. Two more riflemen rose up and matched the first barrage with their own.

Just then, Carson opened fire on the assassins. His shots missed, but he got their attention. That was all John needed.

"I see fate layin' claim to you fools," he whispered.

The deputy rested his rifle on the rock, aimed carefully, and squeezed the trigger.

The rifle exploded. Blue smoke immediately swirled around him, but through it he saw the man's head snap to the side and his body crumple to the rock he stood on.

The other two assassins, surprised by John's superior presence, turned their attention and their rifles toward his position, ignoring Carson's misses.

For the nearest man it was much too late, for John had already cocked his rifle, aimed, and fired again. This time he watched the man's head snap sharply backward before his body dropped like a stone to the rock slab under him.

The third assassin wasn't going to take any more chances against John's skill as a sharpshooter. He tucked away behind the slab of sandstone blocking John's line of fire, and seconds later John saw him scamper down through the rocks. Soon he watched a lone rider, at full gallop, head in the direction of town.

This was not going to be as easy a shot as the first two. The horse was moving fast and dust was rising up quickly to block his vision.

John aimed and fired. He missed. He re-cocked the rifle, aimed carefully, and fired again. He missed a second time. He heard Carson's rifle explode, but the rider stayed in the saddle. Carson had missed cleanly.

In the middle of cocking his rifle a third time, he saw the man lurch forward in his saddle. The report of another rifle shot reached him just as the man tumbled from his horse to the ground in a dust cloud of his own making.

John spotted Lizzie Allen as she walked out from behind the rock, shouldering her rifle. When she realized the man she had shot was not getting up, she lowered her rifle, turned, and waved to John. John stood up and waved his rifle back.

The gunfight was over.

CHAPTER 8

Climbing down off the boulder, John joined Lizzie at the body of the last downed would-be assassin, as Carson hobbled toward them.

"I'm sorry I wasn't much help," he said. "I guess the eyes have gone the way of the body and both ain't much good anymore."

"You did just fine, Marshal," said John. "You okay?"

"Oh, yeah. Nothin' a hot bath and an hour's rubdown won't cure."

"I don't think we can…"

"I'm jokin' with ya, John. I'll be fine. Old bones and rock climbin', though, ain't compatible. You two did a heck of a job."

The marshal reached the body and grunted as he got down on his knees and searched it.

"Help me, John. I got to turn the body over and I'm all tuckered out after playin' mountain goat."

As John bent down to help Carson turn the body over, he glanced up at Lizzie.

"That was a fine shot, Miss Allen," he said.

"Not really, John. He was heading away from me. Your shots were just dandy, though."

"Yes, they was mighty fine," said Carson. "When I stopped hearin' the reports of their rifles, I knew you had done them in, John."

"Thank you both. But like the marshal said, they simply fell to their fate."

John stood up and peered into the distant hills.

"I don't reckon there's any more of 'em up there, or we would've heard from 'em by now."

"Good thing, too," said Carson. "'Cause I don't plan on mountain goatin' no more today."

Lizzie and John laughed.

"Keep your feet on the ground, Eli. You've done enough."

"I have, John. And tonight I intend on snorin' loud all night long to prove it."

Carson turned his eyes toward the woman.

"Before that, Miss Allen, you and me are gonna address your tactical skills knowledge some."

"They were just fools, Marshal. It was plain enough to see."

"Yeah."

Carson turned his eyes downward and studied the body as he grimaced.

"Well, that explains it," he said.

"Explains what?" asked Lizzie.

"What this has all been about. Dowd Campbell. Rides in the Roscoe Tanner gang."

John turned his head and looked down into the face of the dead man.

"Oh, Lord. It *is* Dowd Campbell!"

"Yep," said Carson.

"What does that mean?" asked Lizzie.

"This is all because of Red."

"Who's Red, Marshal?" asked Lizzie.

"Red Darrington. He was the one in the jailhouse when we first met."

"Ah, yes. I recall him. So, these men were trying to kill you because of an outlaw?"

"It's lookin' like that. Although I can't imagine Red bein' so important to Roscoe Tanner to be worth killin' us. But there it is."

In his search of the body, the Marshal reached into the right pocket of the assassin's vest and pulled out two Liberty Head Gold Eagle ten-dollar coins.

"Twenty dollars," said Carson. "Roscoe paid this man twenty dollars to kill us. 'Cause ol' Dowd here never had two pennies to rub together since ever. And now he's got hisself twenty dollars. A lousy twenty dollars."

"That's a lot of money," said John. "Almost a whole month's salary for me."

"It's shameful. Shameful is what it is, but I expect you'll find the same on those two fellas over yonder. At least I hope you do. That'd be sixty dollars in total and it's a real shame. Darn insultin'."

"Why is that, Marshal?"

"Because it's only sixty dollars, John. It's just dirty, darn bad luck, I'm sayin'."

"I don't get it."

"Roscoe hired them to kill us. It don't seem like they was after Miss Allen here. Although I reckon they might've had other plans for her after they was done with us."

"That just gave me chills, thank you," said Lizzie.

"Well, that's just the truth of it," said Carson. "But they was out to kill *us*, primarily."

"Yeah. So what about the money?" asked John.

"So it's all he thinks we're worth, John. Now, I know I'm old and not very important, but darn it all, I've always believed I was worth more than thirty dollars."

"I get it now."

"I'm darn disappointed, John. It's depressin' to know that the worth of yer whole life ain't amounted to more than three Gold Eagles. I mean, there's criminals livin' out in the world that are worth *thousands* dead or alive. It's darn upsettin', I'm sayin'. Heck! Roscoe Tanner hisself is worth two thousand dollars dead or alive. Lord almighty, Red's carcass is worth a thousand dollars. This just ain't right. I'll tell you, me and Red are gonna have words about this when I get back. Darn it all."

"I understand yer disappointment," replied John, chuckling under his breath. "But heck, Eli, I can't be worth more'n ten dollars. So the way I figure it, you must be worth…um…I swear, I just ain't good with numbers."

Marshal Carson finally chuckled resignedly.

"You're good with a rifle and you're a good friend, John. That's worth a whole lot more, by my accountin'."

Marshal Carson was correct. A search of the other two would-be assassins produced four more ten-dollar coins.

The bodies were slung over their horses after John tracked down the last rider's horse, and all six horses were then tied to the branches of a low bush and hobbled for the night.

Carson sat studying the setting sun as he rested next to his deputy on a large flat stone close to the ground. Lizzie paced feverishly in front of them.

"So what now, Marshal?" she asked. "What are we going to do?"

"I reckon we make camp now, Miss Allen. I don't fancy bein' out in the open at night. Not with assassins out here lookin' for us. But here we are nonetheless."

"If there are other assassins out here, then we need to get out of the area and back to town quickly."

"I told you before, nothin' moves quick out here, Miss Allen."

"But it's only two or three in the afternoon, and it can't be more than twenty miles back to town. You don't think we can make it back before dark?"

"No way, no how! Not draggin' all them bodies behind us. Not in this heat. We'll kill the horses if we push 'em too hard. And water is mighty scarce out in these parts. I'm tellin' ya, the desert ain't for fast movin', Miss Allen. Where we are, crammed down in amongst these hills, we're gonna begin to lose sunlight fast. Nope. Here is where we are and here is where we're gonna be come mornin'."

"So you really think there are more assassins out here?"

"Either out here now or comin' for us. I don't know which, but I'm guessin' it's gonna get a mite crowded out here sometime tomorrow."

"I don't much like the idea of spending the night out here, Marshal."

"I don't like it at *all*, Miss Allen, but I suspect if they are out here, you'll come up with a plan to destroy 'em."

"Now, Marshal…"

"You sure ain't the woman I thought you was, Miss Allen. No, sir. You're a whole lot more."

"Now, Marshal. Don't start with me."

"I wanna know how you know so much about fightin' tactics."

"Is it really so strange? I grew up with three brothers. We've been in scrapes together. They knew what to do about it. I learned from them. There you go, Marshal. There's your answer. It's just the result of simple recall. Besides, I had to do something. You two were being too indecisive. I don't abide indecisiveness in men."

"Well, Miss Allen, I stand scolded. It ain't my normal way, but I reckon you're right. I did have a moment of indecisiveness."

"Sorry, Marshal, but there it is."

"No need, ma'am. I'm just glad you was with us when it counted."

Carson eyed the sun again.

"It'll be dark soon enough, and the desert gets real dangerous after dark, exposed like we are. It's also gonna get chilly as soon as that sun goes down behind them hills. John, would you mind huntin' up some wood for a fire while you can still see?"

"I'll get on it, Marshal."

John jumped up and began scrounging.

"And John, while you're out huntin' up wood, you might scout out a defensive perimeter for us just in case we get visitors later tonight."

"I'll see to it, Marshal."

Lizzie continued her nervous pacing.

"Miss Allen," said Carson, "calm yourself. There's no need to be scared. We'll make camp in amongst them rocks yonder. I'm sure everything will be just fine."

"I'm not frightened, I'm angry."

"At me?"

"No. At those men who kept me from being in a nice warm, soft bed tonight. I wish they were alive so I could kill them again for the inconvenience."

Carson smirked.

"Dear Lord."

The darkening skies brought the temperature down quickly. Even with a fire, it was chilly.

Carson was searching through his saddlebags when he looked up at his deputy.

"How many more rounds of ammo you got, John?"

"I got a fresh box in my saddlebag. You?"

"About half a box."

"I have a box and a half myself," added Lizzie.

"Well, at least we can defend ourselves for a bit if we're set upon by another bunch of Roscoe's assassins," said Carson. "How about food?" he asked his deputy.

"Most of it was tied to the packhorse with the other boxes of ammo, but I got a few pounds of jerky."

"Me, too. That's good. We won't starve anytime soon. And I got a full canteen, too."

"Me, too, Marshal."

"So do I," said Lizzie.

"Well, all in all, we ain't too bad off. But since our packhorse had most of our provisions, I'd like it if we could find her."

"Heck, Marshal," said John, "the way she took off when all the shootin' started, she's prob'ly already halfway home by now."

"She *was* makin' quick tracks in that direction," said Carson.

"I wish I coulda put a note on her for Jimmy to come out after us and bring some supplies," offered John.

"With things changin' so fast everywhere, John, I expect someday soon someone will invent a telegraph you can carry in your pocket to send messages to others all over this country."

John and Lizzie laughed.

"That's crazy talk, Marshal."

"Yeah, you're probably right, John. But that horse gettin' back to town carryin' that body on its back is sure to get noticed."

"I expect so. I just hope she gets noticed by the right folks. I don't think I'd care to have more assassins come out at us. I believe I've had enough gunfights to suit me for quite a while."

"True words, John. True words. But in these situations it's best that we pray for the best and prepare for the worst."

"But you *do* think our packhorse will make it back on her own and alert someone, don't you?" asked Miss Allen.

"If she makes it back at all, she'll get back very late tonight — too late to do us any good until tomorrow. Of course, that assumes she won't get attacked by wolves or a mountain lion along the way. Let me tell ya, the desert's a bad place to be on your own. Can't move fast durin' the heat of the day. And at night there's all manner of hungry creatures lookin' to take advantage of them things movin' alone, slow in the dark."

"But you think they'll send someone out looking for us?" asked Lizzie.

"Like I said, Miss Allen, I reckon *someone* will show up out here sooner or later."

CHAPTER 9

The problem with a loud, crackling campfire, made up of the dry twigs and branches Marshal Carson and John had managed to scrounge up, is that it masks any sound outside the campsite.

It was a test now — a test of courage and willpower. For out in the darkness there could have been any number of assassins gathering in preparation for another attack.

From beyond the light of the fire, hidden by the darkness, it would be easy to put down the pair of lawmen and a gangly young woman once and for all with a properly aimed rifle.

This thinking was on the uneasy minds of Carson and his deputy as their wary eyes searched the darkness around them for any hint of an intruder wishing to set violently upon their peaceful night.

Although there are times when adventures do provide some unanticipated excitement, this was not the kind of excitement either of them enjoyed.

Finally, John stirred.

"I can't handle this, Marshal. I don't know what might be out there or what might be sneakin' in on us, and it comforts me none to sit here and think on it. I'm gonna go out and walk around."

"It ain't just men with rifles that might be wanderin' around out there, John. I don't need to remind you that this is mountain lion territory, and coyote land, not to mention all the rattlesnakes that do their huntin' at night. Right, Miss Allen?"

"Right you are, Marshal."

"This ain't my first night in the desert, Marshal. I ain't gonna take any unnecessary chances."

"Okay, then. Just do me a favor and don't go gettin' yerself killed on my watch. It's just bad luck — dirty, darn bad luck, I'm sayin' — that we're here at all."

"Dirty, darn bad luck. You always say that, Marshal."

"And I always mean it when I say it."

"How 'bout I crawl up that boulder over there and see what I can see out yonder?"

"That might work, John, but keep your eyes sharp and your head low if you want to keep it on your shoulders. No tellin' who's out there waitin' for us to do just what you're about to do."

"Thanks, Marshal. That makes me feel so much better."

"Just doin' my part to give you proper encouragement and sound advice."

"Yeah. Thanks for that. I'll tell you, though, I sure wish I had eyes on top of my head instead of down half a mile from my hairline. My big ol' forehead makes one heck of a target."

Carson and Lizzie chuckled.

John didn't wait for a response to his comment. He took off through the darkness and crawled up the face of a nearby boulder until he neared its top.

Stopping just short of the summit, he prepared himself with a few deep breaths, then inched himself up higher until he could see into the distance. He strained his eyes to see, but there was nothing except the silhouettes of rocky hills in the distance against the clear, star-filled sky.

Then he saw a flash of light. A half second later, a bullet struck close, causing shrapnel of rock chips to strike the side of his head. A split second later, the report of a rifle shot rang out.

John ducked his head and slid back down the rock.

"Darn it all, Eli — they almost took the top of my head off!"

"But they didn't, so relax," said Marshal Carson, kicking sand onto the fire until only smoke remained. "And from the report of that rifle shot, he's a long ways away, most likely high up in them rocks out yonder to the north."

"Lordy, we're trapped again by more assassins."

"Only until sunrise, unless they can see in the dark."

"You think that one couldn't? He saw me well enough, I reckon."

"Yeah, he did. Prob'ly got him one of them new telescopic sights on his rifle. Saw you in the backdrop of the campfire light."

Carson looked up at the full moon shining above them.

"Course, the moonlight ain't helpin' none either. He thinks he's got us trapped here."

"Well, he might be right, 'cause I ain't goin' up on that rock again. That's for sure."

"And I'm sure he's countin' on that, too."

"So we wait?"

"We wait. It might be a long night without a warmin' fire, but I don't fancy runnin' around in the moonlight, either. So we're gonna have to keep watch all night long."

"I don't know how you can stay so calm, Marshal," said John.

"First off, I ain't the one that got shot at. In the second place, you think this is the first time I been hid behind a rock with someone takin' a shot at me?"

The marshal chuckled.

"You should be used to it by now as well, John."

"I don't reckon I'll ever get used to gettin' shot at."

"Times like this go with the badge, John."

"Are you gettin' philosophical again?"

"I do believe I am."

"Well, stop it!"

"Who's out there now, I wonder," said Lizzie.

"More of the same that was out there earlier, I reckon — Roscoe Tanner's hired assassins." Carson chuckled.

"What are you laughin' about?" asked John.

"My worth increases with every assassin he hires."

"There's somethin' wrong with you, Eli."

"Sorry, John. Just tryin' to lighten the mood."

"I don't think you're funny, Marshal," said Lizzie.

"Like I said already, I don't think this concerns you, Miss Allen. At least not up front."

"Tell that to whoever's doing the shooting. Those bullets could hit me, too. That raises sufficient concern in my mind for it not to be humorous."

"Yes, ma'am, it's true. I didn't mean to make light of our situation. It's just dirty, darn bad luck, I'm sayin'."

"What I don't understand is why attack us out here at all?" asked Lizzie. "Why not dash into town and free Mister Darrington and gallop away into the night? Why waste time gunning for us all the way out here?"

"All good questions, Miss Allen. And for all I know, Red himself could be doin' the shootin'."

"No way," said John.

"Maybe he escaped and has come out here for his revenge."

"That's crazy talk, Marshal. Ol' Jimmy wouldn't allow Red his freedom."

"What I mean by all of this is I don't have answers for any questions at the moment. Just more questions. But I don't regard it as healthy to create monsters until there's a good need to create monsters."

"That's all we need right now, more of yer darn philosophy," said John.

Four rifles opened fire on their position.

"Well, there it is!" said Carson. "If it's Red, he ain't alone."

John started returning fire until Carson shouted for him to stop.

"John," he called out, "we ain't got the ammunition to get into this kinda fight. Save it. Besides, your return fire is just markin' your position. Don't help 'em."

John stopped firing, but the would-be assassins' bullets continued to strike the rocks around them, sparking as the scream of ricochets echoed through the night air.

"Miss Allen, if you've got any more fancy tactics hid up your sleeves, I'd be open to 'em."

"We need a more fortified position, Marshal. Someplace with limited access that we can control."

"Agreed. How 'bout we move deeper into them rocks over yonder." Carson pointed to a large clump of sandstone boulders.

"That'll work," said Lizzie.

"But we'll never get the horses in there with us," said John.

"We'll have to leave 'em hobbled here."

"But what if them fellers come and take 'em away?"

"Better they get the horses than us, John."

"But how would we get back to town?"

"We'd have to walk. Enough with the questions. Grab all the ammo and water you can carry and let's get outa here."

The three grabbed what they could and made their way through the rain of gunfire to the clump of rocks Carson had pointed out.

Once settled into a more defensible position, they could do nothing for the moment but listen to the unceasing gunfire and the screeching ricochets.

The gunfire continued sporadically for another five minutes.

Finally, it died down to a shot every minute or so. Then it stopped altogether and silence returned to the desert, but the air was filled with the smell of gunpowder and an eerie bluish haze filtered the moon's light over their heads.

The chilly desert night was uncomfortable for them, but they dared not start another fire for fear of giving away their precariously secure position.

"I think we got 'em trapped now, boss," they heard a male voice shout out.

"Hold your positions, boys," yelled a distant baritone voice.

Several more silent minutes passed and then that same deep voice, now closer, called out.

"Send the girl out and we'll let you and your deputy live, Marshal."

Carson was shocked by the request. It certainly wasn't the voice of Red Darrington.

He cut Lizzie a puzzled look. Her eyes met his with equal bewilderment. She shrugged her shoulders.

Then two questions sizzled in his brain. *If it wasn't Red Darrington come for revenge, who was doing the talking? And what did Lizzie May Allen have to do with any of this?* But no answers came forth. He wanted to yell back, but he thought it might be a trick to discover their position, so he held the questions within.

His eyes pierced the darkness looking for any movement at all. He saw nothing but the night.

About thirty seconds passed and then the voice shouted out again.

"Send her out, Marshal. Don't get caught up in this mess. Choose wisely and live through the night. Give her up and light up a nice warm fire, sleep like a baby, and get you and your deputy back to town safely tomorrow."

"What the heck?" muttered Carson. "Get caught up in what?"

His eyes turned once again to Lizzie. She just stared blankly, without a sign of emotion.

"Come on, Marshal," the voice continued. "If you haven't figured it out by now, know this. She ain't who she says she is. Turn her over to us and be done with her. There's no reason you have to die tonight."

"Ain't who she says she is?" asked John. "Who are you, Miss Allen?"

Lizzie's eyelids fluttered. Carson noticed them but said nothing.

"I don't know what he's talking about," Lizzie replied.

"No, no, Miss Allen," said Carson. "You know who's out there, don't ya?"

"I have no idea, Marshal. I think he's attempting deceit. Perhaps he's probing for a point of weakness."

"It's become mighty clear you ain't no kinda ingénue, Miss Allen. In fact, it's more and more like you might be some kinda military strategist — an intuitive tactician. Maybe even some kinda professional warrior-type. We're gonna have us a far deeper conversation about your past, young lady. If we get out of this alive, that is."

"Don't be silly, Marshal. I'm just making considered guesses as to his intent. And I have no idea who he might be."

"That'd be nice if it was true, but I'm thinkin' you know exactly who it is out there. In fact, I'm gettin' thoughts that it's who you been all nervous about this evenin'."

"You don't know anything of the kind," Lizzie shot back venomously.

"Now I'm sure of it," said Carson. "Who are they, Miss Allen? And come clean now. We're in big trouble here."

"Trust me, Marshal," the deep voice shouted. "You're parked in the rocks with a viper. And she'll be the death of you both. If not tonight, then later, but either way, it'll be too soon for your liking. I know what I'm talking about, Marshal. I've got my own scars to prove it."

Carson cut Lizzie a stern stare.

"Divide and conquer, Marshal. He's trying to incite a division between us."

"He's doin' a good job, 'cause I'm beginnin' to doubt everything you're sayin'. Flankin' maneuvers, fortified positions, probin' tactics, dividin' strategies. Them ain't the thoughts of normal womenfolk, Miss Allen."

"You're sliding back into that primordial ooze, Marshal."

"Maybe so, Miss, but at least…"

"Send her out to us," shouted the disembodied voice. "Send her out and I promise we'll disappear into the night and leave you be. We'll even leave your horses for ya. And I reckon all the bodies too. I can see you've been fatally busy. How many of these kills was hers, Marshal? Think on that for a bit."

Carson stared hard at Lizzie.

His thoughts moved to the suggestion. Perhaps, he thought, all of the kills could be attributed to her — her and her flanking tactic, which made the defeat of the would-be assassins possible.

"Miss Allen, tell me now what this is all about right quick."

"Be smart about this, Marshal," the voice shouted again. "She ain't worth dying for. She's a calculating, coldhearted killer, that one. She's already done in one of us."

"Miss Allen?" said Carson.

"Trust me, Marshal. I have no idea what he's talking about."

"Listen, Marshal," the voice yelled. "I'm sure she's been trying to convince you that you can trust her. You can't. Trust me instead. You'll live longer. She's the devil incarnate. As soon as she gets what she's searching for, she'll think nothing of slitting your throats while you're sleeping."

"Miss Allen?" said Carson. "It's now or never."

"I'll tell you, Marshal. Just keep me safe. I'll make it worth your while."

"How's that?"

"Your adventure. I'll give you your adventure. It'll be worth it, I promise. But if he gets hold of me, you'll get nothing but a bullet in the brain."

"I've been patient with you long enough, Marshal. Make your decision. We've got you surrounded. Send her out, or we'll come in after her. Oh, and one more thing…"

Carson waited for the man to finish his sentence, but only silence prevailed until an explosion lit up the sky, deafening all three of them.

Dirt and sand rained down on them as Carson tried to clear his ears.

"You don't want to play this game, Marshal. We're not after you or your deputy. We just want young Miss Adams. That's all."

"Wait!" yelled Carson, feeling instant relief. "We can end this now, mister. We ain't got a Miss Adams here. We only got a Miss Allen. I think you got it all wrong."

Carson heard a laugh.

"Would that be Miss Lizzie May Allen?"

"Yes, it would."

Carson heard more than one person laughing now.

"I thought you were finished with that name, sugar," the voice shouted out.

"Sugar?" asked Carson.

"Her name is Cassandra Ann Adams, Marshal. She's a lying little snake. But she's got some things that belong to me and I'm not leaving without them."

"Can I have a few moments to sort this out, please?"

"Sure, Marshal. I told you already, we ain't got no quarrel with you or your deputy."

"Who you say she killed?" asked Carson.

"I think you know already. It looks like you found him earlier. Did you find the hat and the coin, sweetheart?"

"How do you know this fella?" asked Carson.

"Okay, fine. He's my husband."

"Your *husband*?"

"Yes. My sweet husband. And he'll kill me for what I have. He'll kill us all if he thinks I've told you the secret."

"The *secret*?"

CHAPTER 10

"Let me get this straight," said Carson. "Your name is different. You're a married woman. And you've got a secret on top of *that*?"

"It's not the way he said it is," said Lizzie.

"What way is it, then?"

"Well, it's not the way *he* said it is. That's all I can say right now. You'll just have to trust me."

"Lord almighty. What have I gotten us into?"

"A mighty mess, as I see it," said John.

"It would appear so. It would also appear that we got us a triumvirate of ambiguities growin' up right before our eyes."

"A what?"

"We got us three darn mysteries, John."

"Three mysteries. Yes, sir. We surely do."

The deep voice then boomed out once again. "You've got five minutes to give her up, Marshal, or we'll come in blasting — literally."

"You can't turn me over to him, Marshal!"

"Tell me why."

"I can't."

"Marshal," whispered John, "I see a way out for us. Keep him talkin'."

Before Carson could respond, John slipped out through the rocks and into the night.

"You're hittin' me with a lot right now, mister," Carson shouted, more in an attempt to mask any noise of John's rapid departure than to be heard. "I'd appreciate a bit more time to sort it all out in my head. I'm dealin' with a conundrum here."

"There's no conundrum, Marshal. Give her up and live. Don't give her up and die. Seems simple enough."

"No, sir. It ain't quite that simple. If she did kill her brother, Billy Allen, like you say, I gotta take her into custody for trial."

"Billy Allen? Her brother? Is that who she said he was?"

"Yes, sir."

"Come on, Marshal. You seem like a bright man. He wasn't her brother and his name wasn't Billy Allen. It was Victor Adams. My brother, who was having an affair with my wife — your Miss Allen."

"Oh, my word," Carson muttered. "This hole just keeps gettin' deeper."

"Marshal, please," said Lizzie, "he's lying to you. That wasn't his brother, I didn't have any affair, and I certainly didn't kill the young man. He did."

"He killed the lad?"

"I don't know for sure, but maybe."

"Maybe? But his name ain't Billy, right?"

"No. That's true enough. It's not Billy. But…"

"And he's not your brother?"

"No. He's not my brother. But he isn't Victor Adams either. I can explain everything. Don't listen to him."

"Well, it seems to me he's been more truthful than you so far. You're gonna have to give me a darn good reason why I shouldn't turn you over to him."

"Because of these, Marshal."

Lizzie reached down into her blouse.

"Now, Miss Allen…"

"Oh, shut up," she said, withdrawing her closed fist. "These are what he's after."

She turned her fist over and opened her hand, revealing two halves of a zigzag-cut coin.

"These," she said. "If he gets his hands on these, he'll kill us all. These are all he cares about."

"He's gonna kill us over a little gold coin? Wait! I thought you said your pappy had the other half."

She fluttered her eyelids and then smiled.

Carson noticed.

"Why do you do that?"

"Do what?"

"With your eyes…"

"Come now, Marshal. I think it's safe to dissolve any further pretense as to there being any kind of father involved."

"Marshal! I've given you all the time you need," yelled the voice.

"I'm workin' on it. I'm workin' on it."

"You got two more minutes to finish *workin' on it.*"

"Oh, dear Lord. If there's a bigger fool than me within a hundred miles, I'll be shocked."

"Don't be so hard on yourself."

"Listen to me, Miss. I admit it, okay? I admit it outright. I ain't as smart as you."

"Don't sell yourself short, Marshal. I'll bet there are more than a few men behind bars right now who heard you say those very words just before you slapped the cuffs on their wrists."

"Look, darn it all! We're in a bad way here. I ain't got no more time for your twisty bantering. You lied!"

"Yes, I lied. Okay? I've been lying all along."

"No father? No brothers or farm?"

"I've never even seen a farm, Marshal. I was an orphan, raised in Northampton. In the home of a very rich man. A very rich but stupid man."

"But that still don't make no sense. That coin ain't valuable enough for a killin'. Is it?"

"It's not just a gold coin, Marshal. It's part of a treasure map — to more gold than you've ever seen in your life."

"Oh, my! So, this coin is all he's after?"

"Yes. Well, no. Not really."

"What do you mean, *not really*, Miss Allen…or is it Miss Adams?"

"Well, to be honest, Marshal, it's neither. Actually, my name is Tamara Baxter."

"Lordy, girl! I never saw anyone like you. Heck, I never even knowed there could *be* anyone like you."

"It's complicated, Marshal."

"You're tellin' *me*. So I got yer husband out there in the dark threatenin' me over a treasure map?"

"Well...he's not really my husband."

"What?"

"I used an alias to get married, so technically, I'm not legally married to him."

"Oh, my word."

"Time's almost up, Marshal. I don't intend to wait here all night while she fills your head with more of her lies and nonsense."

"I'm thinkin' on it. Just hold your horses, mister."

"Actually, I'm holding the reins to *your* horse at the moment, Marshal."

"Then just hold on to *my* horse. This appears to be very complicated. I'm tryin' to get my mind around it. This ain't no easy decision for me."

Carson returned his attention to the young woman.

"Tell me this. And darn it all, be honest about it. You said them halves of the coin is only *part* of a treasure map?"

"That's right. Well, two parts, anyway. There's a third part missing."

"What third part is missin'?"

"Well…it's not really missing. I just can't find it presently."

"And what is that exactly?"

"I'm not sure."

"What?"

"I'm not exactly sure what it is."

"I don't believe this. This can't be happenin'."

"I'm sorry, Marshal. But that's why I came out here."

"What are you sayin'?"

"That's why I'm here. To find these two pieces and the third item my father indicated was needed to find the gold."

"I thought you said there was no father involved here."

"Well…that's not exactly true, I suppose. But it is *my* gold, Marshal."

"*Your* gold?"

"Well…sort of."

"Time's up, Marshal!"

Rifle shots rang out, followed by a mad exchange of gunfire coming from somewhere in front of them. But all Carson could see were the reflections of bright flashes off the rocks in the distance.

After some time had passed and several more shots were heard, a man carrying a lit torch plunged into the open and ran toward their position.

"Stop right there and toss up yer hands!" yelled Carson.

But the man didn't stop.

"You ain't getting away with this — that treasure is mine!" he bellowed and continued his dash straight at them. As he drew closer, Carson saw the bundle of dynamite in the man's other hand.

Carson didn't have time to yell out again for the man to stop. He aimed his rifle and squeezed the trigger. The bullet found its mark dead center of the man's chest.

When he fell, the lit torch dropped to the sand. The dynamite dropped from his other hand and rolled toward the torch, igniting the fuse instantly as torch and fuse met.

"Get yer head down! It's gonna be big!" Carson shouted to the young woman.

They had just hunkered down and gotten their fingers into their ears when the dynamite exploded with a thunderous clap. The force of the explosion knocked them onto their backs as sand and shattered stone shot up into the air. Seconds later, a dust cloud swirled around the area like a tornado and soon the bits of destroyed stone and sand showered down upon them as well.

Several seconds after that, with the last of the dust still a fine cloud in the air, masking more of the moon's light, the last bits of stone chips dropped back to earth and all was silent once more.

"Are you okay, Miss…whatever your name is?"

"Yes, Marshal. How about you?"

"My ears is still ringin', but I reckon all my important parts is attached."

"Marshal!" another voice yelled. "Are you okay?"

"Yeah, John. We're still here and whole."

John came running into the area.

"I got the rest of 'em, Marshal. They're all dead. And lookie here what I found."

John walked toward the marshal carrying a telescope-fitted Winchester rifle.

"I'll be. Just look at that," said Carson.

"Yes, sir," replied John. "Ain't it somethin'?"

"Scary is what it is, John. You get the one doin' all the yappin'?"

"No, sir, but that's him there on the ground. At least what's left of 'im. Looks like *you* got 'im."

"Is that your husband…or whatever? Is that the fella?"

"It's him, Marshal. It's Byron. Thank you."

"Don't go thankin' me yet, young lady. We've got a long, hard conversation just gettin' started."

"My Lord," said Carson, walking back toward the campfire. "We got seven horses out there, each one with a body laid over it. One with a fancy telescoped rifle all wrapped up with 'im. The one body we started out with is gone. I been threatened, shot at, blowed up, lied to, and scared half to death. And all of it crammed into one lousy day. I think it's fair to say I've had all the adventure I need — enough to last me the rest of my sorry life. I just wanna get back to town and retire."

"Well…," began the young woman.

"Enough of that, Miss! Every time you begin a sentence with '*well*,' my head goes to achin'. Is there *any* truth within you?"

"Well…"

"There you go again!"

"I told you, Marshal. It's complicated."

"What's complicated about just tellin' the truth?"

"Marshal, in this specific instance, the truth is relative."

"Relative to what? A complete lie or just a little white lie?"

"I was trying to tell you the truth. Well…sort of, anyway."

"Somehow I doubt that, but let's give it a try just for the sake of quackin' ducks. What other *truths* would you like to clear up for me?"

"Can I tell you a story, Marshal?"

"Is it fiction or nonfiction?"

Lizzie (or whatever her name was) giggled.

"I'll tell you and you can decide for yourself. How's that?"

"I don't think I'm gonna like it none either way. But go ahead."

"You touched upon it last night."

"Touched upon what?"

"Just hush up and listen. Last night you told John about the conquistadors coming through the area in search of gold."

"I recall that."

"Well, allow me to get the story straightened out and fill in the blanks. Let me tell you the story of Francisco Vázquez de Coronado y Luján, the Spanish conquistador. He came through the area back in 1541 or 1542. In April 1542, Coronado left the area of the canyonlands, reportedly leaving behind two friars for some reason or reasons unknown, or perhaps just forgotten. It doesn't really matter which.

"As the story goes, the friars harbored a wee touch of larceny in their otherwise sainted souls. Apparently they stole a chest full of gold Spanish doubloons and hid it away prior to Coronado's departure. After leaving the area, Coronado supposedly discovered that the chest was missing and sent some of his troops back to where he had left the friars. The troops discovered, not surprisingly and to their dismay, that the friars had disappeared from the area. Along with the gold, of course.

"From here there seem to be at least two versions of the story. One version has it that a thorough search for the priests by the troops was in vain and the thieving friars were never found. Another version indicates that the friars *were* found and were killed in a fight before they could give up the whereabouts of the chest. Either way, the chest was never recovered.

"That is to say, it was never recovered until my father stumbled blindly onto it the day he was chased by four Apache braves who he later managed to kill."

"When did he tell you this?"

"I've heard the story over and over, ever since I was a child."

"Just hold on a darn minute. You said you was an orphan."

"Well, okay. That was a bit of an untruth regarding my familial status. I lived with my uncle while going to college."

"Your uncle? Would he be the stupid man you mentioned before?"

"Well, yes. My father's brother. He wasn't too bright. Anyway, after I graduated, I returned to my father's home."

"Where's that?"

"San Francisco."

"Oh my Lord," said Carson. "Are you expectin' me to believe this cock-and-bull story now? Or are you just havin' more fun with the old fool before you?"

"I'm telling you the truth, Marshal."

"Somehow I still doubt it, Miss. But it's a good story, I'll give you that. Please continue."

"It was a wonderful story for a young mind. He told it to me as if it were real. I believed him. He said that since he had no way to carry the heavy chest back alone, he recorded its whereabouts and had always planned to go back and get it later. Before leaving it, he was able to take enough with him, filling his saddlebags to the brim, that he became very wealthy.

"Six months ago, while back home, he fell ill. He realized that he would never be able to make the return trip to retrieve the chest, so he told me how to find it. He said there were enough gold coins left in the chest to make four more people exceedingly wealthy."

"I see," said Carson. "And what has befallen your father since revealin' that to you?"

"My father passed away last month, Marshal."

"I have no doubt of that."

"You're passing judgment against me without cause. I did not kill my father. I loved my father, Marshal. And despite what you may believe is true about me right now, I'm just fulfilling his wishes. He wanted me to have the gold. His last words to me were that he wanted me to retrieve it and live happily ever after."

"Happily ever after. Ain't them the words you end a fairytale with?"

"You're being obtuse, Marshal."

"No, I'm just not bein' yer fool anymore. There's a difference, Miss…just what am I supposed to call you, anyway — Miss Adams or Miss Baxter?"

Her eyelids fluttered. Carson squinted at her and muttered, "There they go again."

"Well…"

"Oh, my word. Here we go."

"My real name is Jessica, Marshal. Jessica Abernathy. That's my real and true name. My father was George Abernathy, proprietor of Abernathy's General Store and Hardware in San Francisco. He was a simple man, a down-to-earth man, who lived a simple life until he stumbled onto the gold. Even afterwards, he remained a good man. But can you understand why I have to be so cautious? You've already seen what otherwise honest men will do for a chest full of gold coins."

"Honest men? I admit I don't know nothin' about them that tried to kill us a while ago, but I would not tend to count them among honest men. Not from *their* actions."

"Fine. But honest or dishonest aside, I need to be very cautious."

"On the other hand, they *did* honestly make their intentions known. They was honestly bein' dishonest."

Carson chuckled at his own wit.

"Stop it! You don't know the whole story about those men."

"Sorry, Miss. You're right. Like I said, I don't know nothin' about 'em. But I'm strugglin' mightily tryin' to know anything I can about you. You got some kind of veil up hidin' you from folks. Apparently, I'm one of 'em, cause you're just a mystery. And although I enjoy a good mystery now and then, I don't care for the dangerous sort. And you, Miss, are most certainly the dangerous sort."

"You don't know what you're talking about."

"Here's what I'm talkin' about. I've never heard so many lies spoken at one time in all my years. I'm so confused, I don't know what to believe. But seven men is dead, and right now if you told me the sky was blue, I'd doubt it."

"It's black right now. It's nighttime."

"You're missin' the point. I'm confused about you, but I'm quite certain of one thing. You're a very dangerous young woman. That scares me. And another thing. You know who that boy is we found out in the wash. What I can't figure out is why you won't tell me his name, or what your connection to him is. All I'm hearin' is lies! Just lies on top of lies. You're just a-spewin' lies is all!"

"Would you like me to finish my lies?"

"By all means, Miss Abernathy. Why not? You see, I don't mind listenin' to lies so long as they contain great characters and an excitin' plot. Just one thing, though. Don't ever ask me to accept them as truths, because that insults my intelligence. And I do not endure insults with any affection."

"Have it your way, but I'm going to tell you what I believe to be the truth. You're free to reject it or accept it."

"Proceed, Miss Abernathy, please. I just pray it'll be a good story."

"My father told me that he had several of the coins melted down and recast into one coin with certain engraved information on it. Then he had the coin cut in half. Both sides have clues, but the coin halves need to be brought together in order for the information to be of any practical use in locating the chest.

"My father gave me one half and sent the other half, by special courier, to my brother, Tom, who lived in Ohio at the time. He also wrote a letter which was to be used to decipher the clues on the half-coins. The cipher, combined with the two half-coins, he said, would take us to the chest of gold."

"Where's the letter?" asked Carson.

"Supposedly, my father sent it to Tom with his half of the coin."

Carson chuckled.

"Sounds like your father didn't trust you either."

"He was baked into the primordial man-pie as well."

"For good reason, it seems."

"You're acting the dullard now, Marshal."

"So you *do* know what the third item is after all?"

"Yes, I do."

"Incredible!"

Carson looked over at John and smiled.

"Hey," said John, "I'm just waitin' on the story's end. Nothin' else makes any sense to me."

Carson turned back to the young woman.

"So those two halves of the coin you have now are nothin' without the letter?"

"That's true, Marshal."

"You let me decide what's true or not, Miss Abernathy."

"Have it your way, Marshal, but without the letter describing where the trail to the chest begins, I could search forever and never find it."

"Unless someone else stumbles upon it again, I reckon."

"My father said that would never happen because he moved it to a location that would be impossible to locate ever again without his clues."

"So how did that young fella out at Dead River get hold of the coin?"

"I don't know."

"Why am I waitin' on a *well*?" asked Carson.

"I don't know how he got his hands on it."

"Have you heard from your brother, Tom — or is it Thomas?"

"You *are* persnickety, aren't you, Marshal?"

"I wouldn't say persnickety, Miss. I like to think the appropriate word is *precise*."

"No. *Tom* never showed up and I don't know where he is right now. But I do suspect that evil has befallen him."

The young woman's eyelids fluttered.

"There you go again. Why do you do that?"

"Do what?"

"That thing with your eyes."

"I have no idea what you're talking about, Marshal. You're making no sense."

Carson scratched his chin a moment.

"'*Did you find the hat and the coin*?'"

"What?" asked Jessica.

"That's what that fella asked. Your husband. Byron. Before he tried to blow us up. '*Did you find the hat and the coin*?'"

"Well, we did. Why is that important?"

"I think I know why…now."

"What you thinkin', Marshal?" asked John.

"Well, John, since the moment I found that hat, there's been a question burnin' me alive. Why was the hat layin' on that rock so far from the body?"

"It fell off his head."

"I'm thinkin' no, John. I'm thinkin' now that it was placed there by the killer to be found — a decoy, or bait."

"Why is that?"

"That, John, is the real question, ain't it?"

"I reckon so, although I ain't got a clue, as you can guess."

"Miss Abernathy, why didn't you just tell me all this before?"

"I told you. I didn't know you. I couldn't trust you. I'm sorry. That's just the simple truth of it."

"Didn't Judge Perry vouch for my character?"

"He told me what he could, but I had to discover who you are on my own. That's just the way I am."

"Do you really know Judge Perry?"

"Yes. I told you my father and he were friends growing up in Massachusetts. I was only a child when the judge left for the West, but I knew him. That's the truth."

"You said your father lived in San Francisco."

"You haven't been listening to me. We obviously *moved* to San Francisco later."

"I listen. He owned a general store."

"Correct."

"I do listen, Miss Abernathy. But the jury is still deliberatin' on whether you're speakin' any kinda truth at all. But for now let's suppose you are tellin' the truth. Without this letter, then, I don't s'pose there's any use tryin' to pursue the matter of locatin' the gold coins. Therefore, I find myself returned to my original investigation. Tomorrow we'll get back into town and try to sort out all these killin's. But I'll tell you this. Killin' for gold or treasure just ain't right. Gold ain't worth a life, in my book."

"That's because you don't have any gold, Marshal. If you did, you might think differently about it."

"You might be right, but I think the need to be rich might be some kinda sickness of its own. You see, poor folks like John and me, we keep our minds busy just tryin' to survive. I think needin' to be rich, without the worry of survivin', gives one too much time to think. And thinkin', I reckon, when it's undisciplined thinkin', is what gives birth to all the sickness and worry in the world. Especially when the thought is tryin' to hold onto somethin' as worthless as yellow-colored metal."

"Once again, Marshal, it's easy to think that way if you don't have it."

"Maybe so, maybe so. But I ain't never seen anyone eat gold when they're hungry."

"That's true, but if you have gold, you'll never know hunger."

Carson chuckled.

"I suppose we could debate the issue of rich versus poor all day long and still find no solution to satisfy the both of us. And it certainly wouldn't get us anywhere closer to discoverin' the murderer of the young man neither. To boot, we ain't got no gold to be discussin' over anyway. We do, however, have us a campfire and a chilly night, some jerky and some water. And we got our lives, so after all's said and done, I think we're pretty fortunate."

"Yep," said John. "We're doin' better'n them fellas layin' across their saddles. That's somethin' I do know."

CHAPTER 11

The sun beat down on them mercilessly, the desert hungry for their baked flesh, when John reined his horse to a quick stop and snatched up his Winchester rifle from its scabbard.

He brought it swiftly to his shoulder, cocked it, and aimed it at the distant mirage. There appeared to be at least two ghostly specters on horseback coming straight at them at a slow and steady pace. With the terrain's undulations it was almost as if they were rising up from under the desert sands. But the refraction caused by the heat made it impossible to determine their identities.

Carson stopped his horse next to his deputy.

"Can you make 'em out, John?"

"Nope."

"Well, they must see us as well and they're still comin' slow. I take that as a good sign."

"I do hope so, Marshal."

Jessica Abernathy stopped her horse behind them. She peered at the distant images as well.

"Are we about to receive tribulation or delight, Marshal?"

"I find myself hopin' for a glorious delight, Miss Abernathy, but my hopes so far this week have fallen woefully short, along with my expectations."

"Any idea who they might be?"

"We'll have that answer soon, I reckon."

"Should I get my rifle?"

"I'd appreciate it if you would just sit there and don't make any sudden moves. John's handlin' it."

"I'm not comfortable with this."

"Miss Abernathy, this is the normal way of life out here. Just be calm."

The heat refraction continued to blur his vision of the approaching strangers, but soon Carson confirmed the presence of two riders and a riderless horse walking toward them.

John kept a steady aim on the approaching group, ready for anything.

A minute later, he lowered his rifle.

"Jimmy? Is that you?" he yelled at the riders.

"Yeah," came the answering shout.

Carson blew out a breath of relief.

"I do believe I can start breathin' again," he said.

John heeled his horse into a lope toward the group and Carson could see him shake hands with Jimmy Johnson upon his arrival.

"Is that your other deputy, Marshal? The one I met in the jailhouse?"

"Yes, Miss Abernathy. But I don't know who the other man is. I reckon we'll just have to wait and see."

Within minutes, Deputy Johnson and the stranger came within seventy-five yards of Carson and the young woman.

"Oh no, you don't!" yelled Jessica, pulling her rifle from its scabbard, cocking it, and aiming at the stranger.

Marshal Carson moved like lightning and knocked the rifle off its mark just as Jessica squeezed the trigger.

The shot rang out and the three men in the distance shifted sharply in their saddles.

"That'll be enough of that!" Carson said as he wrenched the rifle from Jessica's hands.

"He's here to kill me, Marshal! You have to kill him!"

"Ain't nobody killin' nobody yet. Now you best settle down, or I'll hog-tie you."

Jessica, however, was determined. She reached for Carson's revolver, but he parried her hand away from it.

"Stop it, darn ya! I mean it. I don't want to bust you across the jaw with the butt of this rifle, but I will if I have to."

"I'd like to see you try, old man."

She wrestled with Carson as if her life depended on it. Her fists flew past Carson's nose, then his jaw, barely missing their mark each time. Then they soared upward, finally connecting with his hat and knocking it off his head. It was apparently a fight to the finish for her, and Carson was battling the best he could, but holding onto the rifle while trying to deflect her wildly flinging hands was almost too much for him.

"You don't understand!" she screamed. "He's a killer. He's an escaped killer. He's been tracking me for months. He wants the gold. He's insane."

"It seems everyone is out to kill ya, Miss Abernathy," said Carson, battling both the young woman as well as for a breath of air.

"And you seemed the likeable type when we first met."

"You don't understand, you old fool."

"Yes, ma'am, and old fool that I am, I'm not understandin' a lot lately. But we ain't gonna shoot nobody just yet. And as far as sanity goes, might all of us be a little bit crazy right now."

John galloped up in a cloud of dust and grabbed Jessica's other arm.

"What is this all about, Marshal?"

"Just grab her so's I can get a breath, John. Get her down off her horse and wrap up her arms tight."

John wrested Jessica off her horse and, despite her kicking and thrashing about and trying to bite a chunk out of his cheek, finally managed to get her under full control by lifting her completely off the ground and holding her until Carson dismounted and got a rope around her feet. All the time, the young woman continued her rant.

"He's going to kill me, Marshal! He's going to kill me!"

"The stranger, John. She tells me he's a killer."

"He said he might be her brother, come lookin' for her."

"Her brother Tom?" Carson asked, still struggling with Jessica.

"I believe I heard him say Andrew."

"He's here to kill me!" Jessica screamed.

"Andrew, Tom, who knows? But she ain't actin' like he's kin."

Before the contest was over, Jessica got two good blows with her knees up under Carson's chin, which brought the stars out early for him.

All Jimmy and the stranger could do was watch the thrashing threesome and be happy to be away from the fray.

Then the young woman began a fusillade of swearwords that would have shocked a drunken sailor.

"Gag 'er, John! Gag 'er!"

John pulled a bandana from his rear pocket and tied it over her mouth.

"Lord almighty, girl!" said Carson. "Where'd you learn words like that?" He put a finger into his ear and shook it hard.

"She was screamin' in my ear so loud, I might've gone a bit deaf."

The lawmen released the young woman to lie on the ground, but she was still thrashing about in an attempt to break free and she continued her verbal assault upon them. Luckily, her words were too muffled to be understood.

With Jessica finally hog-tied and gagged, Carson and John stood up. Then both bent over at the waist, their hands resting on their knees, battling for breath.

John took note of the still thrashing, still ranting young woman.

"You want me to settle her down, Eli?"

"Let 'er thrash, John, let 'er thrash. I'm too tired to care. In all my thirty years of bein' a lawman, I ain't never wrestled a woman like that before. I can't say I regret it none either. She ain't a woman. She's a big ol' cat. And she's got claws like one. I do believe she gouged out a chunk of my back in that fight. In the future, I think it'd be better for me to stick to fistfights with menfolk."

John chuckled.

"I would have to agree with you, Eli. I ain't never been in a scrap like that before neither. She gives it out pretty good for a little gal."

"Don't she, though?"

Carson, still bent over, drew a sleeve across his forehead, then picked up his hat and pressed it back onto his head.

"Whew! I do believe I'm gonna sleep for a week after that fight, John."

"I believe I'm gonna have me nightmares over it."

Carson chuckled.

"Can we approach now, Marshal?" asked Jimmy.

Carson waved the visitors in.

"Yeah, come on in. It's all under control. At least for the moment."

As Jimmy and the stranger moved cautiously toward them, Carson stayed bent over, still searching for one more good breath.

"I think the sun finally fried my brain, John. I don't think I can take much more of this heat. Not with wrestlin' her and all."

"I know what you mean."

"I see you've found my fiancée, Marshal," said the stranger.

"*Fiancée*! This wildcat is your fiancée? I thought you told John you was her brother."

"Yes, well, that depends on how her day is going."

"What *are* you talkin' about, mister? What's your name?" said Carson, finally straighting up.

The man studied the woman, who was still hissing and thrashing about. John straightened up as well, and blew a finishing breath.

"Miller, Marshal. Andrew Miller, and I can see you've got her in a scrappy state right now. She can be a handful when she gets like this, can't she?"

"You've seen her like this before?"

"You bet. She does have her moments. Scratches like a cat, too."

"Yes, sir. I would have to agree with that," said Carson. "So, Mister Miller, explain to me what you mean by you might be her fiancé dependin' on *how her day is goin'*."

"I might be her brother, or I might be her fiancé, or I might be any other number of characters she's cleverly invented in her mind when it has suited her. It really depends on her mood, Marshal."

"Good Lord almighty, Mister Miller, She's got moods?"

"Yes, sir. I'm afraid she has lots of them."

"Sir, I have no idea what you're talkin' about or who this young woman is anymore. She's got more names than a Democrat's votin' list and more stories than a library."

"She *is* my fiancée."

"Somehow I doubt that, sir."

"Well…"

"There's that 'well' again."

"I should say she *was* my fiancée, until she decided that I wasn't who she thought I was."

"Who'd she think you was?"

"It's a long story, Marshal."

"Why am I not surprised about that? Never mind. I don't think I care to know anyway."

Miller looked down at the still struggling young woman, but she was tiring.

"How are you, Becky dear? I see you're making friends, as usual."

"*Becky*?!? Did he say *Becky*?" He looked at the young woman in disbelief.

She glared back.

"Yes, Marshal. Rebecca Ann Middleton. That's who I know her as."

"Jesus, Joseph, Mary, and Cousin Ida. I was just gettin' used to Jessica."

"That would be Jessica Abernathy?"

"The very same."

"Becky, darling, have you been busy creating more characters again? Or just regurgitating the old?" Miller's eyes shifted to the marshal. "Let me guess, Marshal. You've already met Lizzie May Allen and Cassandra Adams, in addition to Jessica Abernathy. Am I correct?"

"You are, sir. And there was a Tamara Baxter in there, too, for a bit."

"Ah yes, Tamara. I see. Then I take it you've yet to meet Janice Bernard, Mary Carter, and Wilhelmina Patterson?"

"Oh, Lord," said Carson.

"And me, Marshal. Since I saw her trying to shoot me, that might make me the escaped bank robber who is trying to exact revenge on her for turning me in to the law?"

Carson shook his head.

"Okay, then perhaps the Pinkerton detective out of Wichita who's been hired by her brutal wife-beating husband to find her and bring her back home."

Carson shook his head again.

"No? Then how about the mad escaped killer who has been tracking her relentlessly for months because of two gold half-coins and a letter with the cipher to break the code to the whereabouts of a chest full of Spanish gold coins?"

The Marshal raised his hand. "That's the one."

"I see. Well, my advice for you is..."

The young woman shouted something, but the gag successfully and thankfully muffled her words.

"She goes on like this for a while, Marshal. It's best to just let her finish it out."

Miller bent down and studied the young woman for a moment, then looked back at Carson.

"Another thirty minutes is my guess. Maybe less. Maybe more."

"Oh my." Carson shook his head.

"Yer packhorse got back late last night, Marshal," said Jimmy. "It still had a body tied to it. I figured somethin' must've gone wrong. And then Mister Miller, here, came into the office to inquire about a young lady that sounded a lot like your Miss Adams, or whatever she's goin' by now. Anyway, I thought I'd bring him along."

"Glad you did, Jimmy. Although we have a real mess here."

"Yeah, looks like it. So, what's goin' on?"

"Jimmy, I have no idea what the heck is goin' on, but I need a bottle of whiskey and a long, quiet night to drink it. And I don't even drink whiskey."

John chuckled. "He was lookin' for an adventure, Jimmy."

"Looks to me like an adventure has done gone and found you instead, Marshal."

"Jimmy, my boy, you ain't heard nothin' yet."

CHAPTER 12

"You don't say, Marshal," said Jimmy, riding next to Carson. "All that happened in just two days?"

He glanced back at the young woman sitting calmly in the saddle, gagged, with her hands tied behind her back, and John holding onto the reins of her horse.

"I'm surprised she let you get her mounted without a tussle."

"Jimmy, this has been a ride to remember."

"Or one to forget about real quick."

"She's been one surprise after another."

"Sure sounds like it."

Carson smiled wryly.

"When we get back to town, I'm gonna disappear for the rest of the day. I'm gonna get good and drunk, and don't no one bother me."

"Well, sir, you need to do what you need to do. John and I can handle things while you find your rest."

"What about Red, Jimmy?"

"I got ol' Jake watchin' him."

"That's good. Jake'll keep him in line. Although I intend to have a nice chat with Red about the assassins that was sent out to meet us. Gave us quite a how-d'ya-do, too."

"I still find it hard to believe ol' Roscoe Tanner would send out assassins on Red's behalf. I didn't know they was all that close."

"Neither did I, Jimmy. But I've been thinkin' on that some. My guess is Red knows somethin' Roscoe don't want him talkin' about. Maybe he thinks Red's already spilled the beans to me and he's thinkin' I might be on to him. Maybe that's why he sent them fellas out — to silence us."

"I s'pose it's possible. But Red ain't said but a few words since you left. And he ain't been a problem neither. He remains of the mind that you intend on sendin' him to Sacramento in a box — an open-top box. Rodney stopped by early this mornin' just as we was about to pull out."

"The undertaker?"

"Yeah. He was simply askin' about you. But ol' Red started bawlin' and screamin' and fussin' about in his cell. He thought Rodney come there to measure him for a box. It was pathetic, I'm tellin' ya. Got me laughin' so hard I thought I was gonna bust a gut."

Carson chuckled. "Ol' Red's been a handful for all of us, but he's the least of my problems right now."

Jimmy looked behind Carson at the bodies draped over horses and shook his head.

"I ain't never seen so many bodies laid over horses, Marshal."

"Jimmy, I swear we're gettin' thicker in bodies and no thinner in mystery. It's just dirty, darn bad luck, I'm sayin'."

"So you got no idea who killed the first fella?"

"No idea at all. But I've got a young woman who's turnin' out to be a bunch more'n I bargained for. She's a crafty one. Smart as a whip, too. She's got a heck of a story, with more twists than a rattlesnake. She's hidin' somethin' big — bigger'n gold, I'm sayin'. I'm gonna have to keep a close eye on that one. Right now, though, I don't know who's killed who. Heck, maybe *I* shot that young fella and don't recall it."

Jimmy shook his head thoughtfully. "I don't think so, Marshal. You was —"

"I was jokin', Jimmy. I ain't that far gone just yet."

"Ah. Well," said Jimmy, chuckling.

"Don't use that word around me right now. I'm all *well*ed out for the time bein'."

"I'm sorry."

"That was another joke, Jimmy."

"Okay, but it's gettin' so I can't tell when you're jokin' anymore."

"Me neither."

"I got it. That was another joke."

"I can't put nothin' past you anymore, Jimmy."

Miller reined his horse back until he was abreast of Carson. John, meanwhile, rode next to the mysterious young woman. Although she was now calm and still causing no further disturbance, John regarded her warily.

"So I suppose you're pretty confused, Marshal?"

"Yes, sir, Mister Miller. I don't mind sayin' it, she's got me totally buffaloed." Carson bobbed rhythmically in his saddle as he spoke. "I'm usually a pretty good judge of character, but this little feline has me questionin' everything I ever knowed to be true. Includin', I think, my own identity."

Miller chuckled.

"She does possess that charm, so to speak. She's done it to me, too."

"How do you put up with that kinda behavior?"

"I'm her fool, Marshal. I love her."

"I find that hard to believe, sir. I ain't yet seen you try to console her, hug her and such."

"Oh, I know better than to try to hug and talk to her when she's in this mood. For my own safety, it's best not to get too close. Know what I mean?"

"Yes, sir. I truly understand."

Carson reached up and rubbed his chin. "My teeth is still rattlin' around in my head from that lesson. Tell me, though: does she really know Judge Perry in Gallup?"

"Apparently one of her characters does. At least there is a daddy somewhere who knows the judge. But I don't know which one's daddy."

"Do you know anything that *is* true about her?"

"I don't know what's true about anything anymore when it comes to her, Marshal, except that I know I can't help myself. I love her. You might think I'm just as crazy for that, and maybe you're right, but I'm so in love with her. When it comes to her, I have no sense at all. But since you've already met Lizzie May Allen, it's a safe bet that you've learned of Smith College, too. Am I correct?"

"Yes, sir. You are."

"Well, from what I could discover, a young woman by the name of Rebecca Ann Middleton was educated there. I can't say that the young woman is our Rebecca, but it does seem to be where Becky came into existence. I could never find any family in Northampton by the name of Middleton that has a daughter around her age named Rebecca. After asking a lot of questions, I now believe that somewhere along the line, while she was at Smith, things began to unravel for her. Who she really is has been lost to time. Apparently, though, she became interested in acting on the stage at the college. I think it fair to say she fell in love with playacting. And…"

"She ain't never stopped her pretendin' since?"

"That's my belief. And the fantasies she's created would rival any stage play on Broadway, Marshal. But it seems they've all been scrambled together in such a way that they've sort of taken over her world. In many ways, I suppose, they've *become* her reality. At least a few of them, anyway."

"Mister Miller. I've got a nasty reality in my face as well. I've got eight bodies to account for. Three of 'em was apparently assassins from an outlaw's gang. I can deal with that easy enough. But I got a bunch more that I can't quite figure out to my complete satisfaction or understandin'. They didn't look to be thieves or desperadoes, but who knows?"

"Well, it doesn't seem like such a mystery to me. As you've described them while telling us your exploits of the last couple of days, the other four seemed dead set on Becky's gold. There's no telling where she met him. The leader, that is; the one she said was her husband. But he obviously became one of her playthings, too. And to tell you the truth, Marshal, there's no telling how many more *husbands* and *fiancés* she has out there who are now looking for her. I've been learning a lot about my beautiful betrothed while tracking her out to here. But the more I discover about her, the deeper the mystery she becomes to me."

"And that don't bother you none? Her havin' all these other men in her life?"

"I won't lie to you, Marshal. It does bother me. But I love her. I don't care about those other men because I know she's only using them to get what she wants. I believe she'll end up loving *me* when all of this is done."

"You're a man of faith, then?"

"Faith in love, Marshal."

"There ain't much about love I'd trust, Mister Miller. But then, bein' lucky in love is somethin' I have not yet experienced. At least not the kind of love you're talkin' about. I only know marshal work, and of late, even that seems to be a mystery. I don't know what happened to our young friend out at Dead River, but I think it's fair to say that he was caught up in the gold coins story just like all them others. I ain't got it worked out in my mind yet what part he played in this mysterious story of hers. I got to admit it, though — she tells a heck of a story."

"I was believing it myself for a while, Marshal. Well, a little, anyway. It has always seemed to me to be a bit over the top, but all in all, it has a ring of truth to it."

"It must've to them others as well, I reckon. They was prob'ly after the cipher letter. That's the key, apparently. If it even exists."

"It does in her mind, at least."

"So you think that's just more playactin' stuff?"

"I don't know, Marshal. I really don't know. I can't explain where the gold half-coins came from. Can you?"

"She says they was from her daddy. But like everything else about her, who can say if that story is true?"

"They do look convincingly real. But as yet I haven't found out anything noteworthy about them."

"She believes in 'em?"

"Oh, yes. She does."

"How did the letter come into it?"

"Darn it all, Marshal, I don't know. But she insists it's real, too."

"And you believe her?"

"You've been with her long enough to know what I've been dealing with over the last several months, Marshal. But I can say this. All fantasy has a basis in reality. And those half-coins intrigue me."

"They *are* unique. And I can't see why someone would go to all the trouble of makin' 'em if there wasn't some kinda truth attached to the story. She makes it sound like she's been trackin' down the other half of the coin and the letter for a long time, but her stories all seem more recent. Like she's only been at it a few weeks. It's confusin' me."

"She was after the other half of the coin long before I met her, Marshal. And I met her just over six months ago. From what I've gathered, she's been at this for well over a year."

"She said her daddy died a month ago and he confessed their existence to her then."

"Marshal, you're a smart man. There's no father mixed into the coin or the letter, as far as I can see. Where those things actually originated is something of a mystery in and of itself. In her more stable moments she gets me believing in almost everything she says, though. So I'm as much a plaything as everyone else is."

"She *does* have stable moments, then?"

"Oh, yes. But she doesn't handle stress very well, I've learned. When she comes into stressful moments, something snaps in her head and out come all the other names and characters she's created over time."

"I don't mean to disagree with ya, Mister Miller, but I've seen her under stress. She didn't seemed troubled by it. In fact, she handled herself pretty darn good. Now maybe that was just how she snapped. But it was darned impressive."

"Maybe so, but I've actually watched the transformation take place. And no matter how you slice it, it's quite odd, but so fascinating when it happens. I've never seen anything like it before or since I've met her. I can spot when she's about to alter her ways."

"Wanna let me in on it?"

"Her eyelids flutter just before a change. The changes aren't always wild and vastly different. Sometimes I had to look closely to see that she had changed at all. It varies and it is sometimes indecipherable. But I will tell you this. Something does change after those eyelids flutter."

"Son of a gun. So that's what I been seein'."

"You've seen her eyelids flutter?"

"I sure have."

"Well, then, you've witnessed her transformations. I'll tell you, Marshal, I've seen all manner of changes in her after her eyelids get to fluttering. Like I said, I can't say they are all abrupt and physical, but there are changes that take place. I can't really describe them any better than that, just that changes do happen. When you see her eyelids flutter, it's best to be prepared for anything."

"Mister Miller, do you think her capable of murder when she's in the midst of one of these transformations?"

"That's a good question, Marshal. I don't know. I'd like to think no. But I can't be sure."

"She took a rider off his horse with one shot, and he was a good distance away. She knows her way around a rifle, I can tell ya that."

"I don't doubt that. She *was* raised on a farm. She has good knowledge of farm life, anyway."

"She told me she ain't never seen a...no matter. Is it true she has three older brothers?"

"That would be Lizzie, Marshal. Lizzie has three older brothers. No, Becky, it seems, is the oldest of four daughters, but she did mention having one older brother."

"You believe her?"

"Not really."

"So, what's his name? Her brother?"

"Carl. Carl Middleton."

"Not Tom?"

"No. Tom is Jessica's brother. That's what she says when she's Jessica, at least. But I don't know if that's even real."

"Good Lord. Well, has *Carl* gone missin'?"

"No. She claims he's managed the store ever since...you know."

"Know what?"

"She hasn't told you?"

"Told me what?"

"Her father was killed. He's gone."

"She did mention her father dyin', but she didn't elaborate on the manner of his death. What happened?"

"He was killed in a robbery. Shot dead."

"Oh, my!"

"She told me that he died while she was away at school. She took it hard. She was apparently very close to her father."

"Like I said before, Mister Miller, she told me her father died about a month ago."

Miller chuckled.

"The father out in San Francisco? The one chased into a cave by Indians?"

"That's the one. You sayin' it ain't true?"

"With her, Marshal, what's ever true or false? All her stories get meshed together in some way or another. They get so convoluted that I don't think any one of them is right in and of itself. She did get a telegram a few months ago regarding the death of someone in her family. But she burned it before I could get sight of who it was."

"Dear Lord. But you don't believe any father exists like that?"

"Marshal, I don't know what to believe. But I do know that something changed in her after she got that telegram. As for the story of a father who used to be a farmer, I simply don't know. The story goes that several years ago he left the farm and moved his family from New Mexico to San Francisco. Made it big in dry goods and such. But anything I might believe about her has been built from small pieces of all the stories. I don't think she knows the truth of it herself."

"Maybe I'm wrong about this," said Carson, "but I'm readin' her different."

"How's that?"

"I think she's extremely clever. Brilliant, even. She's either playin' us for fools or she might be extremely ill — got an illness of the mind. I ain't come to any decision as to which road to take on that. But don't you think it to be an odd story, them movin' from New Mexico to San Francisco?"

"Why's that?"

"From a farmer in New Mexico to a storekeeper in San Francisco: it ain't odd to you?"

"I was born in San Francisco, Marshal. I don't understand what you're driving at."

"There's a big difference between bein' a farmer and bein' a storekeeper, Mister Miller."

"Yes, I suppose there is, but she said her father sold the farm. Made some good money on the sale and the family moved west. It was a dream of his for years to own a store in a big city."

"How about bein' chased into a cave by Apaches? That ain't odd to you either?"

"She insists that he was — about a month before he decided to move to San Francisco. She said the incident really shook him up. She said it made him realize just how dangerous it was out here in these parts for his family. They left for the coast almost immediately thereafter. The ranch was sold from a distance. She said her father wanted them out of the area quickly."

"She told you all this?"

"As I say, I pieced it together over time."

"So her father never stumbled onto a chest full of Spanish coins that made him rich? He was just scared for his family's safety?"

Miller chuckled.

"I have no idea, Marshal. With her overactive imagination, who really knows what the truth of any of it is? She might have heard a story of a man once chased by Indians and turned it into a wild fantasy of her own design involving mysterious half-coins, ciphers, brothers, and Spanish treasure. There might be nothing to any of this except what is in her mind. I just love her and I'm willing to play this out to its conclusion."

"She's intelligent, I'll say that for her."

"Extremely so, Marshal. And witty and charming and captivating. All that when she wants to be. But when those others come to the surface, she can be as mysterious as they come."

"And as devious, Mister Miller. And as devious."

CHAPTER 13

Despite the oppressive heat, Carson and the others pressed on back to Holbrook with the train of horses and bodies in tow.

It was a slow ride and they didn't get back to town until well after nightfall. John, Miller, and the young woman went to the marshal's office to await the marshal and Jimmy's return from the undertaker's office.

The steady banging on the front door of the undertaker's residence finally brought the sleepy old man to the door. Attired in a pair of scruffy long johns and holding up a lantern, he immediately recognized the marshal and opened the door wider.

"Marshal! Glad you made it back safe and sound."

"Sorry to disturb ya so late, Rodney, but I'm afraid I got some bodies for ya."

Carson stepped aside. Rodney Branson's eyes opened wide when he saw all the horses with bodies draped over them lined up behind Carson.

"Lord almighty, Marshal! Did you do all that?"

"They're mostly John's doin's."

"My word. What *happened* to you out there?"

"It's a long story, Rodney. Can we get 'em inside? They're turnin' mighty sour. Been out in the sun all day."

"Sure thing. Take 'em around back. I'll be with you in a moment. Just need to get dressed."

Carson and Jimmy finished lugging the last body into the parlor and set it down on the floor alongside several others, there being only two preparation tables in the room.

"You head on back to the office now, Jimmy."

"Will do, Marshal."

Jimmy departed, leaving Carson to wait for the undertaker.

After several minutes, the undertaker finally came into the room holding up a lighted lantern. He took one look at all the bodies and shook his head.

"It's forty dollars, Marshal; five dollars apiece. That's including the one from yesterday. Who's gonna pay?"

"The government, Rodney. I'll get ya the money tomorrow. Will that be okay?"

"Sure, Marshal. That'll be just fine. Did Jimmy tell you I stopped by your office early this morning?"

"I heard about it. Gave ol' Red a scare, I heard."

"Sure did. Didn't mean to, though. But what about all these boys? Looks to me like they're done being scared."

"I reckon it depends on where they are now."

"I reckon so. The other one, the one that came in with your packhorse, did he belong to the hat you found?"

"It appears so. But I can't say for sure about that right now, or about anything else. There are many more questions than there are answers. The hat *was* in the vicinity of the body, so it seems likely. But I don't know what's goin' on at the moment. I do intend to get to the bottom of it all startin' tomorrow. Did you get a chance to get Doc to look the body over for me?"

"Yes. Doc Martin stopped by and confirmed that the young man bled out from a single gunshot. And he appeared to have been nibbled on a bit, but all that was postmortem. Several of his ribs were broken, too, but it was the —"

"His ribs was broke? I didn't notice that."

"Well, Doc said several were broken. Fractured, he called it. But it was the bullet that killed him."

"Broke ribs? Must have happened when his horse was shot out from under him. Or the packhorse might've crunched up against a boulder or somethin' on the way back to town. We sure didn't notice 'em bein' broke."

"Doubt you would have noticed them, them being only fractures."

"One more piece to add to the puzzle, it seems, or maybe we just didn't take note of 'em while we was movin' the body."

"Maybe. But it was the bullet that did him in. Is one of these others the killer?"

"I really don't know."

The undertaker walked around the room staring down into the faces of the corpses.

"I reckon it really doesn't matter all that much anymore. He won't be complaining about the injustice of it, I reckon."

"No, can't say that he will."

"Well, I'll be," said the undertaker.

"What's that?"

"This here is Jeb Rickson. You killed Jeb Rickson."

"You know him, do ya?"

"Sure do. I buried his pa up in Abilene a few years back. He was a mean one. His son, too. Looks like his mean days is over now."

"Do you recognize any of the others, Rodney?"

The undertaker walked around the other bodies until he stopped next to a badly damaged one.

"Who's this with his head blown apart?"

"Supposedly, his name is Byron. A few sticks of dynamite exploded next to him."

"Never heard the name. Can't say I recognize his face, or what's left of it, either."

"How about the others, Rodney?"

"Nope. Don't know any of them others. But good to see ol' Jeb get his due. He was a bad one, to be sure. Last I heard of him, he was riding with that Tanner fella outa Abilene and Wichita. I wonder what he was doing this far west."

"You say Tanner?"

"Yep."

"Would that be Roscoe Tanner?"

"The very same."

"Then that confirms it. This other one over here is Dowd Campbell. He's one of Roscoe Tanner's bunch, too. And ol' Red rode with 'em. Tanner sent these two and this one over here out to kill us."

"You don't say."

"I do say. It's just dirty, darn bad luck, I'm sayin'. I don't exactly know why he'd do that at the moment, but I got my thoughts on it."

"I reckon you might have some words with ol' Red about it, then?"

"Yep. That's the plan anyway."

"He was a mite twitchy when I saw him last."

"He's gonna be a mite twitchier by the time I'm finished with him. I tell ya, this investigation is gettin' stranger by the minute."

"Well, I'm glad you got ol' Jeb, at least. He was not a good man, Marshal."

"For good men and bad men alike, Rodney, it's been days too long."

The undertaker sniffed the air. "It's certainly been days too long for these fellas. I better get some ice packed around these boys."

"You do that and I'll talk more about it tomorrow with ya, if you don't mind."

"Okay, Marshal. As you wish."

Carson turned and walked out the door.

If cold, staring eyes could kill, Marshal Carson would have been obliterated the moment he walked back into his office. The mysterious young woman now being called Rebecca shot him a glance that could chill the sun to an ice ball.

He stopped just inside the door and stared disbelievingly at the wreckage before him.

His bookshelf had been emptied of books, most of them lying helter-skelter on the floor on the opposite side of the room. The chairs had been tossed about the room, none of them left standing upright. The desk had been twisted around from its normal position.

Jimmy Johnson sat against the wall holding a bloodied cloth to his forehead.

John was tying the last knot to a rope on the chair the agitated young lady sat on. He had tied her to the chair and had then tied the chair to the bars of an empty cell immediately next to the cell containing the hysterically laughing Red Darrington.

The gag in her mouth prevented her from speaking, but Carson heard her muffled verbal assaults clearly enough to gather her meaning.

"What in *tarnation*...?" he said.

Red Darrington howled with renewed laughter.

"Buzzards, Red," said Carson.

Red quieted and sat back down on his bunk.

John finished tying the knot and stood up, turning around to face Carson. His face was bloodied and beaten, and blood was dripping from his nose.

"Oh, dear Lord! Not again."

"Yes, sir. I'm afraid we've had us an *incident*, Marshal."

Red Darrington smirked.

"Red?" said Carson, moving toward his cell. "You strike me as one with a fondness for chucklin'. Well, sir, I got a real chuckler for ya. Jeb Rickson and Dowd Campbell is over at the undertaker's right now with another fella you might know."

"Jeb and Dowd?" Red asked.

"That's a fact. They're about to get prepped and photographed before they get buried. Would you like to be in that photograph with 'em?"

The fun was immediately over for Darrington.

"No, sir. I wouldn't care to do that. You serious, Marshal? Jeb and Dowd is dead?"

"That's right, Red. Jeb and Dowd is dead. Don't know who the other fella is, but he's just as dead."

"How?"

"We shot 'em. Shot 'em all. I believe Roscoe sent 'em out to ambush us on the trail."

Red swallowed hard as Carson continued.

"I believe you met Rodney, the undertaker, this mornin'. I'm thinkin' of sendin' for him, along with his measurin' tape. How 'bout it?"

"No, sir. That won't be necessary."

"Buzzards, Red. Are ya gonna keep yer yap shut and behave?"

Red nodded silently.

"Here's another thing, Red. We're gonna break words in a while, you and me, regardin' your association with Roscoe Tanner. And dependin' on your answers, you just might get to see the measurin' tape of the undertaker danglin' before yer eyes. That is, before the buzzards have at 'em. You catch my drift?"

Red swallowed hard and nodded his head again.

"An *incident*, you say, John?" said Carson, still staring holes through Red Darrington.

"So we goin' after Roscoe now?" asked John.

"What about your *incident*, John?"

"Well, sir. She said she needed to use the facilities. We escorted her out to the privy. I untied her hands and she went inside to do her business. It was all by the book."

"By the book, you say?" Carson turned his eyes toward John.

"Yes, sir. All by the book. Until she come out and we got her back here."

"I'm listenin'."

"She didn't fancy havin' her hands tied again. That's when the incident began."

"And durin' the *incident*, she did all this?"

"I'm afraid she was a mite insistent on not bein' tied up again, Marshal."

"This little girl did all this to my office and to you two as well?"

"I think I heard you say once that you'd classify somethin' like this as an *overly volatile* kinda incident."

"Sorta like what we had with her out in the desert today?"

"Like that, only she was a bit more volatile this time around."

"My stars, Miss. You are some kinda enigma."

"It took some doin', Marshal, but I think we got her under control again. I do believe she's calmed down now."

Carson moved to a point just in front of the woman and bent low, his hands resting on his knees, to look into her eyes.

"Why is the chair tied to the bars, John?"

"She was prone to chair tippin', Marshal. This was my only solution for that."

"I see. And all of this took place while I was at the undertaker's?"

"Just after Jimmy come back. It's been busy here since then."

Carson, still bent over, stared into the woman's fiery eyes.

"She don't look none too calm to me, John."

"I think you'd say it's relative. She's a lot better now than she was before. It's just the chair-tippin' problem that I been workin' on."

"It looks like you achieved the resolution."

"I had to gag her again, too. The words comin' outa her mouth darn near curdled my ears."

"Un-ladylike again, were they, John?" said Carson, straightening up.

"You could say that, Marshal. Some new ones this time around that I still ain't quite got the meanin' of."

Carson shook his head with a chuckle.

"And where did Mister Miller get off to?"

"I believe he's over at Maddie's havin' a drink."

"Was he a witness to any of this *incident*?"

"No, sir. It all began just after Jimmy arrived and he left."

"I do believe I'll join him for a drink myself."

Bending over again to bring his face close to the young woman's, Carson stared deeply into her eyes.

"Miss Middleton, I surely wish you woulda chose to act more ladylike. I gotta tell ya, I'm just plain wore out lookin' at what you did to my office and my deputies. You exhaust me, young lady. And I've done my best to treat you with all manner of respect despite your lies, your pretenses, and your rude behavior.

"You've managed to tax my patience and that of my deputies to the breakin' point. Yes, ma'am, you surely have. But I remain in a gracious mood nonetheless, although I can't for the life of me understand why I feel so inclined. Still, I don't figure it proper to keep you tied to Red's cell knowing he has a history of deviant behavior."

Red's eyes lit up. He raised his head and looked at Carson. Without returning his look, Carson pointed an index finger at Red. Red lowered his eyes again, remaining silent.

"To spare you the likes of that, I, therefore, propose a solution. Seein' what you've just put my boys through and all, I can't exactly condone your actions, nor reward such rude behavior with impunity. But despite your little *incident* here, I'm gonna give you one last chance. Listen to me good. Here's how it'll play out.

"I'm gonna go have me a few drinks with your man friend over at Maddie's Saloon. Maybe more than a few. If you have remained calm while I've taken my rest, I'll cut you loose from your bindin's upon my return, and you can spend a comfortable night in your hotel room. You will have a guard outside your door, of course, and we will revisit your rude behavior and your assault on my boys first thing tomorrow mornin'.

"If, however, you find it impossible to behave yourself, you'll spend the night in this chair with Red right behind ya. You can take yer chances with him and there won't be no more breaks for the *facilities*. You can sit here and wet yourself all you want. And tomorrow mornin', before we visit other matters, you'll clean up the mess, usin' your pretty hair as a rag. Are we communicatin'?"

The young woman stared sharper knives into Carson's eyes, but within seconds her demeanor radically shifted and she appeared calm. After several more seconds she nodded in agreement.

Carson stood up straight.

"Wonderful. I'm glad of it."

"So, Marshal, you say you had an *incident*?" Miller asked as he lifted the jigger of whiskey to his mouth and tossed down the shot.

"That's what my deputy called it." Carson downed his own shot of whiskey with a grimace.

"And what would you call it?"

"Do you recall what we had with her out on the trail earlier?"

"I do."

"Well, whatever that was, we apparently had us another one, only worse than that. It's just dirty, darn bad luck, I'm sayin'."

"An incident. That's quite interesting. I've never heard of her outbursts referred to as *incidents*. Tirades, maniacal rants, fiery torrents of insanity, but never *incidents*. Your deputy seems to have mastered the art of understatement — or he's being quite diplomatically polite. I'm glad I was here instead of there."

"She took us by surprise, Mister Miller. I don't mind admittin' it."

"Don't feel too bad about that, Marshal. You're not the first to say that, and I'm certain you won't be the last."

"It's been my experience that what sets people off like that usually bears the scars of somethin' mighty upsettin' in their past. Can you tell me anything more about her past?"

"I'll tell you what I know, Marshal. As I said, I met Becky a little over six months ago. It was in St. Louis. I was drawn to her immediately. Of course I see now I was attracted to her like a moth to a flame, but she captivated me. Last month I proposed. She accepted, but she wanted to make the engagement official in San Francisco at the home of her father. So we immediately boarded a train for California. She told me that she was excited to introduce me to her family."

"But her father had just died," said Carson.

"She told me, of course, that he had died while she attended school. So you can imagine my surprise...and confusion. But I was also very intrigued."

"As I would be, no doubt. So, did you make it out to San Francisco to meet her newly undead father?"

Miller chuckled.

"I was looking forward to it, just to discover the truth. I never did, of course. She got off the train in Omaha to use the facilities and she never got back on."

"You mean she up and disappeared on ya?" Carson tipped a shot of whiskey into his mouth with a grimace and a shudder.

"Like the proverbial fart in the wind, Marshal. I suppose I look pretty foolish to you, don't I?"

"I've seen men do worse for the curse of love. And you're just now catchin' up with her?"

"Sounds insane, doesn't it? Chasing after a woman who obviously wants nothing more to do with me? Heck, it even sounds crazy to me now that I hear the words coming out of my own mouth."

"As I said, I've heard of stranger happenin's when it comes to afflictions of the heart."

"An affliction of the heart. Yes, I suppose that's what it is. Have you ever been so afflicted, Marshal?"

"Not for a woman, no, but I've done things far more foolish for far less noble reasons."

"Well, now that I've found her, I'm feeling pretty foolish, stupid, used...are there any other words I've overlooked?

Carson laughed.

"Buffaloed, hornswoggled, bamboozled, duped..."

"Okay, okay. Thank you, Marshal. I get the idea."

Carson and Miller both laughed and, after clinking jiggers, threw down another shot together.

"So, what now, Mister Miller?"

"I've been sitting here wondering what I should do."

"Women will do that to ya." Carson smiled. "They have a way of gettin' a man to question everything."

"I'm coming to the truth of that, Marshal."

"So, you ain't never met her brother, Carl?"

"No. Just heard the story of him from Becky."

"Dear Lord. He might be another fart in the wind, then."

"I never thought of it that way, but I'm certain you're right about that, too. I'm beginning to doubt everything she's ever told me. Oh, my."

"'Oh, my' is right, Mister Miller."

Carson and Miller both tossed down another shot.

"Andrew, Marshal. Or Andy, please."

"Okay, Andy it is — until I start callin' you Mister Miller again."

Miller laughed. "That'd be just fine. How about another shot, Marshal?"

"I never cared much for whiskey, Mister Mil…uh, Andy. But after livin' through the last several days as I have, what the heck! There is one more thing troubling me about our young lady, though. Why does she require so many alliances? Or marriages…or whatever else she might call 'em."

"That's a good question."

"I got a better one. How many more husbands are we likely to come across before this adventure is done?"

"Thanks, Marshal. I was trying to avoid thinking about that."

"Sorry, Andy."

"Forget it. After a few more shots, I won't be thinking at all."

Carson and Miller chuckled as Miller filled their jiggers. They clinked them together again and downed the shots.

The marshal walked into his office the next morning rubbing his eyes and moaning.

"Mornin', Marshal," said John brightly.

"Shhhhhh. Shhhhhh," replied Carson.

"Easy there, John," whispered Jimmy. "I think the marshal lost his battle with the bottle last night."

"Havin' a tough mornin', Marshal?" asked Red loudly, grinning devilishly.

Carson flashed his revolver, cocked the hammer, and aimed it at Red, who froze in place.

Carson's hand shook uncontrollably. "You're a real slow learner, ain't ya, Red? Go ahead. Say one more word to me. Please."

Red urinated down his right pant leg, but kept silent despite the puddle forming around his boots.

Carson stood staring icicles at Red, then he finally relaxed and holstered his Peacemaker.

"I'd like to shoot yer eyes out, Red, but the noise of doin' such might explode my head right off my shoulders. You ain't worth an explodin' head, Red. Besides, I wouldn't want to deprive the buzzards of those tasty morsels during the ride to Sacramento."

Red's eyes began blinking rapidly.

Carson looked around his office. Everything had been returned to its proper place.

He nodded to John.

"Thank you, John."

"Welcome, Eli. It just took Jimmy and me a few minutes."

Carson noticed the empty chair where the young woman had sat bound and gagged the night before. He pointed to the chair without speaking.

"I cut her loose 'bout eight o'clock last night. I didn't think you were gonna make it back in time. I put ol' Jake on her door."

"Did Red trouble her any?"

"Once. No trouble from him after that, though."

John pulled his knife from its sheath.

"I made Red a promise if he didn't behave. Ain't that right, Red?"

Red Darrington looked up, but said nothing.

"I don't wanna know more about it. I get the point," said Carson.

"Red pretty near got the point, too. Ain't that right, Red?"

The outlaw dropped his eyes to the floor and refused to answer.

Carson nodded again. "Good, John."

He then moved to his chair, sat down slowly, crossed his arms on his desk, and laid his head on them.

John came close and whispered, "You gonna be all right, Eli?"

"If I died right now, maybe I'd feel a touch better."

"Why don't Jimmy and me walk around town on our rounds and leave you to rest?"

"That would be just fine, John. Do me a favor first. Kill Red before you go, so he won't bother me none."

John looked at Red. The outlaw's eyes widened immediately with terror.

"I can't do that right now, Marshal, but I'm sure Red is gonna keep silent as a mouse while you rest."

Red nodded in frightened agreement, his eyes still blinking furiously.

"Okay," replied Carson, unwilling to argue the point for the sake of his splitting head.

It was two hours before John found the courage to walk back to Carson's office. Upon entering, he discovered two unusual things.

The first was Red sitting on his cot without his trousers and boots. John supposed he had removed them since soiling them earlier. And there was a strong scent of stale urine throughout the room.

The second was Marshal Carson fast asleep on the cot in the opposite corner of the room. John cringed, but he had no choice but to awaken his boss.

Before he did so, however, he carefully removed Carson's revolver from its holster and stepped back a foot or two.

"Marshal? … Marshal?" he spoke quietly.

Carson didn't move.

"Marshal?" he said louder. "I need you to wake up."

Carson didn't move.

John stepped closer and gently poked Carson in the chest.

"Marshal. I really need you to wake up."

Carson remained as still as a dead man.

John gritted his teeth and then shook the old lawman hard and shouted, "Get up, Marshal!"

Carson bolted up, repeatedly reaching for a revolver that, thankfully, wasn't there.

"What? What?" Carson looked around wildly.

"Sorry, Marshal. Are you awake now?"

"Yes, I am, but I ain't none too happy about it."

"Sorry, Marshal, but I had to waken you."

"Okay, okay. We've established that. Now why? What's wrong?"

"Well, sir," John stopped and exhaled hard before continuing. "We've had us another incident."

CHAPTER 14

Marshal Carson was unsteady on his feet as he and John walked to the hotel.

Upon entering the main door, he stopped a moment and clutched the door frame to support himself.

"I swear, John, to a loving god and bowlegged women, not another drop of whiskey will ever pass my lips again."

"I believe you, Eli," said John, laughing under his breath.

Carson released his grip on the door frame and staggered into the hotel, crossing the lobby in unsure steps to finally stop in front of Jimmy and Andrew Miller, who were waiting patiently for him. When they saw the marshal, both men cringed. It was Miller who spoke first though.

"Dying would make you look better, Marshal."

"Make me feel a whole lot better, too, Mister Miller," said Carson, teetering in front of Miller. "So, what is our new incident with Miss Abernathy?"

"Uh, Marshal," said John, "that's Miss Middleton."

"Right, John. If *that*'s her real name."

"She's gone," said Miller.

"She's gone, Mister Miller? Gone where?"

"Just gone, Marshal," said Jimmy.

"What about Jake?"

"Jimmy and I found him on the floor gagged and tied," answered John. "Had a big ol' knot on the back of his head, too."

"He was layin' next to this," said Jimmy.

Jimmy proffered the hat that Carson had found in the desert and given to the young woman thinking it had belonged to her brother. The lining of the hat was torn.

"How's Jake?" Carson asked as he tried to focus his bloodshot eyes on the hat.

"He's over at Doc's office," said John. "He'll be fine. He'll have a whoppin' headache for a while is all."

"Somethin' inside it, I take it?" asked Carson, referring to the torn lining of the hat.

"I suspect it was the letter with the cipher," said Miller.

"Dear me. You mean she had it all the time?"

"She had it, but she obviously didn't know about it until last night," answered John.

"What time did you discover her missin'?"

"About eight this mornin'. Just after we left you in the office."

"Why didn't you come get me then?"

"I thought you needed the sleep more. She was already gone, Marshal."

"Bless you for your amiable consideration, John."

John looked perplexed.

"Thank you for your kindness."

"Oh, kindness. Yes, sir. You're welcome, Marshal."

"Anyone see her leave?"

"Greg Welch did, Marshal," replied John. "He saw her ride out as he opened his store. Said she headed north outa town."

"What time was this?"

"'Bout four this mornin'."

Carson reached for his pocket watch and opened the cover to see the time, but he closed his eyes tight.

"John, look at the time for me, please. It hurts my eyes tryin' to focus."

John looked at the watch. "It's near ten o'clock."

"Six-hour head start ain't too bad. Shouldn't take us long to catch up with her, I reckon." The marshal continued swaying as he spoke.

"Better sit down, Marshal. Before you fall," said Miller.

"I'm a little slow today, boys," said Carson as he tumbled into a nearby chair. "It's just dirty, darn bad luck, I'm sayin'."

"How much whiskey did he drink last night?" John asked Miller.

"I'm not certain, John. I stopped counting after eight shots. But we stayed quite a bit longer."

"Too many. That's how many," said Carson. "Too darn many. Felt like the right thing to do at the time, though."

"Why don't you just rest, Marshal? Me and Jimmy can get on her trail quick-like. We should have her in custody and back here within a few days if we ride hard."

"I wish I could, John. I really wish I could. But I've yet to finish my murder investigation of that young man out by the rock. I believe Miss Abernathy — I mean, Miss Middleton — might be a material witness. I don't understand how that could be just yet, but I do know that hat has some strong connection to all of this craziness. And Miss Middleton is in possession of what might be considered evidence of motive for the crime. I therefore, and with abysmal regret, must go with ya."

"No offense, Marshal, but you're in no kinda condition to ride as hard as we'll need to ride. Why don't you take Red to Sacramento and then take some time for yourself while you're there. Leave the girl to me and Jimmy. By the time you get back, we'll have her back here and secured."

"That's right good thinkin', John. But I need to look in on Jake and get me some coffee to settle my thoughts on the matter."

"May I join you, Marshal?" asked Miller.

"You may, sir, but I'd ask you to keep yer voice low for the next little while, please. I am, at present, a man of many sorrows."

"I understand, Marshal."

"With all due respect, sir, I don't think you do. You'd have to be standin' in my skin to even have an inklin' of what exquisite pain I'm feelin' on this side."

John and Miller snickered.

"You know you ain't gonna hear the end of this anytime soon, don't you, Eli?"

"And I deserve every moment of yer teasin', John, if you should choose to do so. But I'll prob'ly shoot ya in the kneecap if ya do."

John smirked.

Trevor Dunkerton, the managing clerk at the telegraph office, walked into the dining room of the hotel, waved, and yawned as he stopped at the table where Carson was seated with John, Jimmy, and Miller.

"I can see I ain't the only one who could use more shut-eye. Good mornin', Trevor."

"Good morning, Marshal. Yes, sir, I ain't used to sending telegrams so early in the morning. I need at least a pot of coffee to keep awake now."

"What's that?"

"I say I need a whole pot of coffee to stay awake this morning."

"Not that. What you said about telegrams."

"Oh. I said I'm not used to sending telegrams at such early hours."

"Telegrams? Who'd be sendin' telegrams early in the mornin' in this town?"

"Oh, that would be Miss Middleton, Marshal."

"Miss Middleton, you say?"

"Yes, sir. Sent out a couple of telegrams very early this morning. Came banging on my door, all excited. Paid me five whole dollars to send her telegrams each time. I said shoot, I can do that for ten dollars."

"Who did she send the telegrams to?"

"No one in particular, Marshal. She sent them station to station."

"What station?"

"Gallup."

"Explain it all to me, please, Trevor. In order."

"Okay, Marshal. She come to my home about two thirty in the a.m. and had me send a telegram, station to station to Gallup."

"What was the message?"

"It was 'Found it. Stop. C.L. confirmed. Stop. C.C. End.'"

"C.L.?... C.C.?"

"Yes, sir."

"What does that mean?"

"I don't know. That's what she gave me and that's what I sent."

"That's all of it?"

"Yes. Then about an hour later she come again and roused me out of bed to send another one."

"Okay. And it said…?"

"'Leaving soon. Stop. Meet C.L. dash SW 8. Stop. C.C. End.'"

"'C.L. dash SW 8'? That's it?"

"Yes, sir. That's it exactly."

"What does *that* mean?"

"Darned if I know. She paid me to send it that way and I sent it just that way. After she left, I went back and tried to get back to sleep, but I just…"

"Thank you, Trevor. Go get you some coffee."

"You're welcome, Marshal."

Dunkerton strolled away, leaving Carson thinking and scratching his chin whiskers.

John kept quiet and allowed Carson to think for a while. But then curiosity got the better of him.

"Okay, Marshal. What you thinkin' on?"

"I'm thinkin' I'm needin' either a whole lot of coffee or a lot more sleep to clear my head, but I do believe it's all startin' to come together for me."

"How's that?"

"She's got an accomplice. And she's had one all along, right from the start. Oh, she's a joker, that one, fellas. And we're the joke."

After a short visit to ol' Jake and having partaken of enough coffee to float a three-masted cargo ship, Carson sent Jimmy to the undertaker's office with the forty-dollar fee. He then sighed.

"I don't believe I'm ready for this, fellas, but let's give it a try. I'm sure I'm gonna regret the attempt, though."

Carson paid Red Darrington a visit to inquire about his relationship with Roscoe Tanner in the hopes of discovering why Tanner had sent his assassins out after him.

Red, of course, possessed no useful information regarding that issue. And the sound of Red's voice just agitated Carson more than he could stand.

As he had predicted, he regretted his effort to interrogate Red Darrington, and abandoned his quest for discovery. He made the decision to send Jimmy to Sacramento with Red, feeling it was in the outlaw's best interest, seeing that he still favored the idea of transporting Red to Sacramento in a box.

Although Red didn't say it outright, Carson believed the outlaw was glad it was the sober deputy who accompanied him instead of the ornery, hungover, open-box-favoring Marshal.

Even after all the coffee, though, it was still two hard hours out of Holbrook before Carson was able to hold his head up high enough to see where he was going.

Andrew Miller had decided that the adventure was just too great to pass up, though he was now having second thoughts about it.

Marshal Carson and John Slims were more used to the brutal assault of the desert, but even they were beginning to question the wisdom of their effort.

Four hours later had them under the dead heat of the energy-draining mid-afternoon sun. The horses were exhausted, as were their riders. Canteens were near empty, and Carson wondered if he had made a big mistake coming after the young woman.

"What the heck are we doin' out here?"

"Tryin' to capture a young woman, Marshal."

"I'm askin' a larger question, John. I'm really askin' myself the question. Why are we doin' this? She's lighter. She's faster. And she has a real purpose for what she's doin'. As for us, we're just duty bound to track her down because I've got an investigation under way. Does this really make any sense?"

"You're doing your job, Marshal," said Miller. "Does it have to make more sense than that?"

"I suppose not. I sometimes just get to questionin' the sanity of this job, Mister Miller. It gives me pause to consider my own place in all this craziness. And I must be comin' to the end of it all, because I tend to find less reason for doin' this each day. Do you still see the tracks, John?"

"Clear as can be, Marshal. I don't know what she was thinkin' when she lit out on this new adventure of hers. She must've knowed I could recall her horse's tracks."

"I don't think she was thinkin' at all in that regard. I think she has gold on the brain and it's cloudin' her judgment."

"I'll drink to that," said John, smiling.

Carson moaned.

"You have a cruel twist about you, John Slims."

Both Miller and John chuckled.

"Sorry, Eli, but I been bidin' my time all mornin' lookin' for just the right moment to have a little tease at ya."

"I'm glad you got it off your chest, John. I wouldn't want ya to go to perdition without fulfillin' yer need to tease me. But it *is* perdition I wish for ya."

John laughed, then turned serious.

"That girl can ride, I'll give her that. I'm nearin' my end for the day and I ain't even seen a hint of her yet except for these tracks. I don't know if we're catchin' up to her or she's movin' farther ahead of us."

"Like I said, she's already showed me her true colors. So almost nothin' that girl does surprises me anymore," said Carson. "But her willpower is astonishin', I gotta give her credit for that. She is determined. And I believe she's got the skills to pull it off."

"I recall at the time it *sounded* like an exciting adventure," said Miller. "I don't know what I was thinking. You still believe she's on the trail to the gold, Marshal?"

"Yes, sir. But why she's headin' up north like this stumps me."

"Why is that?"

"There can't be nothin' up here, Mister Miller. Ain't no kinda caves up in these parts that I know of. They ain't nothin' up here but rocks and sand."

"Another mystery, then?"

"Out here in this miserable wasteland, everything is a mystery — until it strikes ya dead."

"Then what can Becky be doing up here?"

"I don't know, Mister Miller. I truly don't."

"I honestly can't say anymore that I know her as well as I thought I did, but I do know this.

She doesn't do anything without good reason. I can see now that she exercised good reason in using me the way she did."

"Mister Miller, I think I can speak for the both of us when I say that she's found a good reason for us all. Of course, I don't know presently what that is, but I'm certain I'll have my questions answered sooner or later. I'm not sayin' I'll like the answers, but I'll get 'em just the same."

"She's sure somethin' I've never seen before," said John.

Carson shook his head. "She's either crazy smart or smart crazy. I ain't sure yet which it is."

"What's the difference, Eli?"

"I don't know, John, but whatever the difference is, I don't expect we'll like it either way. Then again, this might all just be the madness come from chasin' after gold. I've seen the eyes of normally sane people go wide with the gold madness."

"You think the story is real, Eli? You think the gold is real?"

"I can't say, John. I believe in her mind it's real. Or might be she's just touched with a general madness. Or she might be on some other adventure and she's bein' keenly strategic about it. I can't rightly say at present who it is we're followin' after. But any way you cut it, it's all in her mind. It's whatever she says it is."

"In whose mind, Eli? The nice lady who talks real pretty, or the crazy woman that tried to bite my face off?"

"I think we all feel a touch of madness now and then, John. I think madness, gold or otherwise, controls its own existence. I believe it chooses when to come and when to go, and when it comes upon you, all you can do is hang on tight and ride it out. It seems a crazy way to live to someone not so afflicted, but I believe it's all normal to one that is."

"Well, from the direction we're headin', I surely can't say a stable mind is in charge. Because this is a crazy way into the canyonlands — a deadly kinda crazy. No one I know ever went this far north before turnin' eastward. Water don't exist for miles and miles. They ain't much shade out here, if you can find it at all. And this trail is normally only traveled by Injuns, and I ain't talkin' 'bout the friendly kind. This is a trail only someone totally crazy would take — or someone tryin' to get themselves killed."

"Or maybe it's a trail only a brilliant strategic and tactical mind might take to put fools to wonderin'. Of course, if it *is* the madness of gold, then it might seem the logical way to go if one is followin' it, I reckon."

"How's that?"

"I don't know, John. I believe that's why they call chasin' after gold a madness."

"Are you feeling better now, Marshal?"

"I am, Mister Miller. I don't relish the jostlin' at the moment, but I'm back in as right a mind as I can be under the circumstances."

"The gold is real! I'm having a hard time grasping that."

"Like I said, Mister Miller, the gold might be real to her in the state of mind she's in. It don't mean that a chest of gold coins actually exists up in these hills. Or we might be followin' after someone who is just filled with a general madness or is on some other kind of adventure altogether."

"I understand that. But what if it *is* real?"

"Then I believe we ain't yet seen the kind of madness that real gold can bring to an unprepared mind."

"If she is unprepared, Marshal."

"True enough, Mister Miller," said John. "And she don't strike me as the unprepared type."

"Me neither. And if she does have the two halves of the coin and the cipher and all of this talk of gold is true, then she might be leading us to it. What worries me most is how she'll choose to protect her gold, should she find it. She could get deadly protective about it."

"Whew! You have a good point there, Mister Miller," said Carson. "Filled with madness or not, she's got tactical skills. And I've seen her shoot. She's good. Too good for us to just run up on her willy-nilly-like."

"She'll have us unsaddled and on the ground bleeding out in a heartbeat if we aren't careful," said Miller.

"You're right, and if my mind was more absent the fog of whiskey, I would've thought about that myself. We might need to back off some and go about trackin' her a bit slower. Otherwise we might find ourselves in the midst of a hail of bullets before we know it."

"You want me to slow down, Marshal?" asked John.

"I think so, John. I don't fancy gallopin' into my next life fulla lead."

Carson looked up into the clear sky.

"It's too hot to run these horses like we have been anyway, John. If we keep up this pace, we'll either run into bullets or kill these horses dead. Let's hole up here a while and let 'em catch their breath."

"Okay," John said as he reined his horse to a stop.

"Let's try to find us some shade, if it's possible," said Carson. "I'd like to think this matter through some more without the sun suckin' my brain dry."

CHAPTER 15

Resting the horses in the minimal shade of the boulders was a good idea. The punishing sun assaulted anything that wasn't in shade. Even objects in the shade suffered from the heat radiating off the sun-baked rocks, which looked as if they could fry an egg. To make matters worse, the men were very short on water.

Carson sat quietly on a rocky ledge, his back braced against a large stone. He was lost in thought until Andrew Miller shattered his peaceful cogitation with a question.

"Marshal, are you thinking or just healing?"

Carson laughed.

"I've been thinkin' about our mysterious young lady, Mister Miller."

"Would you care to share?"

"I ain't thought it all through, mind ya, and I gotta admit my brain is still a bit whiskey soaked, but I've been thinkin' about those telegrams she sent."

"That's funny," said John. "I've been thinkin' on 'em too. In fact, I've been sittin' here readin' the notes I took this mornin' when you was talkin' to Trevor Dunkerton."

"I'd be interested in your thoughts, John."

"Well, Marshal, I'm thinkin' we've been joked with again. 'Cause these notes ain't makin' any kinda sense."

"I think my cynicism is rubbin' off on ya, John."

"Your what?"

"My disparagin' nature."

"Disparagin'. Yes, sir."

"I've been thinkin' the same thing," said Carson.

"I don't follow you boys," said Miller.

"Let's say, for the moment," started Carson, "she ain't fulla no kinda madness. Let's say she's doin' all of this with good purpose and understandin'. Okay?"

Both John and Miller nodded.

"Now, I don't pretend to understand what all them letters and numbers mean just yet. But as I see it, she ain't come out here to meet anyone. At least not right away. The trail for meetin' anyone comin' outa Gallup is through the Dead River wash, where we discovered that young man with the hat. Until the railroad puts in them tracks next year, it's the main stage route between Gallup and Holbrook. It's a common trail, and most anyone out to meet other folks meets somewhere along it."

"Then why is she coming all the way out here?"

"That's the part I ain't got worked out yet."

"Might she soon turn south toward Dead River?"

"No, Mister Miller," said John, "we're too far north and east to get back to the wash now. Well, easily, that is. From here, there's only east into the canyonlands that makes any sense at all."

"Why would Becky go up into the canyons? Do you think the gold is up there?"

"I don't think so," replied Carson. "But I don't think she intends to make the truth of her reason easy to know. It would be my guess that she's followin' the clues in the letter to find the point where the cipher's trail begins."

"So you're saying that if she *were* going to meet someone, she would have just tracked back to the wash — the normal trail?"

"In normal times, yes. But as you can tell, we ain't kin to normal times anymore."

"No. More like we're bastards to anything normal, I would think."

Carson chuckled.

"I think you could say that, Mister Miller."

"One thing's for certain," said John. "So far, she ain't been tryin' to hide her trail."

"I know," said Carson. "That's another part that has me thinkin' hard."

"My guess is she ain't found what she's lookin' for, or I do believe we'd be hearin' the whiz of bullets."

"I think you're right, John," said Carson. "Out here is where you begin somethin' or end somethin'. Other than that, I can't see no reason to be out where we are right now."

"It's clear that the clues to her bein' out here is in them telegrams," said John. "But as I'm starin' at 'em, they's just letters and numbers to me."

Carson nodded.

"To me, too, John."

"I suppose you're used to being plagued by these kinds of obscurities, Marshal?"

"It simply goes with the job, Mister Miller."

"It gives me no comfort, you saying that."

"No, sir. Comfort is another thing lackin' out here."

Andrew Miller picked up a twig and began tapping on a rock. After several minutes, he looked at Marshal Carson and shrugged.

"Marshal, the young man you found out in the wash. Could it be possible that he rode down from the Canyonlands and not from Gallup?

"That's an interestin' thought, Mister Miller. The Dead River wash would be the most logical course to follow comin' down from those lands. I s'pose it's possible. Are you thinkin' that our young woman and that boy is connected with the canyonlands in some way?"

"I'm not an investigator like you, Marshal, but what if where Becky is heading *is* common to both? What if it was where something ended after something began earlier — up in the canyonlands."

"Could be, I reckon. Could be where some kind of partnership or relationship happened. You're thinkin' he was chased or followed out of the canyons and killed at Dead River?"

"This area keeps cropping up, Marshal. Do you consider it just coincidence?"

"Ain't no such thing as coincidence, Mister Miller. Everything happens for reason and purpose. At least that's what I've come to believe. You might be onto somethin'. It's like John said earlier, you don't come up into these parts for no good reason. And as we've discussed before, our Miss Rebecca has got herself a mighty strategic mind. And she's even less a careless person."

"So she's here with a purpose?"

"I do believe so. John, you've been up in these parts a few times, haven't ya?"

"I have. Several times, in fact. Chased a few outlaw types up here."

"This trail we're on, do you know where it ends?"

"This trail splits up several times and goes in different directions. But if you stay on the main trail, it ends up at a place the Navajo call Chi'inili. We call it Chin Lee. There's a good-sized tradin' post up there. It's where most of them travelin' through these parts can get supplies and some rest."

"I see," said Carson. "Ain't never been up there myself. Wait! John, look at your notes again. Ain't there somethin' about C.L. in 'em?"

John scanned through his note pages until his eyes opened wide with recognition.

"Sure is, Eli. 'Found it. Stop. C.L. confirmed. Stop. C.C. End.'"

"That's it!"

"There's more. 'Leavin' soon. Stop. Meet C.L. dash SW 8. Stop. C.C. End.'"

"Very interestin', John. Now we could be onto somethin'. Could C.L. be the initials for Chin Lee?"

"I s'pose they could. But what does 'dash SW 8' mean?"

"How about southwest in eight days?" offered Miller. "As in meeting southwest of Chin Lee in eight days?"

"Possible, I suppose," said Carson. "But there's a problem with that. First of all, there's a lot of land southwest of Chin Lee. How'd you go 'bout meetin' someone without a specific location? Second, why eight days? That seems an awful long time to wait for someone comin' outa Gallup, don't it? John, how long a ride is it from Gallup to Chin Lee?"

"It's about a hundred miles, so on horseback, about three days. Takes less time in winter. Cooler then."

"But not eight?"

"By wagon, maybe. But then it might take ten or twelve days. They couldn't get more'n ten miles a day on the flat with a wagon. And there's lots of steep hills between Gallup and Chin Lee to slow 'em down."

"That's real helpful, John. So most likely they'd come on horseback. And eight days would be at least reasonable."

"Maybe if they was stoppin' along the way for other reasons, it would, Marshal."

"How far are we from Chin Lee?" asked Miller.

"It's about the same to Chin Lee from Holbrook as it is from Gallup to Chin Lee," said John. "About a hundred miles, like I said. But we've been makin' good time despite the weather. I reckon we're about a day and a half out from Chin Lee."

"And Becky, John? How far ahead of us is she, you think?"

"When we stopped, I guessed we was about five hours behind her. More like seven now. Unless she's takin' a break as well."

"I think we oughta mount up and get after her," Carson said as he stood up. "She's the only one who knows the answers to all our questions, boys. We sure ain't gonna get no answers sittin' here on our backsides."

"We sure takin' a beatin' out here, Marshal."

"Yes, John. We are at that. But *she's* takin' a beatin' as well."

He glanced skyward into the clear blue sky and the steady bright sun.

"Everything out here gets beat up. It's just dirty, darn bad luck, I'm sayin'."

After four silent hours of trudging through the hottest part of the day, along a trail made more of dust than earth, Carson stretched his arms wide and yawned.

"I'm needin' some conversation, boys. I think I've thought all the thoughts my brain can conjure up. I'm about to drop into a slumber from all this quiet."

"Then this might be a good time to visit some of what I've been thinkin' on, Marshal."

"Tell me, John."

"I've been goin' over the circumstances of that young man's death out at Dead River."

"Okay, let's have at it."

"I'm still havin' trouble understandin' him bein' so far from his horse at his end. And how his hat ended up on that rock so far from his body. And why was he tied up in the first place?"

"Easy, John," said Carson, chuckling. "Let's take them questions one at a time."

"Fine, but all of 'em have got me stumped so far."

Carson scratched his whiskers and then opened his eyes wide.

"They're all good questions. Let's start with the hat."

"I've seen that look before, Eli. What's goin' on in that mind of yers?"

"I thought before that the hat mighta been set there by someone else. Now I'm thinkin' that I'm right. I think someone put it there on purpose."

"Why?"

"Perhaps as a signal. Perhaps as a marker. Perhaps… Sorry, John. I'm not bein' helpful, I know. It's just another question I can't find an answer to myself. I'm long on questions and short on answers."

"What if the hat didn't belong to him at all?" asked Miller.

Both Carson and John cut him a hard stare.

"Mister Miller! That's a very interestin' notion."

"From what you told me before, it suddenly seemed possible."

"Perhaps likely," said Carson. "That notion never entered my mind."

And while I'm at it," Miller continued, "perhaps all that blood didn't belong to the young lad to begin with."

Carson's eyes opened wide with surprise. "What a terrific notion *that* is," he said.

"Could it be possible that someone else was killed in addition to that young man, and the hat was his?"

"Mister Miller, I'm impressed."

"Don't be, Marshal. I'm just not as close to it as you are. I'm just guessing anyway."

"But it's makin' more sense."

"Wait, Marshal!" said John. "We followed his footprints to and from the rock slab. We only found one body at the end of 'em. If someone else was shot, where'd the other body go?"

"I can't say, but Mister Miller has some good points, John. Most of the blood was near the horse. The bloody crawl marks petered out on the way to the rock. And there weren't no blood at the rock at all. It's reasonable to assume that whoever it was that got shot didn't make it to the rock. As for the lad, he ran away until he was dropped. There weren't no blood on them footprints out to him. The blood was only under the boy's body. It's reasonable, then, to assume that someone shot him from a distance and he dropped where he was hit."

"I see what you're gettin' at," said John. "But the bullet entered him from the front. He had to be standin' and facin' his killer to take a shot like that."

"You're right, John. Perhaps as a last defiant act. Perhaps just from curiosity. Perhaps he was simply talkin' to his killer and the conversation ended with a bullet in the gut."

"That had to be some conversation," said Miller. "Didn't you say you found his body nearly two hundred yards from the rock?"

"I did."

"Then there must have been a lot of shouting before the shooting."

"I see yer point," said Carson. "There must have been some kind of argument that ended with the shooting."

"No matter what caused it," continued Miller, "that had to be a heck of a shot. That's a long way for a forty-four slug to travel in a straight line, let alone hit a man square in the gut."

"If the shooter was standin' on the rock where the hat was," said Carson, "it was an *expert* shot."

"You sayin' the shooter wasn't on the rock?" asked John.

"No. The shot had to come from the rock. No blood trail out to the body. And there weren't no other footprints followin' him out there neither. So it couldn't have come from up close."

"Makes sense," said Miller.

"That's it, then!" said John. "There was another victim shot near the horse who crawled toward the rock."

"Seems right," said Carson.

"Why leave the hat and take the other body, then?" asked Miller. "And whose body is it that got taken? Whose horse was it that got shot? And whose hat is it anyway?"

"Good questions, Mister Miller. Excellent questions! And I think the answer to those questions rides several hours ahead of us."

"The gold, Marshal. Miss Becky's gold. I think all this nastiness is about Miss Becky's gold."

"Could be, John. If there *is* any gold."

"Even if there isn't one coin out here in any cave, Marshal, the killin's have got to be a part of the quest for what treasure might exist, or what someone thinks might exist."

"That's excellent thinkin', John. Sound reasonin', too."

"Could be all about the gold," said Miller. "But it could be much bigger than that, too. I have no idea what drives this adventure right now except the mystery of it. You two are the experts in these matters. Maybe I'm reading far too much into it; I'm used to things being complicated. Being around Becky tends to get complicated, and I'm all manner of confused right now."

"Well, if this adventure wasn't strange enough already, now we got us an even stranger one."

"Yes we do, John."

"But what about those two halves of the coin? They was real enough."

"I don't know, John," said Carson. "I just don't know what to make of it all. Maybe we've simply got a troubled young woman leadin' us on a wild-goose chase out of sheer madness. Maybe she ain't got nothin' to do with any of the killin's out in the wash. Maybe we're confusin' more than one thing with another. Maybe all of this is just dumb coincidence after all."

"But you told Mister Miller there ain't no such thing as coincidence, that everythin' that happens has a design to it."

"I did say that, John. Maybe I was wrong. Somethin' mysterious is certainly at play. And we can sit here and raise all manner of questions concernin' it, but the answers we're seekin' ain't gonna just jump up and make themselves known to us without effort on our part to unravel 'em. They're somewhere out in this miserable desert and we best get after 'em. I reckon our best chance of uncoverin' all this mystery is to start by gettin' our hands on Miss Middleton and go from there."

Three more hours passed silently among the weary men before John asked them to stop and he slid off his horse.

He walked around for some time, studying the prints in the sandy soil.

Finally, he crouched beside a few of the prints and laid his hand down next to one in particular that looked like a boot print.

He stared at it for a few more seconds and then looked up at Carson.

"She got off her horse here. It looks like she was checkin' her horse's hoof. I believe her horse may have a problem. Right here, see it? From the looks of it, her horse is draggin' its left front leg."

"Maybe a stone in the shoe, John. Or just bad in need of water and rest."

"Yeah. Could be either, I reckon. But the horse is in trouble. If she don't slow up, we'll come upon her sittin' next to her dead horse within the next few hours. And these tracks is fresher than the last. We're gainin' on her fast, Marshal. She must have rested quite a while. 'Bout the same time we did."

"Don't that beat all?"

"It riles me, Marshal. Is she really that good?"

"It appears so, John."

"What are you two talking about?" asked Miller.

"While we was restin' and chattin' a while ago, she had eyes on us," said Carson. "She rested her horse right along with ours. She knows we're on her trail. Heck, it wouldn't surprise me if she's got eyes on us right now. And more importantly, she ain't concerned about it."

"What's your best guess on how far ahead she is?" asked Miller.

"The tracks are pretty fresh. I'm guessin' three hours tops, if we can keep up the pace."

"Well, I reckon we keep goin', then, but we really need to get these horses some water soon. As luck would have it, there's a spring pond up ahead. No one knows about it except for a few of us that've been out here before, and the Injuns, of course. It's just a mile or two more."

"I bet she knows about it," said Carson. "She's a sorceress, that one. A tactical sorceress. That girl's got skills I ain't seen in anyone 'cept for them military types. That's got me wonderin' 'bout just who the heck she is."

The three men filled their hats with water from the pond and held them under their horses' muzzles and watched them drink the water dry.

They splashed the backs of their own throats from their filled canteens.

John studied the prints around the area. He shook his head.

"She's been here, Marshal. Them's her boot prints. And them there is from her horse."

"I ain't surprised no more by her," said Carson, shaking his own head.

"But how could she know about the spring, Marshal?"

"I'm guessin' it's mentioned in the cipher letter, John."

"Yeah. I guess so. We're gettin' deep into the canyonlands, Marshal," said John. "We might want to keep an eye open for Injuns. We're about to hit the sacred sites."

"Let's hope they don't know we're here," said Miller.

"Don't get your hopes up too high, Mister Miller. They know we're here already," said Carson.

"That doesn't comfort me any."

"I didn't say it to comfort you, sir. I said it to inform you of the reality of the matter."

"Are they the friendly type?"

"They ain't the friendliest type on good days. We cross into their sacred lands without what they see is good reason, and they can become the deadly type. If you catch my drift."

"Got it."

CHAPTER 16

The bullet that struck the ground ten feet in front of Carson's horse, followed by the report of a very distant rifle, caused a panic in the three riders and brought them to an abrupt stop.

In no time at all, they were safe behind a large boulder and peeking out from behind it to see who had greeted them in such an unfriendly manner.

It was Carson who first caught the flash of light in a distant set of boulders.

"There she is," said Carson. "Up on that top layer of rock."

"You think it's Miss Becky?"

"I surely do. Ya see her?"

"I see somebody."

"Get the field glasses, John. They're in the right-hand saddlebag."

John did as he was told and handed the glasses to Carson.

"There she is, but I think her position might be out of our range of fire."

"I agree."

"And I don't see how we might get up there without goin' straight at those boulders. I sure don't fancy doin' that, seein' as how they ain't no cover between here and there."

"How 'bout we go at her from the flank?"

"You're startin' to think like her, John. You're scarin' me. But it's the only other way I see gettin' there. Nah, it's not good. It'd be a heck of a hike. It could take an hour or more to do that."

"You're certain it's Becky?" asked Miller.

"I am," replied Carson. "But like I said, where she is, they ain't no easy way to get to her."

"I think we're gonna be stuck here a good long while," said John.

"At least we've got shade," said Miller. "It doesn't look like she's got any. Maybe we can wait her out."

"*Maybe* ain't gonna get this done, Mister Miller. We're gonna have to force her hand somehow."

"We got water enough for today, but tonight and tomorrow is gonna be rough on us," said John.

Carson turned away from the rock and squatted down on his haunches.

"I know. I've been on this job for a long time. Sometimes it's best just to go with what's given to ya and not waste time tryin' to figure it out. That's why we're gonna have to do somethin' right now or wait until dark. But I don't consider it wise to be out here without a fire after dark. No tellin' what might come creepin' 'round. Might be a critter. Might be a young woman with a rifle. Either one gets me to wantin' to do somethin' before that happens."

He handed the field glasses to John, who trained them on the woman's position.

"I don't see her anymore, Marshal. I see where she was, but I don't see her or any sign she's up there now."

Carson nodded and then looked up in surprise.

"She wouldn't," he said to himself. He fell silent for a few seconds and then looked over at his deputy. "She would, I bet ya."

"What's that?"

"I swear, that girl's got strategy. She'd do it."

"Do what, Marshal?"

"She knew well enough we was out of the effective range of her rifle. She took one shot at us, knowin' it would get us duckin' for cover. She also knew we'd be lookin' for her, so she stayed right out where we could see her."

"Yes, and…?" asked Miller.

"Right now, I'm bettin' she's on her horse headin' away, grinnin' wide and thinkin' how silly we are, sittin' here bakin' in amongst these here rocks while she's run off puttin' more distance between us."

"You believe that?" asked John.

"Darn it all, she's got a keen mind for stratagems. I wouldn't care to underestimate her."

"I think she's countin' on us doin' just that, Marshal."

"Exactly, John. She knows a predictable old fool when she sees one. We ducked away behind rocks before when them assassins was shootin' at us. Remember?"

"I do, Marshal. She sure is smart."

"She is, John. And she don't forget nothin'."

"Are you willing to test that theory, Marshal?" asked Miller.

"By God and thorny red rosebushes, Mister Miller, I am."

Carson stood up and walked past both men out into the sunlight. He strode directly toward the position of the sniper, certain that it was Rebecca Middleton and even more certain that she had already mounted her horse and left the area.

After walking fifty yards away from any protection, he stopped and stared up into the distant rock hills, placing his hands on his hips.

He stood still for several seconds and then spread both arms wide, boldly daring the shooter to fire again. After several seconds more, he lowered his arms and turned back to the others.

"John," he shouted, "would you mind grabbin' an old fool's horse and bringin' her out to me?"

Moments later, Miller and John trotted out from behind the boulder with Carson's horse in tow.

They stopped next to Carson and waited as he mounted his pony.

"I gotta hand it to you, Marshal," said Miller. "You read that one right — right as rain."

"I'm a mite agitated, Mister Miller. And I'm feelin' sorta doltish at the moment. So if you don't mind, I'm gonna hold any further comments on the matter and ride silently while I work on bringin' my disappointment to a more manageable level."

"I can't say I blame you. She's a crafty one. I never knew how crafty until this very moment."

"If we rush a bit, Marshal," said John, "maybe we can get her spotted again."

"John, I know you mean well, but I'm on the spittin' side of angry at the moment. We ain't gonna rush nowhere. I ain't about to grant her another moment like the last one. We'll take our time goin' up there to pick up her trail. And that's all I'd like to say right now."

John nodded. Carson's mood was as sour as he had ever seen it. He decided to just ride and think on his own.

As they reached the spot where the shooter had been perched, they all spotted the distinct signs in the sandy soil of someone having moved about. The footprints were small — too small for a man. John was quick to point out the direction of a lightly mounted horse. The tracks were not difficult to follow. That fact did not escape the notice of the marshal.

Fellas, I have a question for ya," he said. "Think a bit on this if ya will. Are we trackin' her, or is she leadin' us along?"

John's expression went blank. Miller just grimaced, bowed his head, and scratched the back of his neck.

"Gotcha thinkin', didn't I?"

"Why, Marshal? Why would she do that?" asked Miller.

"I'm guessin' now. And I ain't sayin' I'm right about this, but she's been showin' us just how much of a brilliant tactician and an excellent strategist she is up till now. And I've been fallin' all over myself in awe of it. Fellas, I think she's been playing me like a fiddler plays a fiddle. I believe she's keepin' us right where she wants us."

"I ain't followin', Marshal," replied John.

"She knows where we are at all times. Maybe she's keepin' us in sight so we can't sneak up on her."

"I see where you're going," said Miller.

"Darn it all," said John. "That could be it, Marshal, 'cause I been wonderin' how it is that she ain't tried to mask her trail no better'n this."

"I'm feelin' mighty foolish, but I believe I'm more amused that I'm bein' so expertly toyed with by a little girl. Mount up, boys," said Carson, chuckling. "We wouldn't want to keep her waitin' too long out here in this furnace. I hear it messes a mite with a woman's hair."

John and Miller rode past the marshal as he sat staring down at the tracks in the sand, lost in thought. Finally he stirred.

"It's just dirty, darn bad luck, I'm sayin'."

Rebecca Middleton's tracks continued upward into the hills of the eastern canyonlands in the general direction of the trading post at Chin Lee. After another hour, the tracks turned distinctly more northward along another old Apache trail, its only possible destination the trading post.

Carson, leading them up the trail, stopped his horse and peered down at the tracks. He smiled. Then he shook his head.

"Don't that beat all," he said.

"What's that?" asked Miller, coming to a stop beside the marshal.

Carson didn't answer. Instead, he heeled his horse and followed the tracks, leaving John and Miller behind to ponder the meaning of his words.

John stopped his horse next to Miller, though his eyes followed the marshal up the trail.

"Did I anger him with my question?" asked Miller.

"No, sir. He's just feelin' put out right now. Give him time and he'll get back to his usual self."

"Becky can do that really well — make someone feel out of sorts."

"I think Eli knows that already. I believe he's more disappointed than anythin' else. He tends to put more faith in people than I do. I believe it hurts him to be wrong about folks."

"Is she still heading to the trading post?"

"No question about it now, Mister Miller. This old Apache trail ends at the tradin' post."

"She won't stay there long, I'll bet."

"I reckon not. She'll leave before we get there. You can count on it."

"Where do you think she'll go from there?"

"Only one place to go if she keeps true to the direction she's headin' in — the canyons. We'd best catch up to the marshal." John heeled the sides of his horse and trotted away.

The canyons were deep scars in the earth, three distinct canyons named del Muerto, de Chelly, and, simply, Monument.

They had been named by the Spaniards who'd traveled through the area hundreds of years before. They belonged to the Navajo tribe now, and the Navajo were keen on protecting the sacred lands from all outsiders.

The canyons had been cut over millennia by streams of fresh water rushing from the snowpack in the higher hills known as the Chuska Mountains. The heavy snows that had created the runoff necessary to carve mountains into canyons had stopped falling long before, and now the washes down the length of the canyons remained mostly dry except for the occasional flash flood during the monsoon season.

Thus, water throughout the area was scarce. Even scarcer here than down in the wash of Dead River. There were springs of fresh water here and there, but usually only small pools of standing water could be found, and then only occasionally. It was better for travelers to bring their own water and leave the stagnant pools to their horses.

The trading post was well enough established that one could resupply with the basic needs required for traveling through the area. It was also a place where one could quench a thirst — if drinking cheap whiskey could be considered quenching a thirst.

But the trading post was still a ways off. There was no way they would reach it before noon the next day, if they were lucky. And some of the luck they needed included Rebecca Middleton not slowing them down any further with potshots from the surrounding hills.

The small pool of water was perfect for refreshing their horses, the shade of the large boulder a welcomed relief to the sunbaked riders.

Carson's self-disappointment had eased some by then. He sat on a flat rock, his back up against the face of a large boulder, trying to think like a young, deceitful woman fixated on finding a chest of gold coins that might or might not exist.

All in all, one could conclude that Marshal Eli Carson had his mind fully occupied with questions.

But then he abruptly looked up and squinted at his deputy.

"John, are we still on the main trail?"

"We are, Marshal."

"Still headin' to Chin Lee?"

"It's the only place we can end up now."

"Okay, gents, we need to pick up the pace a mite."

As Carson rode past John, he glanced at him.

"We ain't gonna make Chin Lee, John."

Neither John Slims nor Andrew Miller had questioned the marshal's sudden urge to begin riding at an accelerated pace. John was the ever loyal and obedient deputy, who trusted Marshal Carson's every move, thought, and decision. In the five years they had ridden together, Carson had never given John any reason not to trust him.

Still, John wondered why Carson had told him they weren't going to make Chin Lee. He would have liked to ask the quiet, solemn lawman to explain himself, but he could see that Carson was still in a sour mood and unlikely to want to engage in conversation. John thought it best to leave his questions for later.

As for Andrew Miller, he was just along for the ride, curious to discover what his beloved ex-fiancée was up to. Or so he thought. Carson believed that Miller was actually on this adventure to search for some kind of resolution to his heart's agony-filled desire.

In either case, they all followed in the direction John led them and soon found themselves along the upper fork of the dry, dusty wash of Dead River. They were very deep into the eastern canyonlands, about ten miles from the trading post.

John and Miller rode side by side, engaging in quiet conversation, while Marshal Carson rode some distance behind them, lost somewhere in the murkiness of deep and dark thoughts. John often looked back at the sullen Marshal.

"I ain't seen him like this in a long time," he said. "He's riled up plenty."

Miller glanced back at Carson.

"I don't know. He seems pretty calm to me."

"Trust me, Mister Miller, he's riled up somethin' awful. He's burdened by heavy thoughts."

"Perhaps he's suffering from a bruised ego. Becky's done that to me more than a time or two."

"No, sir. It's more than that."

"I feel for him. I wish *I* had never met Becky. But now that I have, I can't get her out of my mind. I'm doomed. Maybe Marshal Carson is caught up in her mysterious ways as well."

"I can't say for sure, but I do believe this mystery is set hard within him. He's a man who likes to have answers. He likes adventures, mind you, but he don't like mystery. Mystery gnaws at him somethin' fierce. He ain't gonna rest till he unravels it full."

John smiled. "On second thought, I ain't seen him so determined and excited in a long time neither. Maybe he's enjoyin' the heck out of this mystery and it's just got him bedeviled at the moment. Maybe this is just what he needed."

"I'd like to know this, John: Are we following *her* or the mystery?"

John shrugged and smiled.

"Maybe they're both the same thing, Mister Miller."

After another cautious and miserable hour John reined his horse to a stop, dropped down to the ground, and squatted behind a small rock outcrop.

Carson and Miller did the same.

"What you got, John?"

"Over there, Marshal. You see what's by that big boulder out yonder?"

Carson inched forward and looked over the top of the rock and saw what John had spotted. He had been carrying his field glasses around his neck on a leather thong, and he lifted them up to his eyes.

"It's a horse, all right. Don't know if it's hers or not, but I suppose it's logical to think it is."

"It's hers," said John. "Course, the only way to be sure is to go over to it."

"I ain't real keen on gettin' shot at right now, John. Over the past few days I've had my fill of whizzin' bullets."

"I understand that, Marshal. But she ain't gonna do us no harm. She's had plenty of chances already, and we're still here. I'll ride up and see what's what."

Continuing to look through the glasses, Carson said, "Let's not rush into disaster, John. She's got plenty of perches up there in them rocks to spot you comin'."

"Well, heck, then I won't keep her waitin'. Besides, the only other way to get to that horse is wait till dark."

Carson sat silently for a full minute. Then he looked into John's eyes.

"How far is the tradin' post?"

"About eight miles or so. They's hard miles, though. It's gonna be slow…"

"Look at your notes, John."

John pulled his notes from his vest.

"'Dash SW 8,'" said Carson. "Eight miles southwest of Chin Lee, maybe?"

John read his notes.

"Son of a *gun*, Marshal — you got it! So that's what you meant when you said we wouldn't make Chin Lee."

"I suspected, John. She met someone here and is gone already. She ain't up there."

"What about her horse?"

"She's got herself a new one. She ain't up there."

"Looks that way, but we still gotta get up there to find out for sure."

"Her keen mind, John. She seems to always pick a perch where she can control her surroundin's. They ain't no other way I can see to get to the horse except to go right at it. She knew that. She met up with her accomplice and she's gone now."

Through the field glasses, Carson scanned the rock perches one final time for any sign of a shooter, such as the glint of sunlight reflecting off a metal surface. Seeing no one up in the rocks, he dropped his glasses to his chest.

"Mount up, fellas."

Carson mounted his horse and heeled her into an easy lope, passing the others on his way up to where the lone horse was tied.

It seemed like an eternity crossing the open space toward the horse standing still up against the rocks. Carson carefully scanned the hillside before him as he moved closer.

Once he arrived at his destination, he dismounted and walked over to the tied horse. Checking the saddlebags and scabbard, he found both empty.

The two other men rode up and stopped their horses next to his.

"She ain't here, fellas," Carson said matter-of-factly.

"No, sir, she ain't."

"I'm vexed, John. That young woman has me vexed seven ways to Sunday."

"Yes, sir."

"I'm not much of a tracker, Marshal," said Miller, "but I do believe I see two different sets of tracks, both heading off to the northeast — toward Chin Lee and the trading post you talked about."

"I'm certain of it, Mister Miller. She's a witch, that one. She's a witch and she's vexed me almost to the breakin' point."

"Them tracks is heavy in the sand, Marshal," said John. "She's got an accomplice ridin' next to her. I'm sure of it."

"Could the tracks be from a packhorse weighted down?"

"No, sir. But I believe someone came down from the tradin' post with supplies and a fresh horse. They met her here, like you said, and then they headed back together. I'm confident of it."

"Of course you are, John. Some witches have their black cats. This witch has an accomplice. It's all makin' sense somewhere. Not here, mind ya, but somewhere this is all pretty simple and sensible."

John chuckled.

"Come on now, Marshal. We'll catch her. They ain't no way she can outsmart us forever. If she's out here, she's gotta leave tracks from her passin'. We just gotta be patient and more determined to find her than she is determined to leave us behind."

"I told you, John, I believe she ain't tryin' to lose us. She's tryin' to keep us in sight."

John smiled.

"Mister Miller?" asked Carson. "Do you have any idea who she might be partnered with now?"

"I sure don't. It seems the more I learn about her, the more mysterious she's becoming."

"She's becomin' clearer to me," said Carson.

"What about the horse, Marshal?" asked John.

"Grab them reins. Instead of cuttin' it loose, I s'pose it won't hurt us none to have another horse with us. Didn't this horse have a problem earlier with one of its hooves? You better check it out, John, before we go tryin' to drag it along with us."

John checked the horse over carefully, including its hooves.

"No, sir. She's been watered and is rested. She's gonna be fine."

"That woman's a fiddle master and I'm the fiddle. And just so's you both know," said Carson, "I can guess what's gonna happen next."

"What's that?" asked Miller.

"Just you wait. You'll see. It'll be like the partin' of the Red Sea."

"The Red Sea?" John asked.

"Yep."

"Will I like it, Marshal?"

"No, sir, Mister Miller. You decidedly will not like it one little bit. It's just dirty, darn bad luck, I'm sayin'."

CHAPTER 17

"It's just a matter of time before you finally open your ears and hear the world laughin'," said Carson. "Sometimes the world laughs with you. But sometimes the world laughs *at* you. I think your true character can be demonstrated by how you choose to press on despite you ever knowin' which one it truly is."

"What does all that mean, Eli?" John asked.

Carson leaned forward in his saddle, resting his right elbow on the saddle horn, staring down at the tracks in the sand.

"It means this is what I was tellin' you both to expect. She's gotten biblical on us."

John and Miller chuckled.

"The parting of the Red Sea," John said. "I get it now, Marshal. And I think you're right."

Carson stared down at the place where the two sets of tracks separated. One set headed northeast, while a second set headed southeast. Both, however, led deeper into the canyonlands and into Indian territory — territory sacred to both the Apache and the Navajo, territory both tribes wouldn't hesitate to defend if they felt it necessary.

"She's laughin' at me, John. She's testin' my character — my resolve. And she has me near to frustrated tears. So why is it I wanna laugh?"

"She's gotta be on one horse or the other. We just have to figure out which one."

"Look at them tracks, John. They're set about the same depth. She's equalized the weight so both sets don't look no different. Gonna make it hard to know which ones to follow."

"She is a smart one," said Miller.

"You think she's tryin' to lose us now?" asked John.

"She's playin' with me. Havin' a good ol' time with the ol' fool. But if she's after the gold, like I expect, she'll want to put us off the trail sooner or later for good. This might be her move, or at least one of her moves, right here."

Carson chuckled loudly and then continued.

"I just know she's off somewhere, probably close by, gigglin' like a schoolgirl. I guess I might have to giggle too…either that or cry my eyes red."

"So, which one do we follow, Marshal?"

"I'm thinkin', John. I'm thinkin'."

Both Miller and John sat quietly in their saddles, allowing Carson the time to find a reason to choose one set of tracks over the other.

It was several minutes before the marshal blew out a breath of exasperation and sat up in his saddle.

"Do you have the answer, Marshal?"

"I have a guess, John. We continue southeast."

"Why is that?"

"Well, John, because that's the way my bones is tellin' me she's headin'."

"Why didn't she just start out southeast, then? Why ride out this way only to turn back south? It don't make no sense."

"I'm not arguin' with you, John. I'm just sayin' she's trackin' southeast now. Don't go askin' me to tell you how I know. I just know."

"I agree," said Miller. "I don't think she'd head northeast, back to the trading post. She might be seen there, and I think she'd be easily remembered."

"She's followin' the cipher, boys. Now in the end the whole thing might be just a fantasy, but she believes the directions to be true. And my gut tells me to go southeast. So, that's our move."

"Okay, Marshal. Southeast it is."

"Let's get moving, then. I just hope you're right," said Miller.

"So do I, Mister Miller. So do I. I believe I've had enough of bein' her fool."

"You'll be less her fool if you're right."

"That's true, John. But it troubles me some to think I could be wrong. I don't think I could tolerate that."

"With this latest incident, Marshal, I'm gettin' to wonder if she ain't somethin' more than a witch."

"Witch or not, John, I do believe she thinks she's doin' right to follow the directions. And I'm obligated to follow *her*. So, let's get to followin' her. It's just dirty, darn bad luck, I'm sayin'. But there it is."

"I never knew loving a woman could be so complicated," said Miller.

"Like I said before, Mister Miller, it's just a matter of time before a man finally hears the laughin'."

"It's hard to stop believing in someone, Marshal."

"I understand that. I ain't never said it was an easy or simple matter to grasp. All that laughin' sometimes is just laughin'. It don't mean nothin' in particular. Sometimes it's a matter of right and wrong."

"What's wrong with loving someone?"

"Nothin'. But as I see it, ain't nothin' really right about it either. Believin' in someone is just that. You believe in 'em or ya don't. But I'll tell ya this, there comes a time when you have to just go forward not knowin' if what you're believin' in is right or wrong. I believe that pressin' on into the darkness filled with doubt is a courage some lack to their own destruction and others use to discover who they truly are."

"Love isn't always dark, Marshal."

"No, sir. You're right about that. But I'll say this. When you see the blackness, you have to know that the blackness never gets any whiter. Sooner or later, a man has got to stop followin' the darkness. He's got to turn around and head back the way he came to find the light again. You can't keep goin' forward bein' stupid about it forever."

"So you're saying I'm acting stupid? I should give up on Becky?"

"I'm sayin' I hope you'll let her go and discover your own path before you find yerself hopelessly lost."

"That seems a pessimistic thing to say, Marshal. Especially for you."

"I don't mean to be pessimistic, Mister Miller. But some hearts can't be tamed. Some hearts will fight to keep free no matter the cost. Knowin' when the time is right to let go might just be a part of livin'. Not knowin' might be a part of dyin'."

"Those words have the distinct ring of experience."

"Mister Miller, I wasn't born this old and alone."

After following the tracks leading southeast for another several hours, the three riders came upon another horse tied to a tree next to a small brook.

John climbed down off his horse and untied the rope holding the horse.

Marshal Carson removed his hat and slowly wiped a sleeve across his brow.

"Is it the horse that made the tracks we're followin', John?"

"Yes, sir. I'm afraid it is."

"Good Lord," said Carson. "If we keep collectin' horses like we are, we might have to start us a ranchin' business."

John and Miller smiled.

"We could just cut them loose," suggested Miller.

"Not out here in this wretched desert. It wouldn't be right. They're better off goin' with us."

"Look at all the different tracks, Marshal," said John. There's been several horses here, and now there's tracks headin' off in all directions. I think she's beat us finally."

"How did she make arrangements for this many accomplices?" asked Miller.

"This looks well planned, Mister Miller. This ain't somethin' she just threw together willy-nilly."

"What now?" asked John.

"It'll be dark soon. We might as well make camp for the night."

"Okay, Marshal. Ain't no use I can see runnin' around out in the dark anyway. She's got control of us, I'm afraid."

"It would have been nice to make the trading post. We could use some supplies," said Miller.

"She's got hers, you can be sure of it," said Carson. "Someone met her, resupplied her, and then headed back to the tradin' post. I'm positive of it now. Seems to me that she has prepared herself for travelin' into what she knows to be a sparse area."

Carson saw no reason not to have a fire. If they were being spied on, and he believed they were, then their presence was already known. And he hated the thought of spending a chilly night wrapped only in a smelly horse blanket.

Now, lying on his side next to the warm fire, he let his mind go where it pleased. It pleased to go to the mysterious young woman, of course.

He acknowledged that she had successfully teased him along for the entire pursuit so far, and he figured she wasn't finished with him yet. He was certain that his so-called pursuit was a joke to her and that she had regarded him as an inconvenient toy up to this point.

What troubled him most was the issue already raised by Andrew Miller. The closer she got to her goal, the less of a plaything he might become and the more of a problem. And out in the desert, problems were more easily solved with bullets than with trickery. The real problem for Marshal Carson was not knowing when the pendulum would swing from a tolerated inconvenient plaything to an intolerant problem needing to be permanently rectified.

With all these different tracks to sort out, he wondered if she was somewhere close by watching the foolish old marshal stumble around like a lost puppy trying to decide which set of tracks to follow. Then his thoughts were interrupted by Andrew Miller.

"How are we going to find her now, Marshal?" asked Miller, seated next to the fire and staring into the flames.

"Through good reasonin', I expect."

"How can reason help us pick the right tracks to follow?"

"Mister Miller, there's good reason for good reason."

Miller chuckled.

Carson bolted upright.

"Thank you, Mister Miller — that's *it*!"

"What's what?"

"That's the answer!"

"How's that?"

"We don't need to guess which track to follow. The answer to our immediate dilemma is in the story of Coronado. The story says Coronado discovered the chest was missin' about a day's ride out from where they left the priests."

"Do we know where that is?"

"I've read the entire published account and I believe the story indicated that the priests were left near a pueblo, though which one wasn't disclosed. At least it ain't for certain."

"How do we reason with '*ain't for certain*,' Marshal?"

"I'll get to that. As the story goes, his soldiers met up with stiff resistance while lookin' for the priests. Supposedly the natives, friendly with them priests, started a running gunfight with the Spanish soldiers who returned for the gold. Them soldiers was in a foul mood and eager to find the friars and the gold quick-like and get back to the main body of their force. The exact area where most of the fightin' took place, as I recall, was a couple miles due west of the pueblo, in a shallow set of canyons in western New Mexico.

"The Indians lost, of course, and the gold was never recovered, and ain't no one sure of what happened to the priests either.

"I tracked a killer by the name of Zaiman Beauchamp to them parts back in '70. I caught him hidin' in a small cave thereabouts. Had to kill 'im; he just wouldn't give himself up without a gunfight."

"Sorry to hear that," said Miller.

"It was a shame, but I do recall thinkin' at the time that the area would be a perfect place to hide from the world if need be. The whole place is full of caves. And in speakin' with the chief of the local tribe, he offhandedly mentioned the tribe's contact a long time back with men he called "metal heads." I believe he was referrin' to the conquistadors. Now I ain't for certain 'bout this, but I'm bettin' we find Miss Middleton down among them caves somewhere."

"Do you remember how to get there?" asked John, sitting cross-legged next to the fire.

"I do, John. It's about a two-day ride due southeast of here. I've had good dealin's with the pueblo's tribe. They helped me find Zaiman Beauchamp. So I don't expect any trouble from 'em."

"Well, if you don't mind, Marshal, I'll take your previous advice to pray for the best and prepare for the worst."

"That's always good advice, John."

"What's got me bothered," said Miller, "is how she assembled this small army around her and how many of them we'll be going up against in the fight that is sure to come when we do find her."

"She *is* uppin' the stakes, I'll give you that. But if I'm right about her, she'll either give 'em the slip or pay 'em off before she'll split the gold with the likes of any of 'em."

"But there ain't no gold, Marshal. You said as much earlier."

"I said I wasn't for certain. But if there is Spanish gold somewhere, it would most likely be down in that area, not where she said it was. I don't know why I didn't recall this before. But since she seems to be headin' that way, it finally came to me. It seems most reasonable."

"I can't keep up," said John. "Is there a chest of gold or ain't there?"

"I surely don't know, John. Maybe there once was a chest and it was found already, or maybe it's still there. All I know is she's goin' through a lot for somethin' she believes is true. She's headed in a logical direction that matches up with the stories I heard about the Spanish comin' through the area, and I can't say I'm not intrigued by the prospect of a chest of gold coins somewhere out here in this wretched desert just waitin' to be found."

"I bet them soldiers found it."

"Not likely, John. Stories don't come into bein' without some truth at the heart of 'em. I do believe there's gold stashes out here. I believe men have left many treasures behind, always intendin' to return for 'em but never makin' it back for one reason or another. There's lots of Civil War stories about gold bein' stashed and lost because them who hid it died without ever sayin' where they hid it."

"Well, I'll tell you both this," said John. "If sand is treasure, then I reckon I'm already a rich man, 'cause I got it aplenty inside my boots and my hair and my ears."

CHAPTER 18

Twelve miles east of the Arizona–New Mexico border was as much of an oasis as could be found within fifty miles in any direction and thus a welcome sight to the three tired and thirsty men on the hard, hot, dusty trail of one determined young woman.

Although the sign on the front of the small building read *La Taberna del Toro*, The Tavern of the Bull, there was no bull anywhere near the small desert structure.

There was, however, a dilapidated corral attached to one side of the mud-faced building.

Carson recited an old story he'd heard back when he was in and around these parts chasing Zaiman Beauchamp. As the story went, the corral had once housed a giant bull rescued from the bullfighting rings of Mexico City by the tavern's owner decades before.

The story might have been true, or it might have been just a story told to exhausted travelers by a lonely old man desperate for the company of eager ears. It didn't really matter, for the corral now sat as an empty, haunting wreck — a callous reminder of just how hard it was in the desert for everything, living and nonliving.

Carson stared at the old corral and shook his head.

"Nothin' ever lasts out here for long."

Knowing there was nothing more to add, John and Miller said nothing and began walking toward the tavern.

Four other horses were tied to the hitching post. They were sweat-soaked and looked exhausted — they'd been ridden hard. Marshal Carson studied them closely before following John and Miller toward the tavern. He noticed a good deal of blood staining two of the saddles.

"Look here," he called, stopping the men from going into the tavern.

John and Miller walked back to see what Carson was pointing to.

"What do you think?" asked Miller.

"I think we might want to enter slow-like," answered Carson.

All three removed the thongs from the hammers of their revolvers and unseated their guns in their holsters, preparing for a quick draw should those inside find their entry not to their liking.

It was decided that Miller would enter the tavern first; he looked the least menacing of the three. He blew out a steadying breath and pulled the rusted handle of the door, initiating a loud creaking of dried wood that announced his arrival to everyone inside.

The single room was dark and grimy, lacking any colors not found in the desert outside its walls. The air, though deliciously cool, was filled with clouds of tobacco smoke wafting through the room. It smelled of sweat, stale beer, tobacco, and something else, rancid but indefinable.

As Miller entered, all eyes immediately turned toward him. Three men were seated at a rickety table in the far corner, nursing wounds to various parts of their bodies. Another man, a very young man, stood alone at the bar, tipping a jigger of whiskey up to his lips.

John and Carson entered, slowly and cautiously.

Carson's experienced eyes appraised the scene to determine where trouble might come from; he counted four armed men and a Mexican barkeep. His attention focused on the wounded men, and he walked over to their table while watching the young man at the bar out of the corner of his wary eye.

He bent over to study their wounds.

One fellow, shot through the left shoulder, was drifting in and out of consciousness. Another sat with his head cradled in one hand while holding his other hand tightly to his right shoulder over a bloody wad of cloth. A second cloth wrapped around his head covered a wound to his forehead. He was as docile and unaware as the first man.

Carson gently lifted the cloth on the man's head and grimaced at the unmistakable streak of a revolver butt across his forehead. Someone had buffaloed him good. Carson gently moved the man's hand from his injured shoulder to look under the cloth. He saw the knife wound and gently replaced the cloth and the man's hand, noting the man's glassy eyes and empty stare. Punched through his left shoulder was an uncovered bullet hole as well.

The third man had a large bandage over his left ear. His face had been pummeled, his nose blue and swollen. He looked to be the most alert of the three, so Carson chose him to talk to.

"Indians get ya, friend?" he asked.

The man looked up and shook his head, then drank a jigger of whiskey. "Ain't no Injuns did this. It was a skinny blonde girl did this to me. Did it to them, too. She blew off part of my ear."

Carson glanced back at John and Miller. They smiled knowingly.

"Yeah," said Carson. "She *can* aim a rifle, can't she?"

"Yes, she can, I reckon. Wields a knife pretty good, too. Deadly with it, I'm sayin'."

"Did you get her?"

"No. She picked us off from a ways out. Took us right outa our saddles. Then she walked up and stabbed ol' Butch in the shoulder without speakin' a word."

"What, may I ask, did you do to rile her so?"

"It all started simple enough. We seen her campin' by a rock. She's pretty lookin'. We asked for a simple poke. We was all willin' to pay for it, too. That's all, I swear."

"But she wasn't havin' none of that, was she?"

"No, sir, she wasn't. She quick-like pulled her revolver and buffaloed Butch across the forehead. Then she pummeled Jack there in the back of the head, sendin' him to the ground contortin' this way 'n' that. Then she clobbered me right in the nose. I think she broke it. By the time we came to our senses, she was gone."

"But you tried trackin' her, didn't ya?"

"We did. That was our greatest folly. She shot us outa our saddles before we knowed what hit us. I reckon we's lucky to be alive."

"Yes, sir, you are," said Carson, opening up his duster to reveal his marshal's badge. "I've been on her trail for days now myself. I've had me a taste of her sharpshootin' skills, too. Trust me, boys, be grateful for your injuries, because if she wanted you dead, you'd all be dead."

"You take care, Marshal. She ain't one to fool with. I can tell ya that."

"Well, you all look like you'll heal up from your wounds. Rest tonight and travel slow tomorrow. You should make it."

"You keep a good long distance from her, Marshal. She don't miss what she aims at."

"I'm doin' my best to stay outa her range."

Carson turned toward the lone man at the bar.

"How 'bout you, son? You get picked off, too?"

"I ain't with them. And I ain't yer son, old man. Now leave me be, or you'll regret it."

The young man studied the three new strangers for several seconds and then tipped his jigger back up to his lips and drained it. He turned away and refilled his jigger from the bottle in front of him.

Carson chose to let the boy's rudeness go by without a comment. Instead, he stepped up to the bar and tipped his hat to the short, plump Mexican barkeep, and smiled.

"Pedro. That *is* your name, right?"

"Sí, Señor."

"I'm Eli Carson. You were runnin' this place last time I was through these parts back in '70, I believe. But there was another gentleman here then, too, as I recall."

"Sí. I remember you. My father was here then."

"Your father. Yes, I recall him. Where is he now?"

"He is in the ground on the other side of that wall." Pedro pointed toward the right side of the building.

"I'm sorry to hear that, Pedro. My condolences to ya, sir."

"Gracias, Señor."

"You're a mite older now, Pedro."

"Sí. You are older, too, Señor."

Carson chuckled.

"Yes, sir, I'm afraid I am. You still make your own beer?"

"It's swill. Ain't *nothin'* like beer, old-timer," said the youth at the bar.

Carson turned his attention to the youngster.

"I think I remember that, too."

He chuckled again and continued.

"But it's wet, friend. I'll take wet right now."

"We ain't friends, you and me," said the young man without looking at Carson. "I don't know you."

"That's true. My name is Eli Carson. What's yours?"

"None."

"None? Your name is None?"

"Yeah," the young man said, turning to look at Carson defiantly. "As in *none of yer damn business*."

"I see. Well, then, if you'll excuse me, Mister Business, I'll just sit here quietly and enjoy Pedro's fine elixir."

Carson turned his eyes toward the barkeep. "Pedro, could you set us up with three beers, please? We're dry as desert bones."

"Sí, but it is warm. No ice here."

"Yes, sir. Warm will be just fine," said Carson, pulling some coins from his coat pocket and dropping them onto the bar top.

He monitored the young man's movements out of the corner of his eye. Years of experience had caused him to form an instantly unfavorable opinion of the man from the moment their eyes first met.

He was young — not more than nineteen or twenty — and tall. He was angry. He was cocky. His hunched-over shoulders gave off an air of unusual aggressiveness. But what concerned Carson most was that the young man's demeanor was that of a man begging for a fight — and not one he really cared to survive.

Maybe it was because he was hot and weary, like Carson. Maybe it was something else that had him upset. Carson couldn't begin to guess what bothered the lad, but he didn't like him. And he didn't trust him. He sure as heck wasn't going to turn his back on him.

Pedro ladled the liquid passing for beer from a bowl into glasses. He replaced the stretch of cheesecloth over the bowl and then set the glasses on the counter.

He slid the coins off the bar top and into his hands and stepped back, remaining silent but keenly watching everyone with discerning eyes. Years of experience told *him* that most travelers weren't interested in conversation. They came in to drink and recuperate from the bashing of the desert. Some drank quietly, keeping to themselves. There were a few others, however, who came in angry, drank angry, and then got angrier. Pedro's eyes cut to the youngster repeatedly. His mind told him that the boy was like a volcano and it wouldn't take much for him to erupt.

The barkeep cast his eyes to the sawed-off shotgun on the shelf under the bar, confirming it was there and ready should the need for it arise. From the young man's demeanor, he expected that to be soon.

"She was here," said Pedro.

"The young woman stopped here?" asked Carson.

"Sí. Yesterday. In the morning."

"Did she say anything of interest?"

"She did not say much. She was *muy bonita*, very pretty, but she scared me."

"She is a beauty, but yes, she can be scary when she wants to be," said Miller.

"*La hermana del diablo*," said Pedro.

"What was that?" asked Miller.

"'The sister of the devil,' Mister Miller," replied Carson. "That's what he said. But I'm surprised to hear that. I'd a thought she'd be more pleasant-like."

"Sí," said Pedro. "She smiled a lot, but she tells lies like the devil."

Carson chuckled.

"Oh. I get it now. Yes, Pedro. She is possessed of a wild imagination."

Carson shifted on his elbow and leaned in toward Pedro. "How long have them fellas in the corner been here?" he asked quietly.

"They came in early this morning."

"So we're gettin' close to her, then, Marshal," said John.

Carson smirked.

"I don't feel like gettin' as close to her as they did."

"You don't think she'll do that to us, do you?" asked Miller.

"This adventure is gettin' stranger and stranger, Mister Miller. I don't know what to think about her anymore."

"So, what are we gonna do now?" asked John.

"We are become that which we have allowed," said Carson.

"What's that?"

"We become what we've hitched ourselves to, John."

"How's that?"

"If you're feelin' sorrowful, it's more likely than not you've brought that sorrow into your life through some words or action. If you're feelin' guilty, it's likely you've hitched yerself to somethin' dishonorable. There it is, plain and simple."

"Well, it may be plain and simple to you, but what the heck has that got to do with this situation? Are you gettin' philosophical again?"

"I am."

"That's what I thought."

"These are the battles we face, John. Each in our own fashion, I reckon, but each and every battle is of our own makin'."

"Why is that, Eli?"

"To learn."

"To learn?"

"Yes. You learn more from battle scars than you do from books. Because lessons learned the hard way are not carelessly forgotten."

"I don't recall askin' for any battle, Eli. I thought we was lookin' on this as an *adventure*."

"Either way, John, we are learnin'. It has been said that we call into our lives that which we need to learn from."

"So we called Miss Middleton into our lives to learn from her?"

"Yes, John."

"So you're sayin' that Miss Middleton is sorta like a schoolmarm?"

"That's a good way to put it, John."

"So, chasin' after her is teachin' us somethin'?"

"You bet, John."

"All of ya talk too much. And I'm gettin' sick of listenin' to ya," said the young man at the bar. "Just keep quiet and let me drink in peace."

John looked at him and then looked back at Carson.

"I s'pose *he's* teachin' us, too?"

Carson chuckled.

"I reckon he is."

"I told ya to be quiet. I ain't gonna tell ya again," said the furious young man.

Carson turned and faced the man directly.

"A famous Roman emperor once said, '*If you're distressed by anything external, the pain is not due to the thing itself but to yer estimate of it; and this ya have the power to revoke at any moment.*' I see you're angry, young man. I see that plain enough. I don't pretend to know why you're so angry. But I will say it ain't healthy to be so angered. It tends to upset the balance of life."

"Are ya loco or somethin', ya old goat?"

"I'm tryin' to say that you don't need to feel victimized by what life has brought ya. You have the power to change it all."

"Shut the hell up like I told ya! That'll be change enough."

"What's got ya so riled, young man?"

"None of yer damn business."

John tapped Carson on the arm and then whispered into his ear.

"Leave 'im to quietly be, Marshal."

Carson turned his head toward John. A look of regret filled his face as he whispered back. "Too late, John. I fear I've already disturbed the beast in him that won't be quieted. My folly was in speakin' to 'im earlier. I surely regret it now. 'Cause I don't see how this is gonna end peacefully. Best to be ready, John."

"Just leave 'im be, Marshal. That's all he wants. He said as much."

"I wish it was true, John. I truly do. But he won't be satisfied with that. Just get ready."

"You're a rude old dog. Didn't yer whore of a mama ever teach you any manners? Don't ya know it ain't polite to turn away from someone who's talkin' to ya?"

"My most humble apologies, young man. I thought our conversation had ended."

"It ends when I say it ends, ya old coot."

"I am sorry. It was not my intent to be rude."

"Well, I say you *was* intended to be rude."

"No, sir. Just inattentive, I reckon"

"So, ya callin' me a liar now?"

"If it appeared that way, I apologize."

"That ain't good enough."

Carson stared into the eyes of the young villain, studying them intently. The eyes were dead and black — absent anything that might resemble compassion or caring, or even life itself. He carefully considered his next comment.

When he had settled on the words, he spoke them quietly but firmly.

"That Roman emperor I mentioned before, he said somethin' else mighty fittin'. He said,

'There is a proper dignity and proportion to be observed in the performance of every act of life.' I would add this to that: make your choices very carefully, for each choice ya make in this life pursues ya into eternity."

"That badge don't give you no right to go lecturin' me. You look pretty close to yer own eternity. So when ya gonna do the world a favor and die, anyway?"

Carson relished the opportunity for the continued dialogue handed to him — to try again to calm the upset youngster.

"I can't rightly say when it is exactly that I'll expire," he said. "But I expect it'll be sometime near the end of my life." He smiled.

The young man flew into a rage.

"Am I a *joke* to you? A fool standin' here for yer amusement, is that it? Am I somethin' to make easy sport of?"

"Not at all. It was just an awkward attempt to lighten the mood and jerk a chuckle outa ya. No ridicule, nothin' demeanin' intended. You look like ya could use a little laughter."

"I'll laugh at *you* when you're dead, ya old wart."

Knowing that if he lost control of the moment, guns would come out hot and firing, Carson chose to remain upon the higher ground as he responded. "I think a man might appreciate humor more when he's alive to hear it."

"It seems you just can't quit yer mockin' me. Get ready to die, old-timer."

"I don't think anyone can ever get ready to die. I think it just sorta happens, whether you're ready or not."

The young man turned from the bar and faced Marshal Carson. His eyes remained hollow and absent life.

"I'm done with yer mockin'," he said.

Realizing that all his efforts to ease the anger in the young man had failed, Carson prepared his mind for what was sure to come in the next few seconds.

Pedro inched closer to his shotgun. John's hand slipped slowly to his revolver, his finger adeptly confirming that the leather thong was not over the hammer.

Carson made one final plea to prevent the inevitable. "Please think on this, young man. Don't let today follow you into eternity."

By then, the young man had stopped thinking. His hand tugged on his Peacemaker as Carson's hand flashed toward his. But two Peacemakers couldn't bring peace to the moment.

Marshal Carson withdrew his revolver from its holster lightning fast, cocked it, and fired at the youngster's midsection.

The young man's face went blank as Carson's bullet punched a hole directly below his sternum, severing his spine.

The limp body dropped to the wood planks and lay as still as a fallen stone.

Carson returned his revolver to its holster, then stood as still as the man's body on the floor, ruing the results of the tragic and senseless confrontation while the blue haze of gun smoke swirled around him.

It was several seconds before there was any movement. Finally, one of the men at the table, the one with the bandaged ear, stood up and walked over to where the young man lay. He kneeled down and placed two fingers against the youngster's neck and waited.

After a time, he looked up at the marshal and shook his head slowly.

The marshal's face became even more sorrowful.

"Darn it all, I tried to avoid it. I really did."

"You did," said the man on his knees. "We'll all swear to that, Marshal. Won't we, boys?"

The other two at the table, startled from their stupors by the gunshot, nodded unconsciously in agreement.

"Thank you, fellas. I do apologize for disturbin' your peace."

"He came in cocked and ready, Marshal," said the man, standing up. "It was just a question of who it was gonna be that did it. I'm glad it was you. I think I've had enough gunplay for my likin'."

"I'm glad it was, too. At least it was done legal." Carson's eyes turned toward the barkeep. "I apologize, Pedro."

Pedro shrugged his shoulders.

"It happens here a lot. I think the desert makes them crazy and they come in here and die so they don't have to go back out into it."

"Yes, sir. That might just be true," replied Carson.

The man returned to his table just as Carson pulled a notebook and pencil from his shirt pocket.

"Would you all mind writin' down what you saw for the record?"

The man stopped short of sitting down and turned to Carson.

"None of us learned to write, Marshal. But we can tell you what we saw and put our mark to the page, if that'll help."

"That'll be fine. My deputy will write it down for ya."

Carson turned toward John.

"Would ya mind, John?"

"Sure thing, Marshal." John took the notebook and pencil from Carson's hands and moved toward the table.

Carson turned toward the counter, pulled a saltshaker toward him, and tipped it up over his glass of warm beer, shaking several sprinkles of salt into it.

"It's just dirty, darn bad luck, I'm sayin'."

"Bad luck, that's what it was," agreed Miller.

Carson guzzled his beer, set the glass back down on the bar, and signaled Pedro for another.

"He was an angry one," Miller continued. "It was bound to happen sooner or later."

"I wish it was later and somewhere else, Mister Miller. The chance to make a new friend lies failed at my feet, in a puddle of blood."

"He didn't look to be the friend-making kind, Marshal."

"I don't care what he looked like, that lad was too young to die. To die like he did, anyway. What a waste. I believe I'll shed more than a few tears over it tonight."

And he did.

Later that night, huddled around the campfire, Marshal Carson wept for the death of the young man. Despite his usually optimistic outlook, the killing had found a hurtful place within him. A powerfully hurtful place.

After the marshal had stopped weeping, he sat silently, staring into the flames of the campfire, until John spoke softly to him.

"Are you all right now, Eli?"

"I don't know, John. I don't know if anyone can be all right after somethin' like that. I keep thinkin' that somewhere out there is a mother, or a father, or maybe an aunt, an uncle, a brother, a sister, or a cousin wonderin' where that young fella might be tonight. Wonderin' what he might be doin'. Wonderin' if he's safe and happy. If he's okay."

"Maybe he *is* okay, Eli. Maybe he's better off bein' where he is. Maybe you did him a favor."

"Maybe, John. But endin' a life, any life, in any manner unnatural ain't somethin' you should take lightly. There's a special importance attached to every life. Takin' a life should give you pause. It should be painful. It should have profound meaning. Life is an exalted thing. Takin' it should be considered a despicable act for any reason. It should have an insightful consequence on your state of bein'."

"You must have killed many outlaws in your time, Marshal," said Miller. "Have you given each of *their* deaths the same kindness of your thoughts?"

"I have, Mister Miller. Each and every one. Because no one should pass from this life without someone givin' them a thought. It don't have to be no kinda long lament. Perhaps just an acknowledgment that they was once here."

"Even Red Darrington?"

"Yeah. Even that no-account scoundrel."

Miller looked hard at Carson.

"I believe you, Marshal. I truly do."

"I just hate missin' opportunities to heal what needs healin'," lamented Carson.

"Maybe you did do the healing that needed to be done — the only healing that *could* be done," offered Miller."

"I thank you for your kind words, Mister Miller. But every life I take affects me the same way. It troubles me greatly and to no end, it seems."

"Then I reckon you'll have to find a way to make peace with it."

"I always do, Mister Miller. It takes me some time, but I always do."

CHAPTER 19

An hour passed in silence as the three exhausted men lay on their bedding beside the campfire, staring up into the sparkling heavens, each alone with his thoughts.

It was no great mystery what Marshal Carson's mind was doing as he stared into the night sky. It was busy replaying the events at the tavern over and over. The disturbing visions kept his mind active and unable to settle into a badly needed sleep.

Supper had been short and stark, but no one complained. They were just happy to be resting now in the cool night air.

John felt a light movement on his shirt. In the glow of the campfire, he glanced down and saw the scorpion crawling up and over the folds of his shirt and across his stomach.

He calmly reached down and took hold of the scorpion's tail between his thumb and forefinger and raised it up to his face, something he had done many times before. He studied the scorpion as it struggled to free itself. But it was held fast.

John tired of the visit quickly and tossed the insect into the fire. He heard the sizzle of its body cooking in the flame and shook his head.

"Miserable desert," he mumbled.

He folded his arms under his head.

"Time was, not too long ago, when I just hated the desert."

"And now?" asked Miller.

"Now? Now I really hate the desert."

Miller chuckled.

"You take care with the hatin', John," said Carson. "Hatin' somethin', anything at all, ain't ever the right thing to do, as I see it. 'Cause if you hate strong enough and long enough, that which you hate might get it in mind to hate you right back. And I don't s'pose, in the end, that could ever turn out to be a good thing."

"You must still be thinkin' on that young'un back at the tavern, Eli?"

"I am, John. I've been doin' a lot of thinkin' tonight, about a lotta things. Not just about what happened at the tavern, but on what I've learned by way of all the events, good and bad, that have passed through my life durin' my many adventures."

"Tell us about it, Marshal. I would enjoy some conversation. My mind's been busy thinking on useless things. I do believe after what Becky has put me through, I could use some learning myself."

"Well, Mister Miller, I've learned some simple truths throughout my many years. One of them just might lean toward you. It's this. When somethin' is opposin' you, it's tryin' its best to teach you somethin' important. Be it the desert or a pretty young woman, the lesson is the same. Difficult times or difficult people, they both can teach you important ways to live your life — if you have a mind open to collect the lessons bein' handed out."

"If you say so, Eli," said John.

"Look up at that sky, John. Look at all them stars. The desert air gives you a vision like that almost every night. Look at that firmament. It just seems to go on forever."

"Forever's a scary word to me. There's somethin' about it gives me chills."

"I was told once that the sky above goes on forever. Now, it's hard for me to understand what forever truly means. I know there's an end to this desert. I know that if I walk west, I'll eventually come to the Pacific Ocean. I saw it once, you know. When I was much younger. I never imagined forever before, but when I gazed upon that great body of water, I knew it was a glimpse of what forever might be like. It frightened me some, but it was a glorious kinda fright. And I've been thinkin' maybe that's what death is — a gloriously frightenin' forever adventure on a whole other kinda ocean."

"I ain't never seen the ocean, so I can't speak to that," said John.

"Someday, John, I'd like to reach up and punch a hole in that starry firmament and then slip behind it just to see what lies beyond."

"Look, Eli, I don't know what you're goin' on about. I don't know oceans from stars about any of it. But thinkin' on the mystery of dyin' scares me somethin' awful. It's that kinda forever I was talkin' about."

"Don't fret about it, John. You're not gonna die anytime soon that I know of. But eventually you will."

"But I don't wanna die at all, Eli."

"Well, we all die, John. And thinkin' on it tonight like I have been, I've come to believe dyin' is more like walkin' away than anything else.

"Like with that young fella today. I believe at the end of his life, he just walked away. Ain't none of us seen 'im do it, of course, but I believe that's what he did. He looked down and saw his lifeless body and then just walked away from it."

"Well, I expect his steps was heavy after what he did, upsettin' you and all," said John.

"I reckon some walk away in light steps and some walk heavy. Some walk away with a smile, some walk with a frown. Some walk away while doin' somethin' glorious and some walk away in the steps of evil. Some folks just walk away. It's the way of things, I reckon. When it's time to walk, you just set yer legs to movin'."

"For my liking, Marshal, I wouldn't want to be starting that kind of walk anytime soon," said Miller.

"If I had my choice, Mister Miller, I reckon I'd like to walk away from this life while doin' somethin' noble. Now, it might end up bein' that one kind of walk is no different than any other. And I s'pose, when all's said and done, it's all the same for the one doin' the walkin'. But if it is all the same, I would prefer walkin' away while I was on a path toward some higher purpose."

"Well," said Miller, "for a higher purpose or a lower one, if it's all the same to you, I'd rather live a while longer and save that sort of walk for much later."

"Sooner or later, walkin', crawlin', or flyin', it's really all the same. When you're called, you just gotta leave it all behind anyway."

"Let's talk about somethin' else, Marshal. This talk of death and dyin', walkin' and crawlin, it ain't a happy thing."

"Well, then, John, let's have a conversation about gold!"

"Now, there you go, Eli! That's a fine subject. Yes, sir. That's a much finer subject."

"So, where's your gold, John?"

"I ain't got none, Eli."

"Me neither. How about you, Mister Miller? Where's your gold?"

"I don't have any either, Marshal."

"Well, that was a mighty short conversation, fellas."

"That don't mean I wanna go back to talkin' about dyin.'"

"Fine, John. Then let's talk some more about what lessons we might take from this day. That young man didn't have to die today. But the young don't always make the best decisions. I believe it has to do with the fact they ain't had the advantage of years that us older folks have. They don't know how it is that life works. They ain't lived enough to understand the long regrets that come with bad choices. But I do. And I ain't gonna make another mistake like I did today.

"This young woman we're goin' after ain't had the benefit of my years either. So no matter what happens when we catch up to her, I ain't gonna be in no rush to end her life. I intend to give her full advantage to choose life over any alternative. I believe I owe that much to the young man I killed. And I believe I can live with that. Yes, sir, I believe that is the lesson I've been given today."

"I think you're gettin' philosophical again, Eli. That's what I think."

"Yeah, it might just be that. But I think we're all learnin' somethin' on this adventure, John. You'll have to sort that out for yerselves. For now, fellas, time to turn in. We got us another hard ride tomorrow. Good night to ya both."

"Good night, Marshal," said Miller.

John just exhaled hard.

Carson chuckled.

"You ain't dyin' tonight, John."

"You certain of that?"

"No. But if you do die, it would be a kindness to me if you'd go quietly so you don't wake me up. I'm old and need my rest."

Miller chuckled.

Once again, the morning came much too early for Marshal Carson. Rolling out from under his blanket, he let loose a mournful groan.

"Why does mornin' have to come at this ungodly time of day?"

"Oh, oh," said John. "Somebody didn't sleep too good."

"I was sleepin' on a darn pebble that felt like a giant boulder all night, John. I reckon I'm feelin' a mite ornery regardin' it."

"Why didn't you just move away from it, Eli?"

"Don't try to get me to see reason right now, John. I'm in no mood for reason."

"It's gonna be fun ridin' with you this mornin', I can see that."

Carson chuckled as John rolled up his bedding and tucked it back under his saddle cantle.

"I've decided we'll follow the tracks toward the caves where I had that gunfight with Zaiman Beauchamp."

"Fine," said John. "Whatever you say."

Carson chuckled once more as he rolled up his bedding.

"You didn't die last night, John, and you're not gonna die today either."

"I reckon I might — from exhaustion. I didn't get to sleep at all last night, thanks to your jabberin' about dyin' and such."

"Stop frettin' about it. When it's yer time to go, it'll be yer time to go. Hopefully, you'll have finished yer life anyway when the time comes and there won't be nothin' left undone. I'd hate to leave with my life unfinished."

"By God, you're gloomy this mornin'! I don't think I'm awake enough for yer mornin' philosophy. Finished or unfinished, though, what's the difference?"

John began gathering up wood for a fire. Carson and Miller did the same.

"I reckon, with a certain degree of disappointment, that an unfinished life might be like a dead river — a hideous and ghoulish scar left upon the earth, a lamented reminder that once upon a time there was an energy that flowed free, strong, and with promise. Now dry and dusty, the empty carcass of that promise lies unable to speak again the tale of somethin' that was, for a little while at least, glorious and unequaled and now forever forgotten. Yes, sir, I do believe departin' this life before I've finished the good fight of livin' would be a real shame — somethin' I might regret long into my eternity."

"Well, ain't you just a ball of sunshine."

"And what of that empty shell that once housed such a lively delight?" said Carson, walking back toward the campfire pit with an armload of wood and dumping it onto the ground next to the pit.

"What're ya talkin' about now?" John said as he dropped an armful of sticks into the pit.

"I've also been thinkin' about the young gut-shot man back at Dead River."

"Why?"

"Can't rightly say why. But he's got me thinkin' about livin' and dyin'."

"I hate to ask you to explain it," said John, "but I know you're gonna do it anyway whether I ask you to or not, you bein' in such a philosophical mood. So get to it."

"Some people, it seems, live only for the sake of livin' while others die only for the sake of dyin'. It seems like there should be more to livin' and dyin', but I'll tell ya, there are times when even I can't find a good reason in some folks for either. Now, I reckon dyin' is just a part of livin', but I choose to believe it to be more noble to go searchin' for a good reason to live than a holy reason to die."

"What has that got to do with the fella out at Dead River?"

"I like to think he had a purpose as well — a reason for bein', a lesson to teach."

"Maybe he did and maybe he didn't. I know I ain't got no reasons for anything right now and I ain't got no lessons to teach nor to learn. I just got me a whole lotta questions."

"I think livin' creates a lot of questions, John. I think dyin' answers them all."

"You are decidedly not of a light spirit this mornin', Eli. And I have to tell ya, you have me concerned."

John stacked the wood in the pit and lit a match to the dried wood, setting the fire ablaze.

"Calm yourself, John. These are days of learnin'."

"Days of learnin'? What're we learnin', Eli?"

"I can't say at the moment, but more lessons are comin'. I can feel it."

"I'm gonna make sure you have a nice place to sleep tonight, Eli. You're a lot more fun when you're happy."

"I am happy, John. I'm just feelin' philosophical today."

"Well, I'll tell you this, Eli. If you get any more philosophical, I do believe I'll cry myself into oblivion over it."

Carson chuckled.

"Philosophy is a good thing, John. Ain't that right, Mister Miller?"

"Don't draw me into that discussion, Marshal. My thoughts are still on Becky."

"Well, there's philosophy in that as well, I reckon."

"This oughta be good, Mister Miller," John said, pouring water from his canteen into the coffee pot. "Listen up now. Remember, these is learnin' days. Go on, Eli. Tell us the philosophy concernin' Miss Rebecca."

"Don't mock me, John. There is a philosophy about her. About all women, really."

"I don't know nothin' 'bout women neither. Stars, oceans, and women, Eli, they're all the same to me — mysteries, all of 'em."

"I know, John, I know. But women can be a wondrous and excitin' mystery."

"I'd rather talk about the ocean than the mysteries of women. At least I know somethin' about water."

Carson laughed.

"I reckon that's why we're all three bachelors, boys. The whys and hows of womenfolk run too deep for us."

"You can say that again," said Miller.

"I do know this, though, fellas. Mystery exists not to stay your search, but to entice you toward discovery."

"Nicely said," replied Miller. "Women do entice me, but I think they'll always remain a mystery. Thank you, Marshal. These past days have been fascinating."

"You forgot learnin', Mister Miller. These is learnin' days."

"Thank you for reminding me, John."

"You're welcome, sir. Now, Eli, tell us about Miss Rebecca."

"I've been thinkin' on her a fair bit. She's a smart woman; I'd fairly say she's the smartest I've ever come across. I believe she's onto somethin' big. Now I've got lots of whys, hows, and whats goin' on up in my noggin, but I do believe she's onto somethin' she thinks is real. And to tell you the truth, I'm beginnin' to think that chest of gold just might exist."

"Wouldn't that be somethin'? But what philosophy concernin' her are you gettin' at?"

"'What now you struggle against, you might have once struggled for.'"

"What the heck does that mean?"

"Simply put, it means that changes sometimes occur."

"I don't know why you don't just say it straight out simple, then."

Carson and Miller laughed.

"Philosophy ain't always simple, John."

"But it don't have to be so difficult. It's all them fancy words that hide the truth of it."

"You are so right about that, John."

"You know, I think all them philosophers ain't so smart as they'd like us to believe. They just hide somethin' simple behind big words. Makes 'em feel so much smarter than the rest of us. But they ain't smarter. Are they?"

Carson smiled.

"No, John, they ain't smarter than most. They just speak prettier than most. Like Miss Middleton."

"Yes, sir. That's the truth of it right there. Now, what's all this about changin' gotta do with Miss Rebecca? And don't go gettin' fancy with yer words, please."

"There are times when life is one thing and then becomes another. What you once believed to be true becomes totally unbelievable later on, given new information or experiences. Are you followin' me, John?"

"I believe I am."

"Let's take our Miss Middleton. While growin' up, she said, her father told her a story about how he discovered the chest of coins. The story might've been true or it might've just been a tale told to her as a bedtime story."

"But she said her daddy confessed it was true on his deathbed."

"She did say that, John. But with all the changes goin' on inside that girl, what if that story was told by some make-believe father, and in fact there ain't no gold-filled chest at all?"

"You sure know how to take the pleasure outa things."

Carson smiled.

"I'm sorry, John. I don't mean to spoil your fantasy, but we don't know who we're really dealin' with, do we?"

"I s'pose not, but you just said before that you think the chest might be real. Now here you go changin' yer mind about it. I'm all kinds of confused."

"The gold bein' real or not isn't what interests me. What interests me — and to be honest about it, worries me at the same time — is who else might have heard the story and believes it to be true.

"Now, I know she ain't been all that honest with us about it, but she also ain't killed us over it either. I can't say that young fella out at Dead River fared the same. But listen, fellas. The way she's been collectin' accomplices, and I'm guessin' she's got more than one, it's got me thinkin' there might be someone else followin' her that she don't know about."

"You're saying an accomplice of an accomplice?"

"Exactly right, Mister Miller. And that someone out there could be mighty dangerous. They're keepin' low until the time when they think she might be nearin' the place on the map. I think then they might up and do somethin' rash, just in case the chest is real. I believe we need to catch up to her as quick as we can, because I believe her life just might be in danger."

"Wait a darn minute. Are we out to capture her or rescue her?"

"What I'm sayin', John, is that things are changin'. I believe we have to find her before someone else does, someone she might not know about, or she just might go the way of that young man out in the wash."

"What about the other killin' that supposedly took place out there on Dead River?"

"If there was one, I think we'll learn more about that later."

"And I think you've been too long out in the sun, Eli. I think yer brain is fried. How do you come up with this stuff?"

"I've been tryin' to reason it out, John. It's the only scenario that makes any sense right now. Miss Middleton is a strange kinda woman, no doubt about it, but she ain't the murderin' kind."

"Tell that to the man she shot outa his saddle."

"There is the potential within her to kill, I don't dispute that. But she's had ample opportunities to take me out of my saddle on the way out here, and she hasn't taken advantage of that opportunity yet. She's busy with headin' to where the map is tellin' her to go. What she'll find there is anybody's guess, but she's headin' straight for it. We have to determine which tracks are hers and get to her quick."

"I don't understand this. First we're s'posed to capture her, now we're gonna rescue her. I'm so confused, I don't know if I'm comin' or goin'."

Carson laughed.

"I agree with you, Marshal," said Miller. "I don't know about that someone else, but I do believe she could end up in danger. I believe you've got good reason to feel that way."

"Okay, Mister Miller. How 'bout you, John?"

"I don't need any reasonin', Marshal. I'm yer deputy. I do what you say. You say capture her, I'll go capture her. You say rescue her, then I'll do that."

"While I thank you for your loyalty, John, I was hopin' for a better reason."

"Well, I ain't got no better reason than that."

CHAPTER 20

The moment his eyes opened in the morning, John leapt to his feet and rolled up his bedding.

He took the bedroll over to his horse and tucked it under the edge of the cantle, tied it in place with a pair of saddle strings, and then walked back to the dead campfire to restart it.

There was renewed purpose in his steps. He was recharged after a good night's sleep. And there was no secret about it: he was eager to go after Rebecca Middleton.

"Rise up, gentlemen!" he shouted from his knees at the side of the campfire. "We got a full day ahead of us. Time to get coffee brewin' and food cookin."

"Who put you in charge of happy mornin's?" asked Carson, groggily sitting up.

"It's all your fault, Eli."

"How's that, John?"

"You're the one changed our ride from a capture to a rescue. Now we gotta hurry and catch up to her so's we can rescue her. She's helpless out there. Get up! Let's get goin."

"She ain't the helpless kind, John. I reckon she's about as helpless as a rattlesnake."

"No matter, Eli. She needs rescuin' and we're the ones to do it. So get up and go get some coffee from your saddlebag. Get up, Mister Miller. And I mean quick-like."

"I'm up, John. No call to go scolding me for something Marshal Carson did."

"Thanks, Mister Miller. I appreciate the knife in the back."

Miller chuckled.

"Happy to oblige, Marshal. But John's right. You got him all riled up last night about rescuing a damsel in distress. No wonder he's so eager to go."

"I reckon I did, at that."

From their mounts, they stared down at the hoofprints in the sand, discussing which set to follow.

After a while and a hearty discussion with no consensus reached, Carson confirmed his decision to follow the set of tracks that most closely led in the direction of the area where he'd had the gunfight with Zaiman Beauchamp.

The day grew hotter and hotter; there seemed no end to just how hot it was going to get. The trio walked their horses along the trail until a shot rang out and missed, falling extremely short of them in a cloud of sand and dust.

They were off their horses with their rifles and behind a large boulder within seconds.

"How did she miss us so cleanly?" asked Miller.

"I don't know, but I ain't gonna go complainin' about it," said Carson.

"I'm not complaining; I'm pleasantly surprised."

"Maybe it was just another warnin' shot," offered John.

"In that case I consider myself warned," said Carson.

"Where do you think she is?" asked John.

"I didn't take the opportunity to get a good look."

A barrage of gunfire pelted the boulder.

"She isn't up there alone now," said Miller.

"Well, this ain't a good thing."

"No, John, I reckon not."

"How about we get back on our horses and get out of here?" asked Miller.

"Let's get clear of this mess, at least," answered Carson, "and rethink our approach."

"I won't argue with ya, Marshal," said John.

The yip of Indians in the distance was followed by more gunfire and bullets ricocheting off the boulder.

"Well, I'll be," said Carson. "That's gotta be the Acoma tribe."

"You mean she's got *Indians* working for her now?" asked Miller. "Are we going to get scalped?"

Carson chuckled.

"No, no. She ain't with 'em. At least I don't think so. Darn it all, I *hope* she ain't with 'em."

John leaned over to Carson.

"How we gonna find out for sure?"

"Just one way I know of."

Carson held his rifle high with both hands and stood up very carefully.

"No more shootin'!" he yelled. "I'm Marshal Carson...Marshal Carson!"

"Carson?" one of the Indians yelled back.

"Gray Coyote? Is that you?"

"Carson, I Gray Coyote."

Carson stepped out into the open. "Whew! We're gonna be just fine, boys. Put your rifles up like me and come on out from behind that rock. Let 'em see ya clearly."

"Are you sure she isn't with them, Marshal?" asked Miller.

"I don't think she is, or we'd be hearin' about it by now, I reckon. We're gonna be okay."

Carson waved his rifle over his head.

Seconds later, an Indian stood up and waved his rifle, then yipped loudly in celebration.

"Collect the horses, John," said Carson with a growing smile.

The three rode straight toward the Indians, now all grouped together and mounted on their ponies. Carson waved as he approached. One of the Indians waved back and grinned.

As they got closer, Carson called out, "Good to see you again, Gray Coyote. You scared me." He laughed.

The Indian smiled back.

"Good I remember you."

"Yes it is, my friend. It is very good. This is my deputy, John Slims. This man here is ridin' with us. He is called Andrew Miller. Boys, this is Gray Coyote. My friend."

The two men tipped their hats to the Indian. He nodded his head.

"You come to pueblo, Old Carson?"

"I cannot, my friend. We must ride past to find a young woman."

"You look for white witch?"

"Yes, I suppose she might look that way to you. Have you seen her?"

"She pass through last sun."

"Did you talk to her?"

"No. We not have words with witch. We only watch her ride past pueblo. It not good talk to witches."

Carson smiled.

"Yes, I believe you're right. Which way did she go?"

"She go there." The Indian pointed to a trail heading eastward.

"Towards the small canyons?"

"Yes."

"I figured as much."

"You not come pueblo? Caballo Blanco will want speak you."

"Please tell White Horse I will stop by on my way back. I must first find the witch."

"You go, then. I tell Caballo Blanco you come another sun."

"Yes. Thank you, Gray Coyote."

The Indian patrol rode away, toward a distant mesa.

Carson's eyes followed the departing Indians until they moved past them and up to the pueblo.

The sandstone structures supporting the pueblo village rose up off the desert floor some 365 feet to a plateau where hundreds of Indians had lived, worked, and enjoyed their privacy for centuries.

The patrols sent out each day were tasked with maintaining that privacy. The tradition of fervently protecting their isolation grew out of their battle with Juan de Oñate back in 1598, a battle in which over six hundred of their tribe had been killed or maimed.

The Spaniards were cruel victors, forcing the Acoma into slavery and hacking off the right foot of every male twenty-five years old or older

— the Spanish conquerors' way of preventing another uprising.

The persistent erosion throughout the area over several millennia had split the sandstone and allowed caves to form. Some of the openings were so small only tiny animals could gain entrance to them, but others were large enough for a human being to easily squeeze through. Many such caves quickly opened up into larger caverns.

The ceilings contained fractures that allowed smoke from campfires to rise up and depart the caverns, providing excellent ventilation to anyone deciding to make a home in one of those fissures.

It was to such a fissure that the hoofprints led the trio of would-be rescuers.

As they rounded a bend in the trail, they came upon a distant horse tied to a rock. Although it was a few hundred yards away, they could plainly see that it was a packhorse.

"Where'd that packhorse come from?" asked John. "I ain't seen no tracks from it."

"I don't know, John. I reckon she might be a witch after all. Turned her saddle horse into a packhorse."

"Maybe she conjured it outa thin air," suggested Miller.

"Maybe she did, but I expect she had one of her accomplices bring it."

"Okay, so where's the horse of her accomplice? I only see one horse. Where's her saddle horse?"

"Good questions all, John. But I ain't got the answers yet."

John spotted dust rising in the near distance, behind a very large boulder.

"Look! Comes a rider, I suspect."

"I see it."

They remained still and quiet, watching as Rebecca Middleton rode around the boulder and stopped next to the horse.

"There she is!" whispered John.

"Finally," Carson whispered back. "But where was she?"

"Could she have gone for water?"

"Good point, John. If memory serves, there's a good-sized spring over in that direction."

Rebecca answered the question when she pulled her canteen from her horse and drank several swallows.

"That's it," said Carson. "She went to the spring."

John slipped out of his saddle, pulled Carson's field glasses from a saddlebag, and crept closer, crawling at times, toward a large boulder as Carson and Miller backed their horses up until they were out of sight of the cave.

John got comfortable and peered through the glasses, waiting patiently for any sign of who, if anybody, might be inside the cave.

Moments later, Carson and Miller crawled up alongside him.

Carson whispered, "See anyone else yet?"

"No one's come out as yet," John whispered back. "But there's been quite a bit of diggin' done at the entrance. There's a shovel leaned up against the cliff."

A moment later they watched as the young woman grabbed the shovel and began digging, tossing dirt and sand in every direction.

"She's a digger," said Carson.

"Looks like she's been at it for some time, too," added John.

Rebecca dug until the punishing sun sapped her energy. She tossed the shovel to the ground and sat down on the edge of the hole. She appeared exhausted. She reached for a canteen that lay near her, pulled the cork, and filled her throat. Then she resealed it and dropped it back on the ground.

Watching her sitting there trying to regain her strength to continue digging, Carson could almost envision both the excitement and the madness that had led her to this moment.

"She looks whipped," said Miller.

"She don't look like a quitter to me, Mister Miller."

Rebecca picked up the shovel and resumed digging for more than ten minutes before she dropped the shovel to the ground again and sat down. After drinking several swallows from the canteen, she also dropped it to the ground.

"She's determined," said John.

"She is that," replied Carson.

"Is the treasure buried?"

"I believe she said it's in a cave. That fissure must open up to a cave and she must be clearin' the entrance. That's a lot of diggin' under this sun."

"Well," said John, "now the question is, is there somethin' special inside that cave worth all the diggin'?"

"I reckon we'll know soon enough, if we just sit patiently and wait."

Rebecca dropped to her knees and crawled toward the rock wall. Seconds later, she disappeared.

"Do you think it's there?" asked Miller. "Do you think the chest of coins is in there?"

"I find myself hopin' it is, Mister Miller. I hate to think we came all this way for nothin'."

"Maybe we should go help her."

"No, sir. I believe she's earned her privacy. At least for the moment."

Seconds later, a high-pitched scream came from inside the cave.

"Well, I reckon that was the discovery of either a chest full of gold coins or some kinda critter," said Carson with a chuckle.

Loud laughter echoed through the small canyon.

"Well, I do believe someone is mighty happy. I reckon we can rule out it bein' a critter. It would appear our Miss Middleton is a very rich young lady."

"So you think them gold coins is in there?" asked John.

"I don't expect anyone would laugh like that for any other reason. Do you?"

"I reckon not. Oh, my!"

"This doesn't make me happy," said Miller.

"And why is that?" asked Carson.

"She's rich."

"Ah, I understand," answered Carson.

"Well, I don't," said John.

"What I believe Mister Miller is sayin', John, is he was hopin' there would be no chest. That way Miss Middleton might've been more willin' to give up her wasted search and settle down with Mister Miller, here. Did I interpret that correctly, Mister Miller?"

"Exactly, Marshal. Now she'll never know that I genuinely love her. I'm doomed."

"Now, now, lad. I thought you'd surrendered to the lost cause of that notion by now."

"I lied. More to myself than to you, I now realize. I still love her. But she'll never accept me now. I know it. Her life will now be consumed only with keeping everyone away from her gold."

"Well, I think that sounds awful fatalistic, Mister Miller."

"Sounds more realistic to me," said John.

"I agree with John, Marshal. Before the gold, she had nothing to lose taking up with me. But now she's got everything to lose — everything, that is, that's important to her. I'm a fool to even hope she might consider me in her future."

"I'll leave the thoughts of love to your better judgment, then. But I think we ought to pay Miss Middleton a visit now and bring this whole crazy adventure to an end."

John began walking toward the cave. "Hopefully, without any heads gettin' blowed off."

CHAPTER 21

A hat appeared at the entrance to the cave. It was attached to a head that emerged next. Seconds later, the body of Rebecca Middleton made an appearance.

Two sets of hands grabbed her by the arms and pulled her the rest of the way out, startling her.

"Howdy, Miss Middleton," said Marshal Carson. "And may I say congratulations to you?"

Her angered scream nearly deafened them, but it didn't last long, for Miller was quick to apply the gag.

Marshal Carson fingered his ear. "Oh, boy! That was a loud one — loud enough, I think, to call the dead out of their graves."

Rebecca attempted to break their hold on her, but Miller and John had a steady grip.

"Get them legs tied, boys," said Carson, rubbing his chin. "I recall them as bein' mighty lethal."

Miller was instantly at her feet, tying her legs together. Soon, her hands were forced behind her and Miller secured them as well.

Miller and John sat her gently down on the sand and released their grip, leaving her thrashing about wildly.

The three men smiled at each other.

"Well, boys," said Carson, "with the exception of a temporary loss of hearin', I do believe that went better than expected."

"I do believe you're right, Eli," said John.

They stood back and let the enraged young woman fling herself about until she tired enough to stop.

Carson squatted in front of her and smiled.

"We came across some fellas in a small tavern a while ago. I expect you know both the tavern and the fellas I'm referring to. Anyway, they tangled with you earlier and are now the wiser for it. Based my discussion with them, the restraints and gag will come off the moment you can show us that you're calm and not likely to go grabbin' for our revolvers. So, how long you stay restrained and gagged is therefore entirely up to you. But I want to assure you, Miss Middleton, we ain't here to rob you of yer gold. We got more important reasons for bein' out here."

The young woman's eyes were as stilled lightning bolts — flashing wildly, but as yet refrained from striking out. If she'd been able, however, she would have sent fiery bolts straight into their hearts.

Carson stood up and stepped away from her.

"It's all up to you, Miss Middleton. We got lots of time. But you should know that you're the beneficiary of a lesson taught to me by a young man back at that same tavern. I paid dearly for that lesson. So did he. So I'd appreciate it if you'd accept my acts of affability with a bit more refinement."

It took longer than Carson thought it would, but finally Rebecca demonstrated to him that she was completely calm.

He once more bent down and stared into her eyes.

"Are you gonna act like a proper young lady now?"

She nodded.

"All right, then. But let me warn you. If you're lyin' to me, I'll gag you again. And I just might leave you gagged all night. Am I understood?"

She nodded again.

"John, would you please remove her gag? I'd like to have a chat with her before decidin' whether to cut her loose."

John did as he was bid.

"Miss Middleton, would you care for a chug of water before we begin our discussion? I imagine yer mouth might be a bit dry from that rag."

"I would."

Carson stared hard at her.

"I would, please."

"Lovely," he said, motioning to Miller, who offered a canteen.

"Hi, darling," he said. "Miss me?"

"Hardly, dear," she responded. "I haven't even aimed at you yet."

Miller chuckled.

"Are you still sore at me?" she asked.

"Nah. I'm over it, darling."

"Don't fool yourself, dearest. You'll never be over me."

"I'll work on it. Would you like a drink, or should I pour it over your head?"

"Still sore after all, I see."

Miller put the canteen to her mouth and tipped it up. She drank, her eyes flashing at him.

Once she was refreshed, Carson stood in front of her again and did his best to speak calmly and softly to the young woman he guessed was still agitated under that calm exterior.

"You gave us quite an adventure so far, Miss Middleton."

"What lesson were you referring to earlier, Marshal?"

"The lesson is mine. But as I said, Miss Middleton, we ain't here for yer gold."

"Liar."

"I'm a Deputy U.S. Marshal, Miss Middleton. I don't lie, I don't cheat, and I don't steal."

"You'd be the only marshal who doesn't, then. Besides, it's not here. It's gone."

"It's gone, huh?"

"That's right. We can head back to Holbrook now."

"John, would you go into that cave and have a look, please? I suspect she's lyin to me. But if you do find any gold in there, I intend to hold onto it as evidence of a crime. I don't know exactly what crime just yet, but I'm sure to come up with somethin' by the time we get back to Holbrook. In any event, I can hold it for years while I'm searchin' for a crime to go along with it."

"Okay! Okay! It's in there."

"I'm sorry, Miss. Would you mind repeatin' that? I'm a bit hard of hearin' at present."

"You win. The gold is in there."

"That's better. Miss Middleton, I understand your need to protect what you've long searched for, so I'm gonna cut you a little slack. But if you continue to lie to me, I'll hold the gold as evidence. Do we understand each other?"

"We do. You're intending to hold it as ransom."

"I see we still have some trust issues between us."

"How much do you want?"

Carson glanced at John. "Do you see me tryin' to be agreeable?"

"I do, Marshal."

"Is it in my mind only, or is she bein' difficult?"

"Fine, Marshal," Rebecca said. "You're in control. What do you want?"

"I want ya to be honest with me, that's all. Start tellin' me the truth about things and you can keep yer gold, all of it. Heck, we'll even help you get it back to town safely and without anyone else knowin' about it. Do you see this side of the offer clearly?"

"Why would you do that?"

"Let's call it a gesture of trust between us."

"Sounds good, if you're being honest about it."

"We seem to be makin' progress. Now, Miss Middleton, I believe you're in danger. I haven't seen hard evidence of the threat just yet, but I do believe your life is in jeopardy."

"And what would be the nature of that threat?"

"You have someone else on your trail, someone, I fear, not so respectful of your claim as we are. At least that's the conclusion I've come to."

"You've arrived at your conclusion too late. That someone would most likely be my husband."

"Your husband?" asked Miller.

"Yes, dear, my husband. My real husband."

"Miss Middleton, I'm tirin' of your little games," said Carson. "Just how many husbands do you have, anyway?"

"As many as I have needed to accommodate my search, Marshal. Of course, they're all married to women with false names."

"And that goes for the one comin' up behind us?"

"No. He's my real husband."

"He is?"

"Yes. My name isn't Rebecca Middleton, Marshal."

"Why ain't I surprised to hear that?"

"It's Margaret Masterton."

"Margaret Masterton?" asked Miller.

"Yes, dear, I'm afraid so."

"Oh, the fool emerges," said the jilted Miller.

"Sorry, dear. Marshal, my husband, Robert, is most likely who you're looking for. I'm pretty sure it was he who killed the young man. But that man was no innocent. He was bad. Very bad. If he weren't killed already, he'd be killed soon. His name was Arlo Jackson."

"Arlo Jackson?" asked Carson. "The bank robber Arlo Jackson?"

"Yes."

"I got a silhouetted wanted poster of him in my office. There ain't no picture of him."

"You don't need a picture, as I see it. You've got him lying in a box at your undertaker's office, if he isn't already buried yet."

"Okay. How do you know him?"

"My brother isn't missing, Marshal. Mister Jackson murdered him in Omaha. At least I think he did. I'm pretty sure of it."

"Omaha?" asked Miller.

"Yes, Andrew, dear. As I'm sure you know by now, I didn't get off the train to use the facilities. I got off the train to claim my brother's body. I initially heard that he and Mister Jackson had gotten into a bar fight. That fight led to a gunfight. My brother lost."

"What was the fight over?" asked Carson.

"Mister Jackson claimed that he caught my brother cheating at cards. I found that claim to be ludicrous, however."

"Why is that?"

"My brother wasn't a gambler, Marshal."

"Any witnesses to them playin' cards?"

"Not one."

"I see."

"I went to the jail and confronted Mister Jackson about my brother. He restated his claim. I called him a liar to his face."

"You met with Arlo Jackson?"

"Yes, Marshal. He was arrested for killing my brother several hours after the gunfight."

"Any witnesses to the killin'?"

"Yes. Several saw Jackson shoot my brother in cold blood."

"I see. Did you tell Jackson that?"

"I did. He insisted my brother drew first, but the sheriff told me my brother's revolver was found still in its holster with the leather thong drawn over the hammer."

"Then he couldn't have drawn first like Arlo Jackson claimed."

"Exactly. Later, after I went through all of my brother's belongings and couldn't find the other half of the coin and the letter among his possessions, I confronted Mister Jackson about them. He said he didn't have them, but all the time denying it he refused to look me in the eye. That's when I knew he had them hidden away somewhere."

"But you had no proof."

"Call it feminine intuition, Marshal. Anyway, the next day Arlo Jackson escaped from the jail. It took me some doing, but I followed him through Lincoln, then Ogallala, then Denver, through Trinidad, Santa Fe, Albuquerque, and finally down to Gallup. I just missed him every time, but he always left a trail I could follow. I knew he had the letter and was heading to where the trail could be picked up."

"But you had the other half of the coin?"

"Yes."

"Then Jackson wouldn't be able to find the chest without it."

"That's true. But I knew he would go to Gallup because that's where the letter said the beginning of the trail was. Gallup or Holbrook, depending on which direction the searcher began the search from. At least that's what my brother wrote and told me. Then he telegrammed me to meet him in Gallup."

Carson bowed his head in thought.

"You don't believe me, Marshal?"

"Of course not, but I'm confused. Why would Arlo head to Holbrook if he was already at the trailhead?"

"I can't answer that, Marshal. I don't know. But I got word he was heading to Holbrook so I came to find him. You like everything to be explained and laid out in a perfect line, don't you, Marshal?"

"Yes, ma'am, I do. I like things to have order, to make sense."

"Sometimes life doesn't make sense, Marshal. Sometimes it's sloppy, unpredictable, filled with senseless holes — without order. Sometimes things come at you so fast, you don't have time to sort them all out. Sometimes you have to take what comes how it comes, and adjust to *it* instead of trying to force *it* to adjust to *you*."

"You're so right, Miss Midd...er, Missus Masterton. Sometimes life *is* sloppy. And I guess my ways don't fit in with this world no more. Everything moves too fast for me. I don't have the time I used to have to sort things out. This whole country is changin' so fast, and so are the attitudes of most folks. With the comin' of the railroad, where it used to take folks months to travel to will now be reached in only days. The Good Lord only knows what's comin' next to shorten that time. I'm old and worn out, Miz Masterton. My time is fast comin' to an end. I know that. I see that. I'm outdated and rapidly comin' into a time where I'll become completely obsolete. But while I am here doin' my job, I intend to see it through the only way I know how. Now, what about this husband of yours, Robert?"

"After I met Andrew in St. Louis, Robert decided to go on ahead to Gallup and arrange things for our expedition."

"He see the letter?"

"No. No one saw the letter except for my brother and Arlo Jackson."

"You bein' with Mister Miller didn't bother Robert?"

"My husband is a very deliberate man, Marshal. He's not afraid to do what needs to be done. Nor am I."

"What about Arlo Jackson?"

"I sent my husband a telegram about Arlo Jackson whenever I had the chance. Robert was already in Gallup by that time, waiting for me to arrive. He said he would handle it."

"And what did you have planned for *me*, my dear, if I had come out to Gallup with you?" asked Miller.

"We had planned a rope for you."

"You were going to *hang* me?"

"Don't be silly. We were going to tie you up when we got to Gallup and then get out of town, hopefully with the other half of the coin and the letter. It didn't work out that way, though. And I must say, Andrew, I misjudged you. I had no idea you were this clever and persistent. How did you track me all the way out here?"

"You left an indelible impression on everyone you met along the way. You weren't hard to follow."

"Hmmm. I'll have to work on that."

"Lord almighty, Miss," replied Carson. "You're a whole adventure unto yerself."

"Marshal, I've told you the whole truth. I've had to use my wits to get this far, but I haven't harmed a hair on anyone's head doing it. Not physically, anyway."

"I don't think my deputies would agree with that assessment, Miss. You walloped them pretty good during yer antics."

"I suppose that's true. And I do apologize for that. I was scared."

"Try that again, if you will. I don't think you was scared at all. Not for one second. I don't think you know the meaning of fear. I believe you was employing one of yer tactics."

"That sure does bother you, my not thinking like a helpless woman, doesn't it?"

"I don't mind that. I do mind you walloping my deputies for no good reason."

"I apologize, Marshal. There, I said it again. Now, is it really necessary to keep me bound like this?"

"You might want to ask John about that, seein' as he's the one that had to deal with you durin' your little *incident* back in Holbrook."

"I apologize for my behavior, John."

"It's forgotten, ma'am."

"Will you release me now, Marshal? It looks as if I'm going to need your help anyway. That chest is huge. Too big for me to bring out by myself."

"So now you need my help."

"I do. And as I see it, we're partners. I'll split the gold with you if you help me."

"You're hog-tied, Missus Masterton. I reckon I could keep it all for myself, if I wanted it."

"I knew you were crooked."

Carson chuckled.

"Easy now. I'm funnin' with ya. It's yer gold. We ain't partners. And I ain't gonna take no part of the gold for helpin' ya. Will ya just act like a lady, please? That's all I'm askin' of ya."

"You'll really help me?"

"I've said it several times already. It's *yer* gold."

She glance over at John and Andrew.

"It's yer gold," said John.

"I don't want anything to do with it, darling. It's too high a price to pay for me," said Miller.

"Well, then. Thank you. I'll act with more civility."

"Glad to hear it. John, would you mind?"

John untied the young woman's hands and feet. She stood up and dusted herself off.

"Thank you, Marshal."

"Don't make me regret it."

"I won't. Besides, there's no point in it any longer. I've found what I was looking for."

"So you think your husband caught up with Arlo Jackson in Gallup?"

"He did, yes. But it's my understanding that Mister Jackson escaped from him. At least that's what he telegrammed me while I was in Trinidad."

"Trinidad, Colorado?"

"Yes."

"And it's your guess that he caught up to him at Dead River?"

"In some fashion, I believe so, Marshal."

"What about the hat?"

"There wasn't anything special about the hat, Marshal. At least not right away."

"But you identified the hat on my desk as belongin' to your brother. I didn't tell you anything about it."

She laughed.

"People talk a lot in small towns, Marshal. I heard that you found a hat, a dead horse, and a lot of blood out at Dead River. I took the chance that it had something to do with Arlo Jackson, because he never showed up. And if it *was* his body you found, I needed to get to it, and look for the other half of the coin and the letter. The hat simply presented me the opportunity to join up with you."

"And then you found the letter in the hat linin'?"

"Exactly. A very fortunate find."

"I must seem a complete fool to you, Miss…Missus Masterton. You must have had a lot of fun toyin' with me."

"You're wrong. That's what had me concerned at first. You're much cleverer than all the other men I've met on my journey out to these parts."

She looked at Miller. "Sorry, dear."

"No need. I obviously had that coming."

"If it means anything, Andrew, you were the most tenacious of them all."

"Well, that's something, I guess."

"But you, Marshal. I had to think very hard about how to deal with you."

"I see. And leadin' me along the trail behind ya was your solution?"

"Oh, Marshal, you're good. Figured that out, did you?"

"Too late, but I did eventually."

"You're a resourceful man. I decided to keep you close in case I needed you. I found you to be dependable that way."

"You mean I'm predictable that way."

"Predictable, dependable. To me there's no difference. And look how it worked out. I needed your help getting that blasted chest out of the cave and here you are, coming through with flying colors."

"And now your husband is on his way here?"

"That's about the size of it, Marshal."

"How does he know where you are?"

"I left markings along the way until he caught up to me early yesterday morning."

"Where is he now?"

"He left me the packhorse and told me he had some business deals to finish up and then he'd be back."

"What kinda business?"

"He's a private man. I don't know."

"Wouldn't tell me if you did, I reckon."

"Probably not."

"At least you're finally being honest with me. When can I expect him?"

"I don't know. I thought he'd be here by now."

"I must have lived a terrible life before this one, and all my past sins have returned to haunt me in this life."

"Don't be so hard on yourself, Marshal."

"No, it's true. And they're all comin' together in the form of you, Miss…whatever your name is."

"I just told you."

"Yes. Margaret Masterton. Got it. That is, until the next name pops into yer head."

Margaret giggled.

"We are *not* very trusting souls, are we, Marshal?"

"I used to be, I truly did. But then I used to be sane, too."

Margaret giggled again.

"Remember when we met? I told you I could be either your greatest jubilation or your worst tribulation, Marshal."

CHAPTER 22

The second shovel from the enigmatic young woman's packhorse made enlarging the mouth of the cave much easier and quicker.

Marshal Carson sat on a rock watching John and Miller dig, all the while keeping a sharp eye on Margaret.

She appeared nervous, her eyes searching the surrounding landscape for someone expected, but apparently very late in arriving.

"Was it your husband who brought you the supplies up near Chin Lee?"

"No."

"Care to tell me who that might have been?"

"I could tell you, Marshal, but I think I'll let you work that one out for yourself. You seem to be the type who enjoys solving mysteries."

"I'm not askin' outa vain curiosity. I'd like to know if I have to be concerned about unexpected visitors while we're out here exposed like we are."

"I wouldn't worry about Chin Lee, Marshal. It's who's coming that should concern you."

"Why is that?"

"You're not well practiced at being stealthy, Marshal. My husband, on the other hand, well, let's just say that he's the sneaky sort. He's been looking forward to meeting you — you and *those two fellows digging, John and Andrew.*"

"Oh my," said Carson, rubbing his face with his hands. "He's behind me right now, ain't he?"

"You would be correct, Marshal," said a voice behind Carson.

Carson heard the click of a revolver hammer being pulled back and the cylinder rotating into position, readying a round for firing.

"Oh, dear lord," said Carson. "It's just dirty, darn bad luck, I'm sayin'."

"Drop the iron into the dirt, Marshal. Nice and easy does it."

Carson removed his Peacemaker and dropped it into the sand several feet away from him.

At the cave entrance John tossed his shovel to the side and wiped his bandanna across his brow.

"That should do it, I reckon."

"I'll climb in there," said Miller.

"Not so fast, gentlemen," shouted the man behind Carson.

John and Miller looked up.

"No guns, boys, or the marshal won't survive the moment. Drop them into the sand, please."

"Do it, boys," shouted Carson.

Both men dropped their revolvers into the sand and held their hands up to their shoulders.

The man stepped around Carson and motioned for John and Miller to join them.

"Boys," said Margaret once they'd arrived, "I'd like you meet my husband, Robert."

"Is that so?" said Miller.

"I'm afraid so," said the man. "You did say Andrew, didn't you, dear? Or is it Matt?"

"No, dear," said Margaret. "Matt was in Denver."

"Ah, yes. That's right. I get them all confused."

"I know, dear. I know."

"Denver?" asked Miller.

"She's got them spread out all over this country," said Robert Masterton.

Carson studied Masterton. He was tall and good-looking, with jet-black hair combed neatly back and a tanned, chiseled, cleanly shaven face. His bright blue eyes were striking.

"Well, it's fittin', I'll say that," Carson said.

"What's that?" said Margaret.

"You make a wonderful-lookin' couple."

"Why, such kind words, Marshal. You *are* a man of class."

"I'm a fool and we both know it."

"Once again, you're being too hard on yourself, Marshal. Predictable, but much too hard on yourself."

"Well, perhaps so, but here I am, in any case — your prisoner. A pleasure to meet you, Mister Masterton. Although this ain't how I pictured our meetin' takin' place."

"You were right, my dear," said Masterton. "He is the pleasant sort. Exactly as you described him."

"You knew about me?"

"I know a lot about you, Marshal."

"But how? How have you communicated with him?"

"Secrets, Marshal. A woman has her secrets. I can't reveal everything to you. Where's the mystery in that?"

"Well, serves me right, I s'pose. I've never looked too deep into a woman's soul for her secrets. But then, I wouldn't recognize 'em even if I did spot 'em."

Margaret giggled.

"You are wonderfully refreshing, Marshal. And now that I have able-bodied men…"

She turned her eyes to John and Miller. "Would you be darlings and drag the chest out of the cave for me, please?"

"I'll get it," said John. "My name is Slims for a reason."

Margaret chuckled.

"I do like you, John. You do it, then, please."

John undid his empty gun belt and dropped it next to the shovel. He turned his eyes toward the marshal. Carson nodded.

"Here goes nothin', Eli."

"Watch out for rattlesnakes, John."

"Thanks. I needed to hear that right now."

Carson chuckled.

"There are no snakes in there, John," said Margaret.

"I think he knows that already, Miss," said Carson. "I was just funnin' with 'im."

"Oh."

John squatted down and slipped into the cave.

"Holy smokes!" he shouted seconds later. "I'm gonna need some help with this."

"Can you slide it to the entrance by yourself?" shouted Miller.

"Yeah, but we're gonna need a horse and harness to drag it out in the open. It's awful heavy."

Minutes later, Miller, astride his horse, with one end of a rope secured around the saddle horn and the other extending into the cave, waited for John's signal.

"Okay," shouted John.

Miller heeled his horse and it lurched forward, but only a foot or so. He encouraged the horse to pull harder. At his persistent urgings, the mare dug her hooves into the loose sand and strained forward.

The chest finally slid up and out of the hole dug by Margaret and enlarged by Miller and John. Miller reined his horse to a stop when the chest sat on the level.

Carson stared at the chest and scratched his chin. "How did your father get that into the cave by hisself?"

"My father...? Oh, yes. I told you the father story. I have so many stories, I get them confused sometimes."

"No father?"

Margaret smiled back at him.

"Right. No father. Whoever it was, then, how did he — or she — get that heavy chest into the cave in the first place?"

Marshal, you were doing so well. The chest was in the cave already. Mister...ah, almost got me there. He added the sand to cover the entrance."

"You win. Keep your secrets. May I have a look?"

"Of course. I wouldn't want to deprive you of the glory you've helped me to secure."

John exited the cave and sat down next to the entrance.

Marshal Carson moved to the chest and studied it. It was about thirty-six inches wide, twenty inches deep, and eighteen inches high. It was iron-bound, and on each end was an ornate iron handle. The cover was arched in the center and an iron hasp, without any lock, was twisted shut. It looked solid, and ancient.

He reached down and twisted the hasp, unlatching the top. He lifted the cover and immediately stood up, eyes wide in astonishment.

The chest was filled nearly to the brim with shiny gold coins, each stamped with a date. Most were stamped 1535.

"Oh, my Lord," said Carson. "I can only believe it now that I've seen them with my own eyes."

John stood up and walked over to see for himself.

"It's somethin', ain't it, Eli?"

"It's more than somethin', John."

Carson turned to Margaret.

"You're a very rich woman, Missus Masterton."

"I am if you'll keep your word."

"I'm a United States marshal. Like I told you before, I ain't no thief. You keeping it, of course, depends entirely on how you come across the letter and coin. But if it checks out, then it's your treasure to do with as you like. But as I see it, even with our extra horses, we ain't got enough horsepower to get it all the way back to Holbrook. May I ask how you had it in mind to move it?"

"I'm afraid we haven't figured that out yet," said Masterton. "To be honest, I didn't really believe it existed. But Margaret did. She never had one doubt about it."

"Well, we're gonna need a wagon to move this thing. But that's assumin' we can even get it up on the wagon without unloadin' it first."

"Where we gonna get a wagon out here?" asked John.

"It would be easier to build one, I think," said Miller.

"You're takin' this much better than I imagined you would, Mister Miller."

"To tell you the truth, Marshal, I don't think it has all set in just yet."

"Don't feel bad about this, Mister Miller," said Masterton. "I've come to hear that a lot lately. My wife's quite the charmer when she needs to be."

"A charmer, did you say? asked Miller. "I suppose that could be one word to describe her. There are lots of other words that describe your wife, sir: deceiver, liar, cheater…well, you get the point."

"Try not to be too angry at her, Mister Miller. There's quite a few in line ahead of you."

"I'll try to calm myself, then."

"That a boy," said Masterton. "It's better for all concerned if you try to see the lighter side of this situation."

"Oh, I do. I'm laughing wildly on the inside," said Miller.

"Maybe we can construct a beefed-up travois," said Carson. "If we can find poles long enough and sturdy enough."

"Yeah, well, I don't see no forest out here. You think the Acoma might have somethin' like that?" asked John.

"I reckon we could ask," said Carson.

"Is it wise to let them know we're in the area?" asked Masterton.

"They already know we're here, Mister Masterton. And the only reason they ain't bothered you two before is because they think your wife is a witch and they won't have nothin' to do with her. It's bad luck to mess with a witch. They even said as much."

"So, where are they?"

"What do you mean?"

"I haven't seen any Indians. Where are they?"

"You ain't been out here in these parts long, have ya, Mister Masterton?"

"I was raised in Chicago, Marshal. I know nothing about what or who's out here. I can say this, though. It's much hotter than I'm used to."

"Talk about luck of the innocent," said Carson. "You should be thankful we come along when we did, then."

"Darling," said Margaret, "put the gun away. I trust the marshal, and we'll need his help.

Let's just get along and figure out how to move the chest."

"If you say so, dear," said Masterton, sliding his revolver back into its holster. "You can pick up your guns, I suppose."

Carson and the others did just that.

"So, Indians are nearby, then?" asked Masterton.

"On top of that mesa yonder. There's a bunch of 'em up there."

"I had no idea. Why aren't they attacking us?"

"I just told ya. They won't mess with a witch."

"But the rest of us. Why haven't they attacked the rest of us?"

"Because, Mister Masterton, we ain't given 'em any cause to attack us. Despite what you might have heard about the natives back east, they don't bother folks that don't bother them. I've had dealin's with 'em before. They helped me find a criminal I chased out here. They're friends of mine."

"That's a relief."

"Mister Masterton, sir, we need to get you back to Chicago," said John. "You ain't got the stuff to last long out here."

"I won't argue with you."

"If you know them, would they be willing to give us some wood poles to build a travois?" asked Margaret. "Obviously, I can pay for them."

"They ain't got no use for yer gold, Miss…Miss… Oh, heck, Missus Masterton. I swear, just when I think I got your name down to memory, you go and change it on me."

Margaret giggled again.

"Relax, Marshal. You're almost rid of me. But if they don't want gold, what would they take for a travois?"

"I expect blankets, clothin', rifles, ammunition, horses — most anything they can use for day-to-day livin'."

"I got a slab of bacon," said John.

"They won't eat pork, John. It don't suit their diet."

"Well, Marshal, how about the shovels? I don't think we'll need them anymore."

"Missus Masterton, that just might do it. Them and a horse, I expect. I'll take 'em over to the pueblo and see if they'll trade with me. You all sit tight. I'll be back in a coupla hours."

"I'll come with you, Marshal," said John.

"No, you stay here. They don't take to strangers much. I'll be back soon."

Three hours passed before John saw the dark speck of a rider heading toward them.

Fifteen minutes later, Marshal Carson reined his horse to a stop, a solidly built six-pole travois attached to one of the extra horses.

"We was gettin' worried, Eli."

"No need to worry, John. They insisted I take a meal with 'em. And I had to give 'em the other horse. But they was happy to see me again and they loved the shovels."

"You didn't think to bring any extra vittles out to us, did ya?"

"In fact, John, I did. They're in my saddlebags."

CHAPTER 23

"Listen up," said Carson. "We got over a hundred fifty miles back to Holbrook to deal with. It's gonna take us quite a few days to accomplish that. We ain't gonna go gallopin' along draggin' the travois behind us. You might just settle in with the idea of it takin' us two weeks or better before we get back to town. We can't push these horses or we'll be draggin' the travois ourselves. Everyone got that in mind?"

Four heads nodded in agreement.

"Of course, if word gets out we're draggin' this chest of gold coins with us, we might have other kinds of visitors out here right quick — the kinds of visitors you don't want. So keep your eyes peeled. And Missus Masterton, I'm sorry to have to say this, but your gold ain't worth one life. If it gets rough out here, we're gonna leave the gold behind. You got that?"

"I'm not leaving the gold, Marshal."

"Then allow me to rephrase what I just said. I'm leavin' you, your beloved husband, and your beloved gold behind, if I have to."

"Fine. I wasn't planning on you helping anyway."

"Which brings me to another point. Just how was you plannin' to get the chest anywhere by yourself in case it did exist and I hadn't showed up as you had anticipated? Your husband said you two hadn't figured out how you was gonna move it."

"I had a plan."

"Really."

"To be honest, though, I didn't think it was going to be this heavy. But it's really none of your concern."

"Have it your way. But know this: you might have to resort to your plan if I think it's too dangerous for us to stick around and protect you and yer gold."

"I'll be fine, Marshal. Don't worry yourself about it. And I can take care of myself, too."

"Of that, Missus Masterton, I have no doubt. Those three men we ran across earlier with various pieces of their hide missin' will attest to that fact."

"They had it coming, Marshal."

"Yes, ma'am. They said as much. It's not you I'm all that concerned with at the moment. I find myself wonderin' when I can expect them others to show up here that might be more difficult to deal with."

"What others?"

"I suspect there's others comin' for your gold."

"I told you, it was Robert."

"I mean others. I feel 'em. I can't see 'em, but I can feel 'em."

"You're feeling is wrong, Marshal. There's no one else out *there,* except those that might be *there* between your own ears."

"Might be. Might be.... Okay, if you say so, but I know we ain't out here alone."

"I have no idea what you're talking about. But if someone does show up to try and steal my gold, I'll take them out of their saddles. Although…"

"Although?" asked Carson.

"I do suppose…"

"Yeah. You suppose…"

"It could be my husband from Trinidad."

"Trinidad? You got yerself hitched again in Trinidad?"

"Yes. For a short time, anyway. I needed to. It's a long story, Marshal."

"I thought you lost him a while back, darling," said Masterton.

"I thought I did too, dear, but I suppose there's a small chance he might still be looking for me. Although I don't see how, considering the condition I left him in."

"There's an interestin' story in there somewhere, I imagine," said Carson.

"It's really pretty simple."

"I doubt that. If I've learned anything about you, it's that everything with you is anything but simple."

"Well, no matter. I've got my rifle, Marshal. Just in case he does show up."

"What say I hang onto it for a spell? Just to be safe."

Masterton pulled his revolver out of its holster. John went for his, too, but held short, seeing that Masterton had pulled his first.

"Now, now! Everyone simmer down," said Carson. "No need for gunplay. It was only a suggestion. I don't want anyone to get shot unnecessarily. That's all I meant by my words. Calm down."

Masterton thought for a moment. He glanced at his wife, who motioned for him to put his revolver away. He did.

"Thank you, Mister Masterton. I appreciate it. I apologize for makin' my suggestion in such an abrupt manner."

"Everyone has a right to have a gun, Marshal."

"Yes, ma'am. I hold that belief to be true enough, but I also believe everyone who's got one has an equal right to die by one."

"I have a right to protect myself and my property."

"You do, but quite frankly, you might be too quick on the trigger tryin' to protect yer gold. I'd hate for you to go knockin' an innocent man outa his saddle before I can determine who he is and what his intentions might be."

"Well, I don't trust you to protect me. So you'll forgive me if I hold onto it."

"Fair enough, but I'd appreciate you holdin' back on yer sharpshootin' until I give the word to fire. I am the law out here."

"I just know you're going to try to steal my gold."

"I already told ya, we ain't gonna take yer darn gold. But I've got an investigation goin' on. And until it is completed, no one is goin' anywhere except back to Holbrook so's I can sort it all out. After I'm done, if you ain't got no part in any of the killin', you can take yer gold and leave. In fact, I'll be more'n happy to see both you and it gone."

"I don't believe you."

"Well, I ain't the one's been doin' all the lyin'."

"I haven't been lying. I've just stretched the truth a bit to protect my interests."

"Tomato, tomahto. I say you've been lyin'. But I can excuse it some, seein' that chest of gold coins there. Even I might stretch the truth a mite if it was mine."

"Yeah, well, She's only been *stretching the truth* on *you* for days, Marshal," said Miller. "She's been lying to me for months."

"Only because you're so gullible, dear."

"Tell me, if you would, why carry on the lie so long? I mean, you never tried to take anything from me, so what was the reason you led me so merrily along? I'm very curious to know."

"You were great cover, darling. No one would suspect me of anything like knowing the whereabouts of this chest. You were perfect for me. I could travel without suspicion. Actually, it was Robert's idea."

Everyone glanced at Robert Masterton. He nodded his head.

"You were the perfect cover, Mister Miller. Your presence allowed me to stay out ahead and clear the path for Margaret. What more can I say?"

"How was I cover for your wife?"

"Etiquette, Mister Miller. It wouldn't have been seen as proper for a young woman to travel across the country without an escort. You were perfect — so attentive."

"Until Omaha."

"Until Omaha, yes. But I knew she'd align herself with others as she needed to."

"I do want to thank you, Andrew," Margaret said, "for your part in all of this. I'd reward you for your assistance, but I'm not in a generous mood at present, thanks to Marshal Carson."

"Oh, this oughta be interestin', boys. Pray tell, Missus Masterton, what do I have to do with you bein' in a less than generous mood?"

"You followed me and you found me. Do you know how hard I worked to steer you wrong?"

"The way I see it, you worked pretty hard to *string* me *along*. But you did give me plenty of false trails to follow down near the end."

"What finally gave me away?"

"Well, Missus, I know the Coronado story as well. They didn't travel through the eastern canyonlands like you said earlier. They went through this area both goin' and comin'. Coronado's journal even mentioned the Acoma Pueblo natives bein' friendly and helpful. Didn't mention them by name, of course, but I figured if there was a chest of gold, it had to be hidden in this part of New Mexico. Coronado wasn't but a day's march away before he discovered the chest was gone. That didn't leave them friars much time to hide it before them soldiers come back lookin' for it. So I reckoned it would have to be hid somewhere around here. And you, of course, led me straight to ya. As I said before, you ain't all that stealthy either."

"Clever, Marshal. I've badly underestimated you. I won't do that again."

CHAPTER 24

The campfire crackled, sizzled, and danced in the chilly breeze of the night desert.

"Eat hearty," said John, "because you're eatin' the last of our supplies. The next bit of meat we eat we're gonna have to kill first."

"The only meat out here is rabbit and rattlesnake. I don't fancy eatin' either one for the next ten days," said Carson.

"I don't reckon we'll have much choice," said John.

"That's what I was telling you a while back, Marshal," said Margaret. "Traveling with men is like traveling with small children. I suppose we'll eat whatever we have to in order to survive. Let me put this simple for those men minds of yours: we do what we have to do or we die."

"I ain't ready to die," said John. "I got things to do. I don't wanna end my days out here bein' food for the critters we should be eatin' instead. Besides, if ya go dyin' out here, who'll say nice things about ya over yer grave?"

Carson chuckled.

"The way I see it, John, the dead ain't got no use for good words. I think you oughta tell the ones important to you how much you care about 'em while they still got their ears turned on.

Tellin' someone you love 'em after they're dead just seems a poor waste of rich words to me."

"Well, it's a darn poor way of leavin' is all I can say."

Carson smirked. "Death ain't at all a good way to leave this life. In fact, it's a horrid way to die."

Everyone chuckled.

"I reckon we all have our way of leavin' somethin' behind after our journey is done," he continued. "But I think our greatest leavin's are the memories of us we leave in the minds of others. I don't know if it's true or not, but it stirs my heart to great joy thinkin' it might be. And sometimes, I reckon, thinkin' that it might be so might have to be enough. But then, "'*Fame after life is no better than oblivion.*'"

"Stop it, Marshal!" said Margaret. "We don't need you quoting Marcus Aurelius again."

"I understand. But as I see it, you shouldn't put too much emphasis on fame anyway. Because if you get to be too famous for their likin', they'll just send someone more famous out to kill ya."

"Who's that?" asked John.

"*They*, John. The ones who don't like no one bein' more famous than they are."

"Who's that?"

"Them that makes the rules."

"I get it. Them with the gold."

Carson smiled.

"Yes, sir, John. Them with the gold."

"That's real funny, Marshal," said Margaret. "What I wouldn't give for a bottle of whiskey right now and a quiet place to drink it."

"I'm with you on that," said Miller.

"Oh, shut up," said Margaret.

"Is she like this often, Mister Masterton?" asked Carson.

"To tell you the truth, Marshal, I've never seen her this way before."

Carson chuckled.

"We have. It's been our experience that she gets a mite ornery now and then."

"Perhaps, Marshal. But I've never seen her so happy."

Everyone but Margaret laughed.

"I for one think you take life too seriously, Missus Masterton. You need to laugh more, talk philosophy more. You need to bury that gold and go find you some real joy in your life before it's too late."

"And I need you to shut up, Marshal. I need all of you to just shut up."

"I swear, you are just bound and determined not to find joy today."

"And *you* are bound and determined to drive me completely mad."

With that, Margaret jumped up and began walking away.

"Where do you think you're goin'?"

"I'm going for a walk. It'll prevent me from choking the life out of you."

"You ain't goin' nowhere."

"Where am I going to go, Marshal? It's pitch-black out there. So tell me, how far do you think I'm going to get?"

"I was just showin' concern for yer well-bein' is all. No need to go snappin' at me."

"I don't like being controlled. Besides, I've got my rifle."

"No one is tryin' to control you. You wanna go walk out in the night desert, be my guest. Heck with it."

Robert Masterton rose up.

"I'll go with you, darling."

"Stay here, dear. I don't trust any one of them around the gold by themselves. I'll be right back."

Margaret disappeared into the black of the moonless night.

"I gotta tell ya, Mister Masterton," said Carson, "I don't know how you put up with that woman."

"She *can* be a handful at times. Especially after she sets her mind to doing something."

"Well, I can speak for that," said Miller. "And I suppose I'm lucky, if I think about it enough. I don't believe our marriage would have worked out too well."

Carson smirked.

"No, Mister Miller, I don't reckon it would have. But I'll add to that by saying this. I shall welcome the end of this investigation and be glad for the quiet moments once again."

Carson stared out into the night in the direction Margaret had walked.

"Missus Masterton? You okay out there?"

Silence was the only response.

"Missus Masterton?"

Still silence.

"You wanna stop playin' yer games, please? Answer me."

Once again, only silence.

Carson jumped to his feet and started in the direction Margaret had gone.

He had gotten only a few steps when a low voice boomed out of the darkness.

"Stand easy, Marshal."

Carson had his revolver pulled, cocked, and ready the next second.

John, Miller, and Robert Masterton leapt to their feet as well and pulled their guns.

"You're surrounded," the voice said as they heard several rifle levers actuating around them.

"Oh dear," Carson muttered. "It's just dirty, darn bad luck, I'm sayin'."

"Drop 'em to the sand, please," said the voice.

"Do as he says, boys. They got us."

They all dropped their revolvers.

Seconds later, Margaret returned with an extraordinarily tall, muscular man wearing a black duster and black Stetson.

From all around them stepped five other men in like dress, the light of the campfire dancing over them.

"What philosophy do you have for this?" asked Margaret, wearing a devilish smile.

"Well, how about this, Missus? Death has its own time of arrival. But for me, it ain't gonna be today."

Margaret chuckled.

"I told you, honey. He's good."

"She did tell me that very thing, Marshal," said the giant man.

"I'm glad I ain't disappointed either one of you. I take it you're the fella from Trinidad and you've followed us down from Chin Lee?"

"Oh, darling, he *is* good."

"Yes," she replied.

"So how do *you* fit in with this little princess of pandemonium, as if I haven't guessed already?" asked Carson.

"Princess of...," she snickered. "I love that."

"I'm her husband."

Carson laughed out loud.

"Of *course* you are."

"My name is James Cavanaugh."

"Cavanaugh, is it?"

"That's right."

Robert Masterton's jaw dropped.

"Then I'm guessin' Margaret Masterton is not your name, Missus?"

"That would be correct, Marshal."

"Actually, Marshal," said Cavanaugh, "her name is Carolyn. Carolyn Cavanaugh."

"But…but…," said Masterton, bewilderment on his face.

"Of *course* it is," said Carson, laughing again.

"Honey," said Cavanaugh, "have you been playing name games with these boys?"

"Of course I have."

Cavanaugh chuckled.

"But…but…," said Masterton.

"Don't feel bad, Marshal. She did it to me as well for the longest time. She possesses an art for it."

"She does indeed, Mister Cavanaugh. And what about Mister Masterton here?"

"I tried to shake him in Chicago," said Carolyn. "It didn't work. So I married him instead and used him to my advantage until I got to St. Louis and met my loving Andrew. And while Andrew has proven to be the most tenacious, Robert has proven himself to be the most resourceful. And I do very much appreciate that about you, Robert. Your cooperation has aided me immensely, darling. You've been a real trouper."

"But…but…," said Masterton.

"Robert, dear. Get a hold of yourself, please. Think of our time together as an adventure, dear — an exciting and marvelous journey. And be thankful that you'll complete it alive."

"But…but…how could you *do* this to me?"

Miller laughed. "The same way she did it to me, Robert. Join the club."

"Marshal, this has been most entertaining," said Cavanaugh. "And I do like interacting with Carolyn's playthings on a limited basis now and then. But I believe we'll have to relieve you of that packhorse and chest of coins now." Cavanaugh moved to the packhorse and took the reins.

"Well, sir, I'm glad to be rid of it. It ain't been worth the trouble, far as I can see. And I don't expect you'll get it out of the territory without payin' some kinda price for it yerself. Nothin' is free, Mister Cavanaugh. Not even found treasure."

Cavanaugh laughed.

"Sometimes you just have to take what life gives you, Marshal."

"Yes, sir. And sometimes you have to accept what life *takes* from you."

"You are definitely the philosopher she said you were."

"I have my moments, I suppose."

"And what am I going to do with the both of you?" asked Cavanaugh, looking from Andrew Miller to Robert Masterton and back again. "I expect she's done with you now. Will I have to be concerned that you'll seek some form of revenge upon her? You each have that look about you — that *you're not finished with me yet* look. It's a common look. I've seen it on a dozen other faces."

"You don't need to worry about me, Mister Cavanaugh," said Miller. I'll just take the lessons learned and move on. The Marshal's right. The gold isn't worth dying for."

"Good," said Cavanaugh. "Mister Masterton?"

"I never once thought I'd end up as one of her toys," said Robert Masterton. "But I think I'm gonna be like Andrew and leave it be. He's right; nothing here is worth my life. All I can say is good luck to you, sir."

Cavanaugh laughed. "She's wicked about it, gentlemen, I'll say that. But you need not concern yourselves for me. I've got it all handled nicely. How about you and your deputy, Marshal? Need I carry with me any concerns about you?"

"Mister Cavanaugh, like I told your wife, we don't want her gold. And long times in the saddle wear a young man down quickly. To an old man, they're brutal beyond words. I believe I've had all the adventures these old bones can stand. If you don't mind, sir, I'll go back to Holbrook, finish my report — coherently, if I'm able to — and then retire. Yes, sir, I plan to give up my days in the saddle for a few more days in the rockin' chair."

CHAPTER 25

The bubbling conversation had dribbled down to an almost peaceful stillness after several minutes without anyone wishing to be the first to intrude on the silent thoughts of the others.

Carson wanted to speak, but the silence was intimidating. His look into the surrounding eyes saw the effects of churning brains — fluttering eyelids, uncontrolled body twitches, grimacing expressions.

He only guessed at what each person was thinking, but "What now?" was the only question on his mind. Finally, it all became too much for him.

"What are we doin' at the moment, Mister Cavanaugh? Are you plannin' our demise?"

Cavanaugh chuckled.

"No, Marshal. I'm just waiting for my boys to run back and fetch our horses. We left them a ways away so we could make a more silent approach to your camp."

"I see."

"Sorry that my silence alarmed you."

"Well, I must admit I was concerned."

"I wouldn't be concerned, Marshal. I wouldn't let anything happen to your plans for retirement."

"Thank you, Mister Cavanaugh, but before I can retire I have a few bodies back in Holbrook that still need accountin' for. And I have another body, presently missin', that I need to find and investigate. I can't as yet see where you've done anything worth chasin' after you for, Mister Cavanaugh, but if I find out you was in any way involved in Arlo Jackson's murder, you can expect to see me at least one more time."

"It wasn't murder, Marshal. It was self-defense."

"Self-defense?"

"Yes, sir. He got into a gunfight with two of my men while making his escape from Mister Masterton's men. My men tracked him down to a dry river wash. He managed to somehow get a gun from one of them. He shot one of their horses and its rider dead and wounded the other man. Jackson tried to run away, but my man recovered enough to shoot him dead."

"What happened to your man?"

"He's fine now. He brought my other man's body back to Gallup."

"He brought it back?"

"It was brought back to Gallup and turned over to the law. I'm not a criminal, Marshal."

"I didn't say you was, but can you prove what you're sayin'?"

"There's a Sheriff Moncrief there."

"I know him."

"My man filled out a report on the shooting. Sheriff Moncrief can confirm everything I'm telling you. There was a dead-or-alive reward on Arlo Jackson. I've got the poster for it right here."

Cavanaugh reached into his vest pocket and withdrew a folded piece of paper. He handed it to Carson.

The marshal unfolded it and read it silently. He then refolded it and handed it back to Cavanaugh.

"Yes, sir, I recognize it. Same one I have on my office wall. Two hundred dollars. Darn it all. Even he's worth more'n I am."

"What's that?"

"Nothin'. But you didn't collect on the reward?"

"We didn't."

"Why not?"

"My man had no way to get Arlo's body back to Gallup. He only had the one extra horse — the one Arlo rode out to the wash. And it was hard enough to get that body back safely."

"Would you mind fillin' in some blanks for me?"

"If I can."

"Arlo Jackson was bound. Someone cut his bindin's. Someone broke his ribs. How did he get two hundred yards from a large rock in the wash? Can you tell me anything I don't already know about that?"

"I told you almost everything. My man said there was a chase. There was a fight. He cut himself loose and tried to run away. He must have broken his ribs during the fight."

"What about his horse? Why didn't he just mount his horse and ride away?"

"My man had to ride it down and get the reins. Marshal, I think you're expecting this to be much more complicated than it really was."

"Yes, sir, I expect you're right... But he left the hat as a signal? Your man, that is?"

"He just left the hat, Marshal. It was that simple."

"That is darn disappointin'. I was expectin' some reason more excitin' than that."

"Sometimes life is just simple and boring, Marshal."

"Yes, sir. Sometimes it is that."

"Like I said, he filled out a report in Gallup with Sheriff Moncrief. It's all there."

"Well, then, I reckon that's the end of my investigation. The mystery is solved. Wasn't much of a mystery, I don't mind sayin' I was lookin' forward to more of a clever endin'."

"I'm sorry, Marshal."

"You're right, I reckon, Mister Cavanaugh. Sometimes life just ain't all that excitin'."

"Sometimes not, Marshal."

"I'm a mite disappointed, but I'll live with it."

"Maybe you'll find your retirement to be more adventurous."

"Lord, I hope not."

Cavanaugh smiled.

"Well, no harm will come to you. I'm just here for my wife and her chest of coins. Are you going to follow us and make trouble?"

"No, sir, I don't reckon I will. As I said before, I plan to ride a rockin' chair hard. This whole country is changin' faster'n I can keep up with it. I think I might just step aside and let it pass by. I have all the information I need for my report, I reckon. I just need to make it back to Holbrook in one piece and put in my papers for retirement."

A rider rode into camp with two horses. Cavanaugh and Carolyn climbed aboard.

"Well, Marshal, I wish you the best in your restive years," said Cavanaugh.

"Can we pick up our sidearms now?" asked Carson.

"Tell you what. Just to keep it friendly like it has been so far, would you mind giving us a chance to leave before you go gathering up any firearms?"

"I can do that for ya, since we're bein' friendly and all."

"I appreciate it. Goodnight to you, then."

"I wish you a safe journey back to Holbrook, Marshal," said Carolyn.

"Young lady, I wish I could say it has been a pleasure knowin' you, but let's just say it's been interestin' and leave it at that. Although I would add this. It's been a heck of an adventure."

"You are a charmer, Marshal. But let *me* say this. You're a peaceful man. I like that most about you. And you have a gentle soul. Some might look on it as a weakness, though, so you be careful. You were right when you said this desert is mean and unforgiving. I wouldn't want to read in a newspaper one day that the desert killed you just for being the peaceable kind."

"Livin' peaceably ain't the same as livin' weakly. It takes a mighty good deal of strength to live peacefully all the time surrounded by everything and everyone lookin' for a fight."

"I miss the good and peaceful life we once had in this country before everything sped up and became wilder."

"Well, Missus, good life, bad life, peaceful or wild, it don't matter none, I reckon. No kinda life lasts forever. Everything is always changin'."

"But it's the changes coming that I'm worried about. Not every change is necessarily a good thing."

"Times *are* changin'. I feel it in my bones. I see it all around me everywhere. This country ain't gonna stay the way it is right now. One day, I reckon, people are gonna look back on these days and call *them* the good ol' days. By then, they'll have forgot how tough life was on folks.

They won't remember how vicious it was. What horrible things we did to each other just to survive. They'll look back on these days through romantic eyes, givin' no thought to the courage and sacrifice it took to tame this wild and savage land."

"I'm sure you're right about all of that, Marshal."

"Whether I'm right or wrong, only time will tell, Missus."

"Marshal, I have rarely come up against a man of such mindful equality. I shall not ever forget you. It's been quite an experience."

"Yes it has. So, where you gonna go with your newfound wealth, Missus?"

"Somewhere less violent and cooler, perhaps. You'll forgive me for not being more specific, but I'm still feeling the need to be protective. Try to live well, Marshal."

Carson chuckled.

"I'll do just that. Thank you."

"John, I hope you'll forgive me for not being able to teach you all the words you wanted to learn."

"Aw, shucks, ma'am. I wasn't gonna hold you to it anyway."

"And I again apologize for my behavior back in Holbrook."

"It's forgot. You travel safe, now."

"Andrew," she said, "I…"

"There's nothing to be said. I got the learning I needed from the experience. I'll be just fine."

"I have no doubt about that, Andrew. No doubt about that at all. Robert, what can I say?"

"Good-bye would be nice."

"Good-bye, Robert."

"Missus," said Carson, "I have just one more question, if you don't mind."

Her eyes fluttered.

"There go them eyelids again."

She smiled.

"I had to practice that fluttering hard for Andrew's sake."

"You mean it's not you changin'…?"

"Changing my personality?" She giggled. "What do you think, Marshal?"

"Well, I'll be."

"What's your question, Marshal?"

"Why so many accomplices, marriages, or whatever you might call them? Why so many? How were you able to communicate with everyone?"

The young woman laughed.

"I could answer those questions for you, dear man, but then there would be no more mystery for your magnificent mind to ponder. And a sleeping mind was never meant for a man like you, Marshal. Consider my refusal to answer as my parting gift to you."

Carson laughed.

"How well you have come to know me. Gift accepted, then, with gratitude."

"Marshal," said Cavanaugh, "in the spirit of honesty, because you do appear to be an honest man, I have to tell you one more thing."

"What's that, sir?"

"Our last name isn't Cavanaugh."

Carson laughed out loud.

"Of *course* it isn't."

The mystery man and the even more mysterious young woman reined their horses away from camp with the packhorse in tow, and within minutes even the sound of the travois being dragged over the hard, sandy ground fell to silence.

"Well, boys," said Carson, "time to get some sleep and head on home. It should go quick now that we don't have that chest slowin' us down."

"So that's it, Eli? We're done?"

"We're done, John. Sometimes you discover truths, sometimes you're just left with the mysteries. You win some battles, you lose some battles. We got out alive, fellas. I'm gonna call it a win."

"Is the adventure over, Eli?"

"We ain't got back to Holbrook yet, John. I reckon anything can happen along the way."

"Oh. I was hopin' you was just gonna say yes."

Carson chuckled.

CHAPTER 26

The morning sun peeked over the horizon to find four riders following the marks made by a heavy travois.

Carson decided it would be fun to follow the tracks for a while just to see in which direction the mysterious couple would head with their chest of gold coins.

After a few miles, they came upon four flour sacks stacked together and lying in the middle of the tracks.

John slipped from his saddle and inspected them. Tucked in between the bags was a handwritten note. He read it aloud: "You *are* predictable, Marshal. Enjoy your retirement."

"Dear Lord!" said John. "They're filled with coins, Eli! They're completely filled with coins. All four of 'em! What d'ya make of that?"

"I'd say that pretty much makes me retired, John. How about you, Mister Miller?"

"I'd say my feelings aren't hurt so much anymore, Marshal."

"How about you, Mister Masterton?"

"My heart is already healed."

Carson chuckled.

"I believe you. What do *you* say, John?"

"Well, to be honest about it, I was sorta hopin' she was gonna keep her word and teach me the words and numbers. But I reckon I can hire someone else to do that now."

Carson laughed.

"You've got enough money there, John, to have them teach you all your words in different languages if you want."

Carson walked through the door of his office.

"Welcome back from Prescott, Marshal," said John. "How'd yer retirement meetin' with the governor go?"

"Just fine, John. Thank you."

Carson strode over to his desk and plopped down into his chair. He lifted his boots and set them down upon his desk. He then turned his eyes to Red Darrington's empty cell and sighed before looking to his deputy.

"It's been a month since ol' Red left us, John, and yet every time I walk into this office I expect to see him, grinnin' back at me like the odd fool he was and ready to toss some rude comment my way."

Carson smiled as he continued. "I think I miss him a mite. He did keep things lively around here for a time."

"He did that, Eli. They sure did him fast, though. Tried him one day, hung him the next."

"Where's Jimmy?"

"He's makin' his rounds."

"Good. So tell me, John, what did I miss while I was gone?"

John picked up a short stack of paper.

"A few telegrams arrived for ya."

"Read 'em to me, if you please."

"Okay. This one here's from Mister Andrew Miller. Says he's settled in and doin' fine back in San Francisco. This one here's from Mister Masterton. He just wanted you to know that he settled in Chicago and all is well. Both gentlemen send their good wishes to ya."

"That's fine. That's just fine, John."

"This next one is from Judge Perry. He apologizes for the tardiness of his response to your inquiry regardin' the identity of the young woman."

"Oh, this should be good. What did he say?"

"Basically, he says he never heard of her, but he wonders how she could know how he got his nickname."

Carson laughed.

"Of course."

"This other one's from Sheriff Moncrief. He points out that while Dead River isn't in his jurisdiction, there *was* a body brought into his office resultin' from an incident out there. The report was signed by a William Owens, the wounded man who brought the body in. Mister Owens' description don't match Mr. Cavanaugh's, though."

Carson shook his head.

"Interestin'. Continue, John."

"This last one's also from Sheriff Moncrief. He says his deputies killed Roscoe Tanner and his boys in a gunfight up in the eastern Canyonlands eleven days ago."

"Well, that's a bit disappointin'. I reckon now I'll never know why he sent his assassins after me. I guess I'll just have to settle for knowin' he won't be tryin' for me again and move on."

Another week passed quietly and uneventfully until a handwritten letter arrived from Sheriff Moncrief briefly describing how a stagecoach had arrived in Gallup, delivering a man dressed only in torn and soiled long johns. He said that the man was found by Ben Jonas, driving his team out near the Dead River wash. It seems the man was wandering around aimlessly along the trail when they came up behind him. He was dehydrated, hungry, tired, and mumbling incoherently about Carson, gold coins, and a vanishing wife. He gave his name as James Cavanaugh.

The marshal dropped the letter onto his desk and walked out of his office laughing.

Four days later, Marshal Carson left Holbrook, Arizona, for the last time. The whole town turned out for his departure. It was a momentous farewell.

EPILOGUE

"You have a good mind, John. It's an active mind. It's always seekin' answers to good questions. I think that teacher was wrong about ya. You *can* learn. And I think you can learn everything you'll ever want to learn. Don't listen to anyone who says you can't become a *man of the mind*. Because I've seen the gift within ya. I've seen the desire to learn burnin' strong in ya. Don't ever settle for less than the very best you can be."

I took those words to heart. Marshal Eli Alva Carson spoke them to me the day he retired and moved away, and the marshal never lied.

I took the opportunity and put the money given to me by that mysterious young woman to good use. I left lawman's work and went back to school. I finished my lower studies with a private tutor and then went on to college, where I graduated as a lawyer.

A while ago I began writing about my experiences riding and enforcing the law with Marshal Carson. I finished my first book based on those amazing true-life adventures with a wonderful friend and mentor. You're reading that book.

The whole world has changed so much since those wondrous days together, though I'm not sure all the changes have been for the best. But Eli Carson knew that the changes were coming nonetheless and had the good grace to step aside and let them take place without his interference. But then Eli was always gracious.

I last visited with Marshal Carson on January 25, 1920, on the occasion of his ninetieth birthday celebration, in Los Angeles, California.

Although his long years had him looking tired and slightly bent, he was as happy as I had ever seen him. And his eyes lit up brightly when I stepped in front of him. In greeting, I held out my hand to him, but he hugged me tightly instead. Then he stood back with wet eyes and smiled widely. He was as delighted to see me as I was to see him.

To my utter amazement, another legendary lawman was in attendance and standing right beside him. Wyatt Earp. He'd just *stopped by* to visit with an old friend, he said. I had no idea Eli had ever known Earp. He never told me about their early lawmen days together in Dodge City. But then, it was not like Eli Carson to mention such things. And seeing the two men exchange affectionate words, I recognized just how truly blessed *I* was to have been his friend and colleague during those few precious years we were together.

"You can make everyone in the world happy that they knowed ya if given enough time and chances. But that ain't the way of this world.

So make happy those who you can. For the rest, well, they'll have to get by without ever knowin' just how grand their life mighta been if they'd only had the chance to get to know ya."

Those words from Marshal Carson rang in my ears as I looked at those two amazing men standing together and chatting. These great men knew each other and they were happy about it. And I knew Marshal Carson. That made *me* very happy.

We spoke on many topics that day. He was delighted that I was able to hold my own in our conversation, *havin' finally learned them big words*. I believe that is what pleased him the most.

I did ask him if he'd ever found answers to the myriad of questions the mysterious young woman had left him as her parting gift. He just smiled at me and winked.

"I'm still enjoyin' them gifts. But I wanna show you somethin' special, John."

He left the room with a slow, shuffling gait and returned a few minutes later carrying a perfumed envelope and grinning from ear to ear, his eyes sparkling with delight. He opened it and withdrew a short letter. He carefully unfolded it and handed it to me to read.

I was shocked to see that it was from that mysterious young woman, who was not so young anymore. The date on the letter was only two days before. The letter read:

My dear Eli,

Although our time spent together was short, you left an indelible impression on that long-ago young woman. I have never ceased thinking about you, nor will I ever forget the kindly, tolerant, and courteous man that I see you still are.

I have kept close track of you over these many years and in fact live very near to you right now.

I want to wish you a very happy birthday. It's not every day one gets to wish someone so admired, respected, and loved a wonderful ninetieth birthday.

I hope you're still enjoying all the little mysteries I left you with and that your magnificent mind is still pondering all the answers. You deserve it all.

Please give my regards to John when you see him next.

With much love,
Mrs.…well, you know

All I could do in response was smile and nod with acknowledgment and appreciation. She really *did* understand him.

"*Alone of the emperors,*" wrote the historian Herodian of Marcus Aurelius, "*he gave proof of his learning not by mere words or knowledge of philosophical doctrines but by his blameless character and temperate way of life.*"

Such words, I believe, could have been written about Eli Alva Carson, the philosopher marshal.

But those words could not begin to complete a truthful characterization of a man like Marshal Carson. For not only was he a great philosopher, he was a wonderful teacher as well. He taught me about life. About the kind of life that only a man like him could understand and pass on to a young man like me. And treasure. He taught me the value of treasure. Not gold or silver, but the kind of treasure that sees a man gently into his old years. The kind of treasure that lies in a man's mind and shines brightly in those years when all that is left for him to do is think — the adventure of life and all that goes with it, the good, the bad, the beautiful, and the not-so-beautiful. And I lived through some of it with the most adventure-loving man I've ever known.

"*I'm goin' lookin' for a new adventure, John. And to go someplace new you gotta leave someplace old. To greet the mornin' you gotta leave the night behind.*" Eli spoke those words to me on the day he left Holbrook for his retirement. And it was on March 12, 1920, that a gentle heart stopped beating during the night so that a remarkable soul could greet a new morning — to begin its last and greatest adventure of them all.

Standing next to Eli's casket with my hand resting on that now still chest and my tear-filled eyes staring at that charming and restful-looking face, I daresay that although the adventure may have been the final one for him, it just had to be far from the darkness he had always expected it to be. I can't imagine a man so full of light ever coming in contact with darkness again.

But sometimes, during the darkness of night, when staring up into the twinkling firmament above that had so fascinated him, I imagine him traveling past all those stars with his ever-questioning mind filled with a joyous and forever wonder, and then slipping behind that veil that he had finally punched a hole through.

And somewhere down in the desert, along a dry and stony, occasionally flowing riverbed wash, I am certain that the wind still blows unmercifully, the sun still bakes the living, and the sand still flies about like clouds.

For me, though, no place on this earth will ever be more precious nor hold more meaning, or more truth. For it was there, among all the waste and scatter, death and torture, dread and doom, where *my* life's adventure truly began. It was a wondrous place where an old, tired man set a young, hopeful man upon his path, leading him toward his own old age gracefully and with some measure of worth.

Yes, sir, it was wonderful, darn blessed luck, I'm sayin' — the luck of astonishing and splendid adventures down there on that dusty wash known as Dead River.

~ John Kevin Slims, Esquire
Former Lawman Colleague
and Grateful Friend
of U.S. Deputy Marshal Eli Alva Carson
1921

THE END

Marshal Carson's Philosophy

******

"Some might say don't bother to load a gun if you're not intendin' to shoot it. But I'd rather say don't bother to live a life if you're not intendin' to live it as gloriously and completely as possible."

******

"Accept an offer of a free dinner very cautiously. Because what they're probably not tellin' you is that you're most likely to be the main course."

******

"Never hold onto anything so tight you can't let it go, if only to see what it might do after it's set free."

******

"I can't imagine wantin' anything more from life than just the chance to live it."

******

"You gotta get the most out of life you can while you're here and able, because you never know how many chances you're gonna get to mess it up and start over."

******

"I've learned not to accept every gift as a kind offerin', for there have been moments in my life that have arrived as sweet assurances of heaven, only to turn bitter as if delivered by hell."

******

"As for my bein' a touch cynical, I am. But bein' a touch cynical has so far kept me from bein' stuffed and served up on a platter."

******

"You can't expect to find any peace without that it first ain't been found within."

******

"Philosophers often start in the dark. But that's how they discover the light."

******

"If you give power to someone who don't deserve it, don't be surprised when they smack you over the head with it later."

******

"Fools are often intrigued by foolishness."

Marshal Carson's Logic

******

"Hirin' an idiot to manage anything is like hirin' a blind man to pitch horseshoes in a tournament."

******

"Expectin' a politician to protect the people is like expectin' a rattlesnake to protect a mouse."

******

"Lessons learned the hard way are not carelessly forgotten."

******

"Good life, bad life, peaceful or wild, it don't matter none, I reckon. No kinda life lasts forever."

******

"There's a certain logic to gettin' through life, and it's really very simple. Battle discord when you must. Repose in accord when you're able."

Marshal Carson's Humor

******

"Yesterday is a part of who we are today. But hang on to yer hat. Today will be a part of who we are tomorrow. And if that don't get ya to drinkin' hard liquor, I don't know what will."

******

"Just remember, things don't always have to be this or that. Sometimes they can be that or this."

******

"It's best not to anger your captors when you're wanted dead or alive."

******

"If you ain't certain that those attackin' you are Indians, just wait for the arrows."

******

"Simultaneous occurrences work best when they arrive at the same time."

******

"If you can't avoid it, try to resist it. If that don't work, try runnin'."

******

"If you've got yourself too far in to get out, try walkin' backwards."

******

"Life demands a certain degree of intelligence. Might be that some of you should check your pulse."

About the Author

Dillon Garrison (Val Edward Simone) was born in Seattle, Washington, and has been writing since 1980.

Val has published adult-themed action/adventure novels; historical fiction; western novels; short stories; a collection of thoughts, musings, and observations; a collection of children's short stories; and several children's picture books. He continues to work on many other novels and short stories.

He is also a strong advocate of early childhood reading and continues to work with schools, local libraries, and directly with children through parent-assisted workshops, helping children to discover their own creativity through reading, writing, and drawing.

Val currently lives and works in Arizona.

His websites:
www.ekidslandpublishing.com
www.morningsidepublishing.com

Other Books by Val Edward Simone

Morningside Publishing, LLC
Novels/Novellas
Blood Trackers: One Crazy Love Story
Blood Trackers 2: Revenge of an Angel
About Things I Lost Long Ago ... scribblings from a foolish heart
The Wondrous Life of a Long-Ago Man
Comes the Devil to Crooked Creek
Captain Delightable's Magical Tales of a Minchon Warrior
A Minute of Forever
The Firestone ... Is Mankind Ready?
The Story
Adventures at Dead River
The Art of Living Between Hell and Breakfast

Short Stories
Manifest Destiny
The Secret Life of Goner Andling
Love Bytes
Dragons Within
The Problem with Dragons
The Unfortunate Dragon

Ekidsland Publishing, LLC
Children's Picture Books:
Felix
The Gingerbread Pony
The Littlest Bell
Mean Muley McGrudge
Otto and Kevin
Proton Gator
Sammy Sparrow Spy

Short Stories
The Fairy Collection
Through the Waterfall
Fairy Forgotten
Emily's Wish
Kaylee's Secret
The Wizard of Sebastianville

Children's Coloring Book:
Proton Gator & Friends Coloring Book

www.ingramcontent.com/pod-product-compliance
Lightning Source LLC
Chambersburg PA
CBHW061314170626
46817CB00001B/173